A Man Named Baskerville

Jim Nelson

First edition published in 2022

Hardcover ISBN 978-1-80424-605-4

Published by MX Publishing
335 Princess Park Manor, Royal Drive,
London, N11 3GX
www.mxpublishing.co.uk

The Bridge Daughter Cycle

Bridge Daughter
Hagar's Mother
Stranger Son

Other books by Jim Nelson

In My Memory Locked
Man in the Middle
Edward Teller Dreams of Barbecuing People
A Concordance of One's Life
Everywhere Man

Visit the author online at j-nelson.net

Evil indeed is the man who has not one woman to mourn him.

– *The Hound of the Baskervilles*

Hound Of The Baskervilles, Sidney Paget

Editors' note

The journal this book is translated from was penned in a mixture of Portuguese, Portuguese Creole, Spanish, and English. Its multilingual author changed languages between sentences, and even between phrases and words. He perhaps did this unconsciously, as the handwriting of the document suggests a harried writing schedule.

The editors have endeavored to translate every passage into English with the utmost fidelity to the original.

Sunday, the Twenty-first of October, Eighteen hundred and eighty-eight

One

Let this journal stand as the one true account of the events in and around Dartmoor and the estate known as Baskerville Hall. Undoubtedly, the exploits there of Sherlock Holmes and his biographer Dr. Watson will command a worldwide audience once published. I hope this modest diary will serve as a corrective to Watson's inevitable fabrications and omissions regarding the circumstances surrounding the curse and terrible hound of the Baskervilles.

*

Where to begin? Last night, I fled home and hearth to plunge headlong into the treacherous bog of Grimpen Mire with only self-preservation in mind. In dinner coat and spats, I raced across the mire without a lamp to guide my way. Feverish in my escape, fearing being struck by a bullet from Dr. Watson's military pistol, my footrace into the mire was almost animalistic in instinct.

Crossing from the hilly moors into the bog-mire was signaled by the fetid stench of Grimpen, its miasmas and decomposition saturating the foggy night air. The foul, rotten-egg stench is evidence of a cycle of renewal. All that comes from the earth returns to the earth. Muscle and skin and eyeball and brain matter are mulched down by the mire from their exquisite forms to a muck of fetid goop. From this stew comes new life reconstructed, as it were, nourishing off the death of that which precedes it.

Once in the mire, my progress reduced to a near crawl for fear of plunging into a muddy bog pit and twisting a knee. Worse, I feared encountering a sink pit and being drawn whole into the thick, churning sludge, sucked under like a giant anaconda devouring a fawn. In some parts, I resorted to advancing on hands and knees to test my way with full assurance.

I reckon it was near two in the morning before I reached the tin mine, now long-abandoned and quite desolate. The mine is on an island within the mire, with a mere thread of solid ground acting as a natural bridge to cross and reach it. Even in daytime, the crossing is treacherous. The moat about the island is blanketed by a thick mesh of bog-peat and grass, a great rug hiding a massive trapdoor capable of killing horses and mules, kings and queens, barons and baronets…even pretenders to the throne.

Sopping wet, covered in mud, bitten up by mites and bog fleas, I stood among the mine's abandoned structures with a cocked ear. I waited for the distant sounds of the men of Dartmoor mobbing and thirsting for blood—my blood. No sight of torches dancing in the fog-ridden moonlight. No baying of bloodhounds, no shouts demanding I surrender myself. My inflamed mind cooled as I recognized my pursuers had not made even basic progress to the mire's edge. Grimpen's reputation as a watery grave for calves and dogs has become my first line of defense, and a formidable one at that.

Exhausted, I retired to a concrete bunker at the rear of the island. This was once the explosive depot storing the miners' detonators and TNT. The depot does not compare to the great explosive storehouses I've seen in South America, where mining tends to be dry rather than wet, and the mineral veins deep rather than shallow. For now, this depot serves just fine as a refuge from the elements.

Although the events of last night remain a shock to me, I can at least prove I was not ill-prepared for them. Over the course of months, I have assembled here a humble camp. In this storehouse, I keep a cot, dry goods, spare clothes, wool blankets for the fog-soused nights, hardtack and salt pork, fresh water, Caribbean rum, a small cache of tobacco and its accouterments…all the necessaries for fire, light, and warmth. Perhaps I should have stocked more in the way of self-defense. Save for a buck knife and a Colt Single-Action Army—one of the few mementoes I've kept of the New World—I am defenseless and alone. The men of Dartmoor are armed, savage, and legion.

Although I earned an appetite after my swift campaign across moor and mire, I took no meal. The rum shot a little fire into my belly and cooled my panicked head. I shook out three wool blankets from my cache. After starting a meager fire in the rear of the storehouse, I arranged my wet clothes to dry. I draped one of the blankets over my wretched self and stood at the fire, teeth chattering and tucked-in arms shaking, wondering if I had caught my death.

No, wondering what my next moves should be.

More than the frigid water, I shook with bitter outrage. Here I stood, in the center of a damp, godforsaken bog, only able to count the simple blessings of a wood fire and a roof overhead. An entire county beyond the bog's borders waits to slaughter me in my socks. To emerge from Grimpen Mire was tantamount to tying off the thirteen loops of the hangman's knot and slipping the noose about my own neck.

I am a Baskerville, born into aristocracy and raised with a proper education. I've traveled from New World to Old, enjoyed the hard-earned weight of a fortune in my purse many times, and watched it slip away just as often. My raven-haired wife, known across Central America for her soul-weakening beauty, is a turncoat. My closest friend has abandoned me. Nero is dead. Agrippina is...unknown. Turn thee unto me, and have mercy upon me, for I am desolate and afflicted.

How did I arrive at this position? Last night, a magician walked on stage, employed his world-famous sleight-of-hand, and—poof!—I disappeared. His act was so convincing, not one audience member raised a hand to request my return.

Of course, the illusionist I speak of is the damnable Sherlock Holmes.

After the botched events of last night, I must now consider the possibility that matters will never sufficiently cool for me to leave this place. Not only is all of Dartmoor on their guard for my presumptive exit from Grimpen Mire, by now, Scotland Yard has undoubtedly placed a watch for me at all ports. Never could I have foreseen an international light like Sherlock Holmes becoming involved in this matter, nor the presence of his faithful spaniel Dr. Watson, who will undoubtedly polish and buff the account of his involvement to exaggerated effect.

In my many treks across the bog, humping in food and supplies to this old tin mine, I managed to include a pocket leather-bound notebook, as well as two fountain pens and traveling bottle of India ink. This provision was not to maintain anything like a journal or memoir. In my travels, I've learned that a bit of paper and a ready supply of ink to be invaluable in a pinch. Now I find another use for these tools: To record my version of the events in and around Baskerville Hall, which concluded so unjustly last night.

*

When I awoke this morning and glanced about this abandoned explosives storehouse, in my bleary daze, I thought I'd been transported to a gray windowless prison cell.

I revived the fire I'd made in the wee hours and brewed coffee from a small tin of Costa Rican beans I stashed here. Crushing the beans and boiling the water reminded me of the fine morning meals we used to assemble on the muggy floor of the Amazon before a day in the banana fields. It's a simple luxury, these brief memories.

Today, I abandon the dowdy English costume I adopted of a naturalist, the chaser of butterflies, the absentminded bachelor of Merripit House, running around the moors with my trusty net flapping behind me like a regatta's sailing flag. There will never be occasion again for tie and dinner jacket. My father taught me there existed an upward path in this world, if only I could locate it. The truth is plain to me now. All paths lead to this watery, bog-ridden island, surrounded by snapping turtles and parasites eager to burrow into your scalp.

I don the clothes I cached here. They are more suitable for this dank environment. The dungarees and denim bring with them a renewed nostalgia for my years in the fields of Brazil and Panama. Hands in the dirt. Shovel handles and machete grips. The songs shared as we moved from tree to tree gathering nature's yield. From the earth I came, to the earth I return.

*

After the tin miners' abandoned their claim to Grimpen Mire, nature reclaimed the island. Peat and mud have begun to overtake the island the miners toiled so hard to develop. Someday the cottages and storehouses will sink into the bog, be digested whole, and forgotten.

As with the explosives depot, the mess hall was emptied before the mine was abandoned. Not even a footstool was left behind. It is there I kenneled Nero and Agrippina, the Hellhounds of the Baskervilles. Their cages remain, as do their water and feed bowls. Sticks and leashes, chokers and collars, the muzzles they chewed through like so much jerky. Steak bones for rewards. Leather crops across their snouts for simple punishments. Training a beast requires steely resolve, make no mistake.

From the refuse, I produce the pair's first harnesses and muzzles, all blackened leather with the seller's name embossed in ripe gold print. The gold embossment is long destroyed—Nero and Agrippina fought any restriction I placed on them.

Holding the leather to the morning sunlight, I locate the faint outline of the seller's name impressed into it: Ross & Mangles, Brompton Cross, London.

Two

The indefatigable energy of Londoners buying and selling; the hansom cabs and the growlers trotting past; the shouts and cries and merchants and hawkers; it all overwhelms my country boy senses so. I feel displaced and disjointed merely writing about it. The great plazas of São Paulo and Salvador compare timidly to London's vigor. The dour weather—I have witnessed no other in London—dampened only mildly the activity at Brompton Cross.

Such was my mood when I engaged with one of the proprietors of Ross & Mangles. The kennels were arranged in a tented lot backing onto Fulham Road, all surrounded by a neglected perimeter fence topped with barbed wire. Among the cries of chippies selling their fried feasts and the *clop-clop-clop* of horses drawing cabs came the din of caged dogs whelping and barking.

"You'll 'ave no better guard 'ound than this one 'ere, sir," Mangles told me in a thick southeastern accent, and dropping all his aitches which followed as well.

"Do not call me 'sir.' I work for my money."

"And earn every farthing, to be sure." He led me across the pound to a bear of a canine, with a ruddy-brown coat and the forehead and jaw of Neolithic man. "This Mastiff is about as faithful as they come—"

I offered the beast the back of my hand. Its piercing black eyes tracked my moves. When my hand drew close, he snapped his jaws at me with a voracious snarl. I retracted barely in time.

"...But its loyalty is only superseded by its ferocity," Mangles said with a smothered grin.

"I require the largest pitch-black hounds you can offer. This one is not merely coated wrong, it is also too small."

"Too small!"

"I require a hound a half larger than this, one with an indefatigable sense of smell, who could track his prey miles away across a bog in the dead of a fog-drenched night, and capable of snapping the neck of a deer in an instant. I also require an older bitch of the same breed."

"Impossible," Mangles said. "You ask for an animal which don't exist." He nodded at the Mastiff. "This here is the largest I could offer, and at a fair price. Now that is a fact you cannot deny."

I surveyed his other offerings, fully anticipating this merchant would be unable to fulfill my needs. Ross & Mangles sold canines to landed gentry and city sophisticates. Not lap dogs or toys or poodles, mind you, but petite hunting dogs for chewing up foxes and purebred collies for gentleman farmers who raise three sheep and a goat and call them a herd. This lot was the best London could offer me, and it was not up to my standards.

Pencil and paper—useful in a pinch when traveling. "You will wire this kennel." I jotted the particulars down. "You will place an order for two *Fila*."

"Filly what?"

"*Fila*. I require a pair, a dam and her grown son. Not a whelp, mind you. The bitch should be in her prime and the son at least eighteen months old. Twenty-four if possible. He should be thirty-three inches at the withers, and at least one hundred and seventy-five pounds. The pair must be black as pitch, without a single contrary coloration on their coat. Not even along their underside or as socks, understand? I would prefer they were shipped in separate pens, although with trade across the Atlantic being what it is, that may be unfeasible." I thrust the paper into his hands.

"What's this about the Atlantic?" He flicked the paper with a fingernail. "This here says Brazil!"

"The seller is in São Paulo. Do not worry, they comprehend English as well as Spanish and Portuguese." What with the admixture of cultures that is Brazil, and its feeding of the world from its bounty of fruits and cash crops, fluency is a must when trading. "In your wire, you are also to request that they obtain and ship with the canines this fungus." I thrust at him a second sheet of paper.

"A mushroom, you say?" The Latin on the page only confused him further. "Four pounds of…a Gardener? Feed for the fillies, then?"

"Absolutely not. The fungus must be shipped separately, sealed in a wax-paper box with a soil of coconut wood chips saturated with water. This is most important, do you understand?" I pointed out my detailed instructions on the paper he held before his nose.

Mangles scoffed and thrust the papers back at me. "I'm not in the business of importing alien canines and contraband and such."

"The animals you offer here are all bred and raised in England?" I made an amusing motion at the international cacophony of barks and growls around us, as chaotic as the moment the Tower of Babel workers realized they could no longer comprehend one another. "You are most certainly an importer of livestock, Mr. Mangles, and I now require your business acumen to import a species of canine perhaps never before seen in Britannia. All I'm asking of you is to stretch your horizons and also acquire four pounds of a fungus found only in Brazil." I held my palm to stifle his mounting objections. "I assure you, this fungus has no ill effects. It induces neither euphoria nor hallucination, nor does it contain an exotic poison. All I request is for you to use your considerable contacts and understanding of international trade to locate an exporter who can acquire my fungus and ship it with the canines. I've even supplied you the name of the kennel there."

"Importing hounds is the nature of my business." He was stewing. "Importing breeds I never heard of is another thing. And to throw toadstools into the mix…"

I produced from my coat pocket a folded pack of bank notes. "This advance should cover your time and expense, with the remainder a bonus for your considerable professional efforts. I assure you, you will have no customs trouble with the importation of either beasts or botanicals."

With a scowl, his hand gobbled up the bank notes and squirreled them away in one of his trouser pockets. This was the little game playing out. I was a man of station buying my way through the world, and he was a man who'd resigned himself to being bought. It is a game as old as the Neolithic tors dotting the Devon moors.

"Leave me your name and how to contact you," he said. "Your articles should be at the dock in eight weeks, give or take."

Principal matters concluded, I took my leave of Ross & Mangles. I made two more stops while in London, one of them being a visit to Harrods. On the North Devon express, I carried a bow-tied box of Ecuadoran chocolates and a small bag of Costa Rican coffee beans for my lovely Beryl, who waited patiently for my return. Our mutual love still held a spark then. Fond memories.

Three

Spent the remainder of the day humping supplies out of the mining camp and to my new abode. Although I know the eastern end of Grimpen Mire well, my understanding of the western side is far less complete. The work of moving supplies has been slow-going.

Grimpen Mire is a Harrods for an entomologist as myself. I'm more properly classified a lepidopterist, although I prefer the archaic term for the passionate student of butterflies and moths, an *aurelian*. And while I have not been conferred a degree on the subject, I am not being immodest when I express my expertise on the subject.

Be aware, dear reader of this journal (pray it should survive), that the British Museum has on public display a singular moth I discovered in Yorkshire while mastering there. The day I patronized Ross & Mangles, my other stop was at the Museum to admire my achievement. Adjacent to the great glassed atrium, encased under glass itself, is my discovery. Its broad cloud-gray wings are pressed wide, a crucifixion in miniature.

If you like, you may view the moth yourself. Beneath its pinned corpse is a small card bearing the name of the discoverer, *Vandeleur*, one of many assumed names I've taken. Among the other names I'm known by—Jack Stapleton, Rodrigo, Rodje—who am I today? If there were justice, I would be Sir Rodger of Baskerville. No doubt Holmes and Watson and the police are still calling me Stapleton. Well, toiling here in the mud today, perhaps I have found my true name.

On my final return to the tin mine to claim the last of my necessities, men's voices approached. My Colt held six bullets. Each would have to stand and be counted, if they were of any service to me today.

I slipped into one of the watery peat-covered holes surrounding the island. An ignorant man in Grimpen Mire might slip into a hole as deep as a lake, be caught in the tangle of vines growing beneath the surface, and find himself drowned, snagged by Neptune's net. I know better. I crouched in a shallow one with my pistol ready.

Soon the men materialized in the distance. The tall man's shouts and peals would have scared fowl in the next shire. The shorter, stouter man bellowed questions and thrashed his walking stick through the dense underbrush. Both were covered in mud and dreck. The stubby fellow had apparently fallen face-first into a puddle of the stuff. He had only managed to wipe clean the thick ruddy mud from his glasses and around his eyes and mouth. The gaunt chap in the seersucker hiking uniform was mud-caked from the neck down. He must have slipped into a sinkhole toes-first. The only reason he survived was thanks to the other being there to pull him out.

Enter Mr. Sherlock Holmes and Dr. John H. Watson.

Thanks to Dr. Watson's walking stick, the pair located the narrow path of firm ground to the mining camp. I watched in hiding as they trod from one abandoned structure to another. Holmes led the way, gesticulating wildly to add flourishes to every pronouncement he made, like a ham actor told a newspaper critic was seated in the front row. From the mess hall came Holmes' unmistakable shrill "Ah-ha!" upon the discovery of my makeshift kennel. Holmes shrieked similar eurekas from the explosive depot. He emerged brandishing my butterfly net as trophy, the fisherman returning home with a broken line and wild tales of the big one that got away.

As swift as his emotions percolated up, they would cool equally as fast. "Hold," he told Watson with one hand raised. "There was great evil located here. This place…it dampens rational thought. It encourages a man's baser impulses." He glanced about, as bird might when startled. "Perhaps it is corrupting my judgment as well."

"What is it, Holmes?"

The detective dismissed his own hesitation as suddenly as it had struck him. "Nothing. A groundless possibility."

Here was an opportunity primed and gilded. Before the two would know it, I could rise from the dreck, level the Colt, and put down Holmes and Watson like the dogs they are. Two well-placed bullets would fell these esteemed men. They have grown soft from English roast beef and gravy dinners, and from the warm snifters of brandy consumed with their evening tobacco. Even if the first volley did not set them down, the element of surprise guaranteed I could get a third and even a fourth shot off, if need be. Watson was armed, but his sidearm was holstered and strapped. Surprise was mine. To the earth they go, from the earth rises new life—egg, larva, chrysalis, imago.

A few gunshots at the mine would not attract attention from the village. But unlike a wayward tramp wandering into the bog by accident, Holmes and Watson were most certainly expected in Coombe Tracey before dusk. Were they not to return, more men would arrive, including police and Scotland Yard. It will not be a mere two-man party my six-shooter must contend with.

With great dismay, I am forced to record here I remained hidden in my watery hole, head and gun down, while Holmes and Watson completed their survey of the tin mine. Thanks to my forethought, I had already transported the bulk of my supplies to my new location, otherwise, they would surely have destroyed the remainder to flush me out of the mire. Seething, hands figuratively bound, I could do nothing more than await their departure. The advantage is theirs, at the moment.

"Come, Watson," I heard Holmes cry as they left the island. "We've heard the last of Jack Stapleton."

"Devoured by the bog?"

"A grisly coda to your story for the papers." His blaring voice trailed off as they managed their way back. "Almost Biblical, wouldn't you say?"

"Holmes, in all the years I've known you, you've shown neither familiarity nor curiosity of the Holy Scripture."

"Still, a most righteous ending for the antagonist of our story! Have I told you of my private researches into animal decomposition in humid and temperate environments?"

Their voice faded off, but even with considerable distance, Holmes' exclamations carried across the bog. When I emerged from the watery pit I'd hid in, I cursed myself up and down. Holmes and Watson were not the only ones made soft by English beef and gravy.

Given the opportunity once more to kill Holmes, I vow here and now not to squander it. I might just have to create such an opportunity.

Monday, the Twenty-second of October, Eighteen hundred and eighty-eight

Four

The prehistoric men who resided in the mire had no dry fertile land for planting or herding. They undoubtedly made up for it by feasting on the abundant amphibious life. Frogs, turtles, and snakes can make fine meals if one is brave, or desperate, enough. The bog is also home to a number of berry species, including whortleberry. Not a succulent fruit as one would buy at Harrods, mind you, but plump berries produced by plants low to the ground. It would take hours to pick enough for a meal, or even enough for the beginnings of a dessert, but they do add variety to the diet.

And the butterflies and moths here—I could fill this journal writing only of the wondrous varieties to be found. Damselflies, Double Line moths, march fritillaries…my time in Grimpen Mire would be so much more pleasant if I could devote all hours to observing and cataloging its profusion of winged subjects.

I have spent too much time in England. The English gravy and their oily battered fish have fattened me. My brain soaks in a pool of Anglo-Saxon suet and my tongue has become batter-coated. I so miss the vivid diet of my Brazil. The English, they find *Portuguese* cooking exotic (!), which only bespeaks the dietary desert I have been living in for years now. The Portuguese, with their flavorless fish bakes cooked in cream and unsalted cheese, garnished with a single black olive—you insult my country when you think that since we share a language, so must we share a cuisine.

"You are Brazilian," my father told me when I was young, "but you are also English. And you are a Baskerville, heir to a baronetcy. Never let anyone else tell you otherwise!"

My father worked in the fishing village at the end of the dirt road we resided on. My mother managed the house and took me to services every Sunday. I made myself useful picking up small jobs here and there in between classes taught by the Colombian sisters of a local nunnery.

My father's Portuguese was passable—he seemed to know only enough to get by. His Spanish was even more rudimentary. I never heard him say to my mother "I love you" or any of the other affections a husband shares with his wife in the privacy of their home. He was most proud of his native tongue. He spent hours every week teaching me the Anglo-Saxon language. I memorized Wordsworth, Tennyson, Ben Jonson, and

Shakespeare. When I returned home from the clapboard schoolhouse I took religious instruction in, he would halt me at the door and demand I recite the opening to Coleridge's *Kubla Khan*.

"Incorrect," he scolded me, although I had recited it perfectly. "Back straight. Chin level with the floor, tilted only slightly toward the sky. Pronounce your *a* again. Again. Now your *e*. Again…"

Every syllable had a single correct pronunciation, and he would drill me until I mastered them. It was not enough to imitate him. Proper pronunciation had to come by instinct. I did not understand it then, but I know it now: He was wrestling back the Romance languages I had conversed in since I was but wee. Portuguese and Spanish, they are soft languages with round O's, supple S's, and buttery N's. He hardened me with the syntax of his public schooling and the strict pronunciation of his father and forefathers. The distinction between *shall* and *will* was hammered into me, as well as *may* and *can* and *who* and *whom*.

"There is no article of clothing nor piece of jewelry more valuable than proper English speech," he told me. "Doors will be thrown open for you if you are well-spoken, mannered, and groomed."

Other lessons lacked the rigor I'm suggesting here. He spoke enigmatically to me of his upbringing in Baskerville Hall, and his time in a prestigious boarding school in Bristol. *I'm a Baskerville,* he proclaimed to no one when inebriated, as though shooing off ghosts hovering about him. *My family battled in Ulster!*

For all his pronouncements on Empire and tales of Merry England, his mythical Baskerville Hall remained but an abstraction to me. The devout describe Heaven as a perfect place, but if pressed, they are able to offer few specifics. My heaven, Baskerville Hall, was a gleaming castle atop a verdant green hill, with azure skies and edifices covered in sweet pea framing its opulence. Horse riders marched in formation on the grounds around its parapets. Dames in chiffon and tiaras of woven daisies frolicked on the grass.

"He is Brazilian," my mother told him. "There is nothing for him in the Old World."

My memories of my mother are only of a woman exhausted. Her father's livelihood was as a servant in a city down the coast. Her future there was servitude as well, which was why she abandoned her family and married my father. She was not a beauty and she did not bring with her a dowry. I believed my father's situation was such that she was a prize. He was a broken man, although I was too young at the time to formulate such a phrasing on my own.

"A Baskerville," my father bleated from his chair at the window. "A descendent of the Cavalier class."

I would lie on the bare rug and listen to his upright English accent for hours. He looked out the window while telling me stories, facing northeast as though capable of seeing the majestic British Isles on the far side of the Atlantic. He sometimes spent the entire evening at that window wordlessly smoking cigarettes and pacing. Other nights, he stared at Britannia across the waters with a bowl of cut limes and a bottle of rough tequila at his side. Those nights, the stories of Baskerville Hall grew more intense.

"Call me an Atlantean," he announced one of those drunken nights. "My island sunk ages ago. I am as Cain, forsaken by my brother and wandering the world," he declared in a confusion of Biblical stories.

"Tell me about boarding school again? You and the other nobility?"

"Tennyson! 'Tears, Idle Tears'!"

With a heave, I rose to my feet and assumed the speaking posture he had browbeat into me. "'Tears, idle tears, I know not what they mean…'"

"School? School…" He drew in a deep breath of air. It revived him from his tequila stupor. "I boarded with the sons of barons. Sons of the peerage."

"Did you school with knights?"

"Knights, of course! And sons of lords, and sons of dukes. We dined in halls of fine oak cut from forest primeval. The hall was lined with the portraits of forefathers who'd dined and sang and schemed in those same halls…"

"Including Baskervilles?"

"Of course Baskervilles! Our family is one of the oldest in all of England. We fought for the Stuarts and we fought in Ulster." He grinned an evil grin. "On the crisp green Bristol fields we learned to hit each other—hit hard, strike 'em down." He smacked his fist into palm, making my mother at the sink shake with a start. "I fought them off with as much fight as a Baskerville can give."

"Who?"

"School chums and school bullies. They hit me hard! I hit back harder. The teachers hit the hardest. Shut up—quiet down—stand—sit—no lavatory for you—no trifle for you—shut up—stand—sit—two across your backside for defaming the Lord, one more for defaming the Queen—" Slapping his hands, he mimicked the sound of a paddle striking buttock flesh.

"You're scaring him," my exhausted mother called from the kitchen.

He washed down his glass of *reposado* and poured another. The bowl of limes was now a bowl of spent wedges sucked dry of their juice. His eyes wandered and glistened with a seething nostalgia.

"The teachers could be brutes," he said. "Some were soft with me. They made Rodger feel…cared for." I had returned to lying on the floor.

He leaned down and let his alcoholic breath wash over me. "School was fa-aaa-ar away from Baskerville Hall. No one in Bristol to look over me. No big brother to guard me from the older boys. Or from the teachers."

He stared out the window longingly. Above the Atlantic stretched an obsidian field of stars.

"No one to watch out for you. School could be a lonely place." He spoke with care, as though the words were stepping stones leading across a rushing river. "Some of the teachers, they…cared for me. Others only said they cared." And he began crying.

You are a Baskerville.

The more he repeated it, the less of it I believed. My childhood curiosity for his tears evolved into the impatience of a young man, and then outright disgust. This delusional, bent man had given up—a pathetic resignation compared to the lives of American men who rose from meager situations to domination, men such as Carnegie, Rockefeller, and Vanderbilt. My father came from title and family, and witness what he'd cobbled together: A clapboard hovel with floors made of planks of old fishing boats, a wife who did not love him, and a bowl of spent lime wedges. When I was seventeen, headstrong and thirsty for dignity, I left home with my nose upturned and my back arched. I never spoke to my father again.

Five

Truly a fright since laying down the ink of my last entry. Once more across the mire came the shouts of gathered men, this time at least a dozen voices, as well as the baying of dogs. I managed to come within eyesight of the party without detection. I lay low within a clutch of gorse bushes arrayed around several upright stone slabs planted in a semicircle by our Neolithic forefathers.

The party was composed of men from in and around Dartmoor. They carried hunting rifles, handguns, and other surplus from the Boer campaigns. They navigated the mire in an apparent attempt to locate and surround me.

Farmhouse dogs know of rolling plains and the thin mud after a rainstorm, but not the dangers of a mire. Pheasant hounds can navigate marshy lands, and even swim across the easy waters of a lake, but again, the perils of the bog are beyond their ken. The peat-covered sinkholes of Grimpen Mire would have dragged them under howling and clawing if not for their masters yanking them out by scruff or collar. These dogs may have fine noses for tracking birds, but the florid odors of decay and renewal led them into the mire's traps one after another.

This inept search party was a tangled mess. Dartmoor is a pathetic coven of villages populated by small men of small ambitions and gossiping church wives baking fruit pies and keeping up appearances. If this is the best Dartmoor can muster, then safe I am indeed.

Enjoying the spectacle and not minding myself, I was caught unawares. A burly man with a thick blond mustache emerged from a thicket to one side. His knuckled hands were wrapped around a double-barrel shotgun.

"Gotchya." He held the shotgun at his waist. "He's here!" he cried out.

He was a hunter who lived and plied his trade on the far side of Princetown. Rare was it to see him near Grimpen. The men of Dartmoor no doubt summoned him for his expertise in tracking, and it had paid off.

The hunter made a simple mistake. In no way would a seasoned man of his trade take the time to signal to other hunters in his party he had cornered an animal. Confronted with the opportunity to kill a man rather than beast, he wasn't quite as ready as he'd imagined himself being when he left his cottage this morning.

"He's alive all right!" He raised an arm to catch the attention of the blinkered party a hundred yards off. "Got him right—"

I'd been crouched, with my back to him. I turned and squeezed off a shot from the Colt. He flailed backwards. From the end of his shotgun bloomed a mushroom of gunpowder smoke. The boom erupted in my ears; they're still ringing. The aim was way off, sending the discharge high overhead.

He fell on his back empty-handed. Blood spurted up from his left thigh.

As he cried out in anguish, I approached with my Colt trained on him. He kicked his legs as though trying to right himself, but the heels of his boots merely sliced troughs into the mud.

The wound was not superficial, but not life-threatening either. Even a medical fool like Dr. James Mortimer could have dug out the slug and bandaged him up before teatime. The hunter would walk with a limp the rest of his life, but he would have survived. If only he'd thought to go hunting near a doctor's home and not out here in the mire.

He managed to spit out between groans of pain, "You're one sonovabitch—"

Using the flat of my heel, I nudged his side. I did not aggravate the wound, but even the touch of my boot caused him to spasm. I retrieved his shotgun and lorded it over him.

"What you did to your family—" he sputtered. "The Baskervilles was good to ya—"

I relieved him of a box of buckshot cartridges and the buck knife strapped to his uninjured leg. Harder now, I began rocking him back and forth on his side. His flailing hands slapped uselessly at my foot.

"Your own wife, you treated her like a common whore—"

With a sturdy push of my heel, I rolled him over and into the muddy bog he'd fallen beside. He thrashed about in the muck, flailing his arms and screaming for help. The tan mud in that part of mire bubbled like a cauldron, each belch sending up the florid smell of decomposition. With each exertion, more of the muck's watery fingers clung to him and drew him deeper into its embrace.

I fled before the men and their dogs could reach the scene. They huddled around the pit that had become the hunter's wet tomb. They tested the mud with their poles and walking sticks, yelling for him to grab hold. The hunter never emerged.

"Stapleton!" came a cry from the party. It was Dunn, a Dartmoor busybody who owned an inn and kept himself involved in the local councils and such. "Stapleton! We are coming for you! All these years, you paraded around Dartmoor pretending to be our superior, but you are not! Sir Charles was good to this village and its people, and you took him away from us! In the name of the Baskerville family, we are here to put an end to you!"

From my vantage, I counted nine men and four dogs.

"Your friends Sherlock Holmes and Dr. Watson have departed for London!" he called out. "As has Scotland Yard! They all believe you're dead! We did not acquiesce so easily, and our rightness is now manifest!"

I could not stand it. "They are not my friends!"

Dunn, ear cocked, conferred with the other men. They pointed around in an attempt to come to an agreement of where I might be concealing myself.

"Oh, they were your friends all right!" Dunn called to me. "They would have put you in a warm cell with three hot meals a day and a soft pillow for your guilty little head. You might have seen the gallows, but you would have enjoyed the benefit of a long trial first! You'll get no such consideration from us!"

After a moment, he continued.

"We're not notifying Holmes of what we've found here today, nor any authority to speak of! Let them close the book on you! It makes our hunt all the merrier!"

"Tell me about Agrippina!"

From the looks about the men, I realized I'd confounded them.

"My dog, dammit! My dog!"

"You ask about your dog before your lovely wife? After you beat her so?"

"You treat her well! She had nothing to do with this!"

I sensed I'd squandered too much time hiding. Sure enough, when I counted their numbers again, only eight men were within sight. To be ambushed twice in one day is to admit defeat. And so I beat a retreat to my little castle on the verdant hill, this Stone Age tor built upon a swamp.

Six

The first penurious years away from my family were harsh and I do not wish to recount them here in detail. My shifts in the port town factories alternated between hellish and grueling. Long days of toil without the reward of a single nourishing meal or warm shelter shakes me even today. There were days I thought I might not survive to sundown, either dying from exhaustion or going mad from assembly-line repetition. Our intellect may distinguish us from the animal kingdom, but it is nothing more than economics that separates us from its savagery.

Scratching around the town of Santarém with my knapsack over one shoulder, and failing to secure my labor for compensation or barter, I gave in to desperation. I had saved a bit of money working at a rubber plantation outside of Prainha. It was time to invest in myself and trade in on my esteemed lineage:

> *To whom it may concern,*
>
> *I am Rodger Baskerville II, son of Rodger Hugo Baskerville, and of direct ancestry to the Hugo Baskerville who fought honorably for King Charles I and in Ulster. I am writing from the Empire of Brazil to open a line of communication with my esteemed family and to inform them that Baskerville blood flows in the New World.*
>
> *I make a minor request for your time. Although the peoples of Brazil are respectful of British peerage and titles, due to its distance from the isle, the name Baskerville does not carry here the esteem it so deserves. I humbly ask to return to me, care of Santarém post, a notarized statement of my lineage to the baronetcy of Baskerville.*
>
> *I assume it is unnecessary to explain the usefulness of such a document, as I am now of age and eager to better my place in the New World. In Brazilian society, introductions and references are paramount to securing a position proper to the man and his station.*

Your precious time is much appreciated in this matter. Yours,

– Rodger Baskerville II

The sum required to post this message to England was exorbitant, but my desperation won out over my hunger.

*

Black enough boots and you stop looking men in the eye. You spend all your time looking at their *boots*. Dirty boots, muddy boots, boots covered in manure, boots sticky with beer and piss. I reclined in the shade of a carriage on the street, sleepy from the heat, when a boot coated in Santarém's tawny dust clapped down on my blacking box.

"Boy—shine, on the double."

I confess I did not jump to attention with as much briskness as I should have. I shook off my sunstroke and began to clean his boot with a rag and knife.

"You do not appear from these parts," the man called down to me. "Are you a *Confederado*?"

I confessed to him I did not know the term, although I speak Portuguese as well as any native Brazilian.

"The *Confederados* would never let one of their own work the street as you do," the man said. "Are you an orphan? Where are your parents?"

"I am a Baskerville." Still I had not looked him in the eyes. His boots were tooled leather, but not overly ornate: A *vaqueiro*, perhaps, or a ranch foreman. They were working boots, fine and expensive but well-used. His denim was faded and frayed at the hem, but pressed with a sharp crease. It all told of a man who works in the field, but who does not *work* the field.

"Never heard of 'Baskerville.' Is it a Protestant sect?"

"It is a baronetcy," I snapped in English. "The letters patent were issued by the crown."

"The name means nothing to me," he continued in Portuguese. "I would think it means nothing to anyone for five hundred miles in any direction."

"I am heir to an aristocracy," I said in English.

He let out a great laugh into the air. "You have a fire in your belly, I give you that. Who taught you that accent? A British card sharp?"

"What difference does it make to a yokel like you?" I said in the lowest Portuguese I knew.

His boot came off the box. On my knees in the dirt, dizzy from the heat, I stared down at my shine box for a long moment, waiting for him to cuff me across the head. Finally, I reclined backwards in the dirt. I looked into his eyes for the first time.

"Where did you get that mouth?" he demanded.

"From my father," I told him.

The stranger had a handsome face. He had a jaw of straight lines and a dark mustache underlining perceptive eyes and squared-off cheekbones. From his demeanor, he seemed much older than me. I was young and cotton-headed, and did not understand a man in his thirties is very much in his prime.

His temper cooled. "If this is the best confidence trick you can muster, I suggest you improve your ruse. This English fairy tale of yours carries no weight in Santarém. Claim you are the long-lost heir to a *visconde* or *barão* in Lisbon. The crown has created so many new *viscondados* in the past two decades, you could draw a name from a hat and be believed—"

"I am a Baskerville, heir to the baronetcy in Devon."

"Then speak the English," he said suddenly in my father's tongue, albeit falteringly. "Not your street patter. Speak to me in your aristocratic tongue."

"My father spoke only Standard English in our home," I parried, in the words just as I've written here on the page. "I am an Englishman first and foremost, to the bone, a Brazilian by chance of birth. I am Rodger Baskerville the Second, descendant of Hugo Baskerville, who fought for King Charles I and in Ulster."

My outburst silenced him again. In wonder, he asked, "Are you educated?"

"My father impressed upon me a proper education in the classics. He taught me poetry and oration, as well as the Greek forms of Rhetoric and Logic."

"Poetry?" He laughed. "You know poetry?"

Oration is posture, diction, and focus. Standing before him in the dust, I began reciting *Kubla Khan.*

"Stop," he cut me off, mouth agape. "Your Portuguese is most common, but your English is elevated. It's one thing to speak fluently in these parts. But to speak the English of aristocrats, that is quite a valuable skill, my friend. Where are your parents?"

"I make my own way."

"How would you like to work for a landed family? American aristocracy…by their own reckoning, of course. I can guarantee a bed, a roof over your head, and three hot meals a day. You will even earn a few *reais* of your own."

A young man boot-blacking on the street learns there are many confidence tricks in this world, and all manner of confidence tricksters.

"It is legitimate," he assured me. "I manage a banana plantation south of here. The manual labor is considerable, but it involves standing and walking, not hunching over a box and crouching in the filth of the street. There will be travel around the countryside and into the jungle. You will find it far better than any opportunity here in Santarém."

"I would rather work for and improve myself than be stuck under the thumb of another man."

"My employer, they are *Confederados*. You know of them? No? They came here from the United States twenty years ago." He took up my box and led me to a waiting wagon. "You will see. They live in a dream that died with the end of the American's war of their states. They also say their forefathers emigrated to the Americas from England, just as you peddle your little tale on the street here."

"I am peddling nothing."

"Except boot shines."

I could say nothing in return.

He clasped my shoulder. "Do not fret it. No one believes the *Confederados* either, at least their claim on gentility. They own land, though, and because of that, they command a bit of respect, so the locals put up with their puffery. They might like you. If you're lucky, they'll take you in. You can teach their daughters proper English. Maybe you can exorcise from them the strange drawl they've carried with them from their Mississippi..."

This was how I met Antônio Almeida Melo.

After an hour's travel on rutted jungle roads, we arrived at a plantation. Its stately whitewashed mansion made a grand first impression. Columns lined the front of the house like centurions standing at attention. Round staircases leading up from the roundabout reached a regal double-door entrance. A trio of flags mounted along the balustrade snapped overhead in the wind. One honored the American Confederacy, the next the State of Mississippi, and the last the Empire of Brazil.

Upon approach, the facade grew apparent. The whitewash had grown dingy and cracked after years of exposure to the jungle. More damaging was to discover later that, of the stately three stories facing us, only the bottommost floor was constructed and could be occupied. The chessboard of windows above was a front, making the mansion more like a stage backdrop.

"Welcome to Far Oaks," Antônio told me. "Built by Major Leland Harris after his arrival in Santarém twenty years ago. His family joined him later. Those are the stables. The Major practices military formations with the other *Confederados* around Santarém."

The domestic help were locals. They wore the service garb of the American South, costumed much as London stage actors might appear when playing butlers and maids from a bygone age. When the Major strode out from his estate's double doors at dawn every morning, he never emerged wearing anything but his military uniform. He carried himself about the plantation in its gray stiff coat with epaulets and sashed at the waist. Medals and ribbons festooned his breast. As old and gray as his coat, he rode stiffly about the property inspecting the day laborers' progress from atop his warhorse Jupiter. When the other *Confederado* families arrived for the balls and masquerades assembled by Mrs. Harris and their daughters, Maj. Harris would holster a long sword under his belt and mingle with their guests.

All this was to come, though. My first night was in the bunkhouse with the other fieldworkers. Antônio assigned me a bunk and ordered the others to ensure I minded my manners. He left me with a promise to meet again in the morning.

Around a crackling campfire surrounded by banana plants, the field men cooked up a pot of beans and pork scraps and root vegetables. Underripe bananas were mashed and cooked into a starchy-sweet paste. I carried a tin plate of the vittles and a chunk of stale bread into the shadows to eat alone. Around the fire, the *lingua franca* spoken was as thick as the stew. The men conversed in a mélange of Portuguese Creole, the Spanish of the countries surrounding Brazil, a Caribbean patois, and a smattering of American English. They shifted between the dialects effortlessly. It took a few months for me to converse with them as naturally.

In the shadows, I hoped my plea to my family in England would be answered soon. They would be shocked to see one of their own in this situation, and they would relieve me of living among these coarse men. In my bunk, itchy from the burlap blankets I was given, I recited Wordsworth to myself until I managed to find some semblance of sleep.

Seven

When the tin mining company pulled out, they carried off almost all of their equipment and goods. They did not strip the place clean, however. In the debris of the old metalworking shop, I located a workable hacksaw handle. From an otherwise bare cabinet, I discovered a pack of machined hacksaw blades wrapped in brittle tobacco-brown paper. A sturdy workbench remained behind, and with it, a vise all but rusted shut. From these meager resources, I managed to saw off the Winchester's barrels just past its pump handle. With a little sandpaper, I smoothed off the metal filings around the breech. The process took hours, but the expense of my labor rewarded me with a new means of self-defense.

I turned my attention to the old mine shaft. The frame of a great waterwheel, the wheel now removed, stood beside the mouth of the mine's adit. An iron fence barred entrance to the mine shaft, but without a padlock it was easily managed open.

I moved carefully along the passage without the aid of a light source, hunched to avoid scraping my scalp on the rock ceiling. No Stone Age man made a home in this cave, only 19th-century men with pickaxes, shovels, and explosives.

In the depths of the shaft I had stashed one reserve I dared not store in the old explosives depot. While losing my hardtack and rum to thieves would have been a hardship, I could not risk losing the belt I'd smuggled into England. Sewn into it were Brazilian gold *reais* and several California gold dollars. This represented insurance should the need arise to flee this sodden country.

The dampness of the mire was not present that deep into the tunnel, but the mire's coldness was twice as severe down there. The brimstony stench was also doubly concentrated. To be one of those miners of yore, forced to breathe the fetor while descending toward the gates of Hell itself, all for a little tin to beat into cheap pots and bad jewelry.

When I detected the slope of the tunnel tilting downward toward the exhausted deposits below, I crouched and searched around my feet for my funds. I spent a fair amount of time in the dark attempting to locate the belt. Cursing my incompetence, I realized I would need to return to the tor and retrieve a lamp. It was only then my nose detected an odor amiss, the faint but unmistakable aroma of pipe tobacco—

A voice pierced the darkness. "Got you, you shifty-eyed scoundrel."

There came the *schick* of a wood match being struck. Its flame wove through the darkness like a moth. It landed on the wick of a kerosene lantern hanging from a peg the miners had hammered into the shaft wall decades before. When the warm light settled and my eyes adjusted, it was Barrymore standing at the lamp.

"Don't you get any ideas," he said.

He wore the proper black jacket, vest, and trousers of an English butler, one who'd been trained in the domestic service by his father at a young age. Unlike any butler I'd met or seen before, Barrymore brandished a hunting rifle with considerable menace.

"No, no, no." It was like he had to wrestle the words out to speak through his thick brogue. "Stay on all fours like the dog you are. Like the cold-blooded hound you released upon Sir Charles and my brother-in-law, you bastard."

Strapped diagonally across his chest like a bandolier was my money belt, heavy with its own ore.

"Take that gun you got there and set it aside. Then back off."

I placed the sawn-off shotgun on the rock floor. Barrymore kicked it down the slope of the mine shaft. The *clackety-clack* of it tumbling into the murky depths of the tin mine echoed from below. In the darkness, he did not make out my holstered pistol.

"So good of Cousin Henry to give you a day's leave," I said.

"Sir Henry has dismissed Missus Barrymore and me-self. Our household services are no longer required. We brought a considerable bad light to the Baskerville name, what with my escaped convict of a brother-in-law being found dead on the moor not far from the estate. And wearing the master's fine Canadian suit, to boot." He menaced me with the rifle. "Dead by your hand, that is. Your hellhound would have ripped out his throat if Selden hadn't broken his neck in the fall."

Against my protests, he cried, "Quiet, you! Selden is dead by your doing and my wife grieves so. Do not deny it!"

The sudden inflammation of passion ran counter to a lifetime of domestic training. He composed himself with as much composure one can muster in a cave while directing a hunting rifle at a helpless man on all fours.

"Sir Henry promised excellent references, as any gentleman would. But the events around Baskerville Hall have been disseminated across the country due to the newspapers. And, of course, thanks to the involvement of Mr. Sherlock Holmes. The Barrymore name is sullied for good due to you."

I started to protest again, but he would not hear of it.

"Oh, Sir Henry's severance was as generous as could be expected. And your uncle's will left us with a goodly amount as well." He gripped my money belt with one hand. Only briefly, though, before returning to keeping the rifle trained on me. "As you can see, I've acquired a significant source of funds to hold us until I can arrange a new situation." He spat when he said, "A severance for my grieving wife, whose brother you had slaughtered."

One hand on the wall of the shaft to steady myself, I gradually rose to my feet. Barrymore menaced the rifle barrel at me with a threatening grimace, as though perturbed I would stand without his permission. He did not prevent me from rising. The man was a butler, after all. He was not in the habit of giving orders to anyone other than the lower domestic staff.

"Put that pistol of yours down," he told me, now aware of my holster.

"You'll have to remove it yourself." I minded my hands, careful to keep them up and away from the Colt.

"I believe I'm in charge now." He brandished the rifle at me. "No more 'Barrymore, this, Barrymore, do that.'"

"Mind yourself. I am Rodger Baskerville the Second. Henry is my cousin. Charles was my uncle." With a hand out in warning, I chanced a step toward him. "You are not going to harm a Baskerville."

This is a technique common to dog training. A firm and even voice. No sudden changes in the dynamic or volume of your speech. You draw a verbal line in the sand between you and canine. Eyes on the beast's eyes to exert your domination. A single hand out as you approach, creating space around you while closing the distance between yourself and the canine. Legs spread to distribute your weight, as a boxer does. If the dog lunges, it will lunge at your hand and not your neck or leg, and you can retract your hand much faster than the others. If it strikes, not only do you retract, you cuff the beast across the head with your other. It will fall aside, flummoxed. You will be standing and it will be cowering from the blow. This will flummox it further.

You cannot read a dog's mind, but you can limit its options. This is the secret of training and mastery.

"Selden was my wife's little brother. She held him in her arms when he was born." Barrymore was staring down the rifle barrel at my outstretched hand. "He had a good heart led astray by the wickedness of this world."

Barrymore stood erect and forthrightly, as a proper butler would at all times. His trim pepper beard outlined his mouth and underlined his face's round Anglo-Irish features. In the many times I visited Baskerville Hall as

Jack Stapleton, I observed how he mannered himself as an older gentleman, although he was not old by any measure. The men of Dartmoor, the gentry who visited the estate, even Holmes and Watson: They all underestimated Barrymore, as British upperclassmen would and always will. Only I recognized he was a fit and virile man who'd grayed prematurely. He harbored the character and mental strength of a man a decade younger than they supposed him to be.

"They told me you were quite pleased to see his dead body on the moor," he said. "They told me you were smoking a celebratory cigar over Selden's cooling body."

"Who told you this?"

"Why, the doctor himself."

"Dr. Watson?" I cried out. My voice boomed down the depths of the shaft. "You would believe a word from that man's mouth or pen?"

"I trust him as much as I trust Sherlock Holmes himself."

"I was aghast when I discovered Selden dead. It sickened me to see him lying on the moor. No, man, listen: It was Sherlock Holmes dancing the devil's jig over his corpse."

"The good detective? I do not believe it!"

"I witnessed it with my own eyes. A more revolting sight I cannot name! For a man who claims to represent justice and reason, for him to rejoice in the death of another—there is no name for such immorality. And as for the good Dr. Watson, well, within minutes of your brother-in-law's death, he was reasoning aloud that Selden deserved what he'd gotten as penance for the crimes he'd committed."

"You lie!" Now Barrymore's voice echoed down the shaft to its depths. "You've lied to all of Dartmoor, calling yourself Stapleton—you told us your wife was your sister! And you permitted Sir Henry to woo her in public!"

His protests were nothing more than a wild-eyed dog baring his teeth and barking ferociously up at me. With one more step, I was within striking range. I'd pressed my luck as far as it could be pressed.

"You hear how I speak of Selden. I was aghast to see him dead on those rocks." I returned to the even, firm voice I used for training canines. "You know I am speaking the truth."

I could hear his breath whistling in and out of his nose. He ground his jaw as though chewing up the choices before him.

"Leave here with the belt," I said. "In a day or two, I will be gone."

With a great expulsion of air, he nodded grimly. "No, you will not." He retreated backwards three full steps, quite out of my reach. He drew the hunting rifle's sight to his eye and trained the bead on my forehead.

"Far as the world knows, you're already dead." And he cocked the hammer.

Eight

Even in the dancing light of the kerosene lamp, I recognized the hunting rifle. Uncle Charles displayed a matching set of them behind glass in the library. They were long-bore percussion rifles with engraved nickel-plated locks and deep chocolate-brown stocks of New England walnut. It surprised me to see him handle one so adeptly. Now I realize Barrymore would have accompanied my uncle on his hunting trips. He would have been responsible for oiling, loading, and storing the rifles.

He was no hunter, though. He was a servant. And he needed to work up the nerve to pull the trigger. His gaze remained focused on my outstretched hand, just like any trained and leashed dog would. Dogs and butlers. Both eat from bowls in the kitchen while the master dines at the table.

With my other hand, the hand normally reserved for cuffing the hound across his snout, I swept the kerosene lantern off its hook and flung it Barrymore. He reacted as any sane man would, by floundering and shrinking away. Thank heaven he didn't fire the rifle, as he would have dropped me dead then and there.

The lamp smashed on the rock floor. The oil splattered and the fire went up his trouser leg. He smashed at the flames with the flat of his hand. Crying out, he barreled past me and out the tunnel toward the entrance. Stupidly, the faster he ran, the more he fanned the flames.

In chase, I emerged from the mine tunnel unbuckling my holster. He'd raced across the island and jumped into the water at the edge. When I approached him, he was climbing up from the muck, wet to the bone. Along the way, he'd tossed aside my uncle's hunting rifle.

Teeth chattering in the cold mire air, he alternated between damning me and sputtering damnations at himself. In the mine shaft, he could not keep his eyes off my outstretched hand. Now he could not stop staring at the end of the barrel I leveled at him.

"Tell me news of Beryl."

"Your sister? Or, I should say, your wife?" He shook a disdainful head. "The shame you laid upon Sir Henry. He was mortified to learn he was wooing a married woman."

"Cousin Henry will live, and he will live well. Where is Beryl now?"

"They were planning to take her to London. It appears they have acquired enough information from her for now, however, for she remains at Merripit House."

"Free?"

"Confined under house watch, as is Anthony, your playacting manservant."

"Does she speak of me?"

Hands stuffed under his armpits and shivering, he snapped back, "How would I know of her state of mind? Do I have any business with your wife? I was in the service of Sir Henry, and now I am even without that. The Barrymores served the Baskervilles for generations, and to be dismissed under this black cloud—"

"And they still believe I am dead?"

"Mr. Holmes and Inspector Lestrade? Yes, yes. They departed Dartmoor believing you met the Maker in your escape across the mire." He regarded me for a moment. "You certainly fooled us with your butterfly net and that ridiculous straw hat you donned. When Mr. Holmes suggested you bred an enormous cross of Mastiff and English bloodhound, and trained it to kill on command, I laughed aloud! 'Mr. Stapleton? The scatterbrained catcher of butterflies?'"

"What of my dog."

"Dead. Mr. Holmes and the good doctor shot it down. As they should have!"

"Is he buried?"

"What say you! Should we have held a service for it as well?"

"And what of my other dog?"

"The bitch? I do not believe Scotland Yard knows of the female. The men only discovered her after the men from London departed."

"Are they feeding her?"

He regarded me once more. For the first time since emerging from the pool, he made himself erect again, standing as a butler should, although his numb fingers and hands remained tucked under his armpits.

"I do believe you care more for the dog than your wife. I shan't be surprised, a man who treated his wife as a lady of the night."

"Are they caring for her?"

"They can't get near the bitch. She's Fury incarnate. Anyone who gets too near her risks losing a hand or his face. Some speculate she knows her son is dead, although I cannot fathom how a dumb beast locked in a cellar could sense such a thing."

"Because she is an animal of pure instinct. Humans reasoned instinct out of our breed long ago. We treat it like a disease to be cured. It is to be nurtured." To myself, I absently murmured, "She is in hell."

He studied me for a long while. "I liked you better as Jack Stapleton, witless chaser of moths. A grown man living with his sister because he's incapable of securing a bride. Mrs. Barrymore would be scandalized to hear me say this, but—" He licked his bluing lips. "Your wife is one of the most beautiful women I've come across. And your manservant Anthony, well, he did not fool me at all." He sniffed. "He was never of the butler service. There has been in this isle neither a valet nor a footman as careless and slothful as your man."

"Tell me of your reasoning, then."

"Your stagecraft was over-planned. He was to be your manservant, but in your haste to play the part of an absentminded academic, you left the house with morning stubble and unkempt hair and tie knotted askew. A bachelor with no staff may have made such unseemly errors, but not one with a domestic on his payroll." He sniffed again. "Mrs. Barrymore said, whenever she crossed paths with him, he had whisky on his breath."

"It would have been rum. And he's…an old friend."

"You have poor taste in friends."

I raised the Colt. "Your tongue is growing lax. Where is my belt?"

Grudgingly, Barrymore motioned toward the thick muddy pool he'd doused himself in.

"What, you lost it?"

"It came off my shoulders. I was treading water. It is deep in there."

A small fortune at the bottom of a bog-girt.

"I followed you into the mire a few weeks ago," Barrymore said without prompting from me. "Mrs. Barrymore heard some scuttlebutt in town that you were prowling around Grimpen Mire. A few of the women in town suspected you were chasing more than butterflies. What manner of lady would meet a man in this godforsaken place, I cannot imagine—"

"And you wished to spy on us in the act?"

"You carried a pack quite laden down, I noticed. From a distance, I gathered you were hauling supplies to the old tin mine for some reason. By chance, I spied you enter the mine shaft with an oil lamp. I returned days later with my own lamp and found the belt. The moment I took it up, I surmised what it contained."

"You could have taken it then."

He was, as a butler would be, offended. "I am no thief. I surmised you planned to leave Dartmoor for some reason, perhaps to run up debts and leave bills unpaid. But," he admitted, grudgingly, "neither I nor Mrs. Barrymore ever learned of a significant debt associated with your name. So, I bit my tongue and told no one. I regret it mightily."

"Does your wife know of your suspicions? Did you tell her you discovered my stockpile out here?"

He refused to answer.

"Mrs. Barrymore might not hate you as much as she hates me," I said, "but she would most definitely turn you out of bed if she was to hear of your foreknowledge."

"Ridiculous," Barrymore muttered.

"You could have saved your brother-in-law's life, Barrymore."

"Are you threatening me?"

Now it was my turn to brandish a gun. I let it answer his question.

"You're going to retrieve the shotgun you kicked down the mine shaft," I told him.

"I am not going back in there."

I waved him toward the mine entrance. "You have matches, yes?"

"Completely wet."

"Did you bring another lamp?"

"Why would I do that?"

"Well, we're going to find that shotgun, one way or another, even if it means crawling around in the dark."

Still sopping, he began toward the mine entrance. He trudged slowly, obvious in his intent to make time for himself. I urged him along with the Colt.

Oily kerosene fumes washed out of the mouth of the mine shaft. He spun around and confronted me at the gate.

"This is not about a gun. You plan to execute me."

I waved him on.

"Murder!" he screamed, ducking away from me. "Murderer!"

He plunged headlong into the mine shaft before I could do anything. His screams ended as soon as he broached the shaft entrance. I scurried in after him.

In my earlier trips down the mine shaft, I'd noted several narrow forks leading off toward branches of the tin vein. Barrymore could have scampered down any of them. On occasion, I stopped in the dark and listened intently. His plodding footsteps echoing off the walls gave me some clue, but I could not be certain.

More so, I worried I would lose myself in the maze of forks and tunnels. To die down there was unfathomable. I'd survived this long. I would not perish chasing a butler around in the dark.

*

The gray light of the half-moon was dispersed by the mire's mist. At night, the sounds of the mire grow to a symphony of clacks and chirps and buzzes and rustlings. The heavy wings of owls passing overhead sound as mighty as the great flying lizards of antediluvian history.

A faint dark blotch appeared against the outline of the mine shaft entrance. The motion was mild, but against the utter stillness of the nighttime, it would only be missed if one were not waiting for it. Gently came a creak of the rusty gate being pushed open with gradual patience. Into the scattered and dim moonlight emerged Barrymore in silhouette.

With only outlines and splotches to work with, I had to guess, and I guessed well. The percussion cap exploded. The butt of the rifle kicked my shoulder. The outline fell to the ground in a slump.

The slug passed through his head. I doubt Barrymore felt anything. He gambled I'd given up on him and moved on. He gambled wrong.

I had waited six hours for him to appear. He'd spent a good while down in the mine hoping to find another exit. It's miraculous he managed to find his way back to the surface.

Exhausted from the long day, and with midnight approaching, I dragged his body into the mine tunnel. At the start of the steep descent, where the miners of yore had to tie themselves to a mounted rope to prevent from falling, I rolled his corpse until it began tumbling on its own. Down Barrymore went, past the depleted diggings and into the very lobby of Hell itself.

Nine

Rain was plentiful in the deep reaches of the Amazon, cleansing showers, fresh and purifying. In certain seasons, it comes down as warm as a lady's bathwater. Work in the fields did not stop for rain. Mud and mosquitoes were the order of the days. And the bunkhouse, constructed of packed clay, timber, straw, and burlap, did little to keep out the elements. Wasps would build nests in its walls, and we would have to periodically smoke them out. I toiled eight hard months in those fields, eating every meal outdoors.

Mrs. Harris required all field workers attend Sunday services at the Baptist church the *Confederados* built in Santarém. Our service was under a tent in the mud, while they communed in a whitewashed steepled house of worship. Although it rubbed against the others, most looking to Rome for their faith, it mattered little to me. My father's Anglican faith was not represented well on the north coast of Brazil. My mother's Catholicism, no matter her strenuous attempts to impress upon me a strict devotion, failed to weigh on my conscience. The Baptists and their love of brimstone and damnation merely taught me that any book, no matter how great or inspiring, can be turned against its own intentions.

After services, Mrs. Harris and her daughters served a fine Sunday luncheon on the expansive rear porch of Far Oaks. The family dined on the porch while us workers sat in the field, our backs against banana plant trunks, devouring the Americans' fried chicken, turnip greens, stewed beets, and chess pie. The servants pushed a spinet onto the veranda, which Mrs. Harris played while her daughters sang hymns for the family and workers. To catcall the young ladies was to invite a beating from Antônio, who administered it without so much as a glance at Maj. Harris for permission.

After one of the services, Antônio called me over to the porch. "Major Harris, this is the precocious young man I spoke to you about."

The Major eyed me up and down, his bushy gray waxed moustache twitching. "Antônio here says you speak the Queen's English."

"Rodger Baskerville the Second," I introduced myself. "Heir to the baronetcy."

Maj. Harris harrumphed. "I do say, you possess a parrot's skill of mimicry, but I will not have such bald-faced fictions propagated before me or my family."

"Major, please, there is more here." Antônio prompted me: "Recite for the Major 'The Charge of the Light Brigade.'"

Feeling uncomfortably like a trained poodle, I did my best in my overalls and filth to stand at attention and narrate Tennyson's opus. Halfway through the third stanza, the Major shook his head and stopped me.

"It's most impressive," he told Antônio. "His command of the accent would have fooled me had I not known the truth of the matter. But how can you suggest such a rough creature come into my home and teach my fair daughters their forefather's literature?"

"He can do more than recite poetry," Antônio said. "He's cognizant of English history, and well-versed in Shakespeare's plays. He knows of Aristotle and Euclid, and speaks Latin—"

"How do you know?" he demanded of Antônio. "Do *you* speak Latin?"

"Major," Antônio said sheepishly, "I am a practicing—"

"A Papist, yes, yes." The Major retreated toward the house, the foot of his walking stick tapping with each step. He called over his shoulder, "No more of your fictions, boy! Not on this estate!"

Antônio scolded me after the Major was out of earshot. "I told you: No more of your Baskerville nonsense."

"I never asked to teach his dainty flowers a damn thing." I spat on the ground. "To hell with him."

He struck me upside the head. "Never speak ill of the Major or his family again. Hear me? Back to work."

*

One morning, as we toiled the banana fields in a stifling heat, a giant butterfly as large as a prayer card circled me. It danced round my head and before my face. It fluttered over to the field hand nearest me, a broad-shouldered bald man named César. Rugged as a granite mountain and chestnut-brown, he gently offered the butterfly a perch on his outstretched hand. The delicate creature faced him and flexed its wings occasionally, much as a ballet dancer might stretch her legs after a performance.

"Behold God's majesty," César said in a strong Ecuadorean accent.

With skin calloused from a lifetime of hard labor, and fingers flattened by years of being smashed between farm equipment and tools, he gently took the butterfly in his boxing-glove hands and spread its wings. The butterfly, strangely sympathetic to his fascination, lay back and allowed him to pin back its wings. Spread wide, it was over eight inches from tip to tip. The Amazon's lusty humidity made everything more magnificent.

"*Mariposa tigre,*" he said, named so due to its dark stripes against the gold background of its triangular wings. I should add I do not believe this particular specimen has yet to be categorized. If I'd known then to collect it for scientific study, I would have named it *Baskervillius* after my heritage. Even after six months of waiting, I remained naive enough to believe a letter would arrive any day greeting me from Baskerville Hall and welcoming me back to the fold.

"Look at the color of its wings," César murmured. "No oil master in Europe could mix such shades on his palette."

And with that, he released the insect, which resumed its chaotic dance across the field and up into the jungle canopy.

"You can spend a lifetime admiring their beauty," César said as he returned to his work. "Each is unique, just as we as God's children are."

*

When Antônio needed an extra hand around the plantation, I made sure to volunteer, thinking I might prove myself at a task that would lift me from the banana fields.

The task I proved myself in was handling the dogs. Maj. Harris' pride was Jupiter, his warhorse, but the real money came from Augustus, a Brazilian *Fila* who sired numerous whelps the plantation trained and sold to neighboring farms and ranches. Antônio showed me how to approach the dogs, how to make them respect me and how to make them fear me. He taught me how to distinguish between breeds, and what to look for when evaluating one: Its gums, its posture, its stance. The clearness of its pupils. The smell of its breath, not too sweet, not too foul.

He was not a dog trainer by trade. He simply understood them well. Antônio was more than a jack-of-all-trades, he was a soul capable of doing anything well. If we managed to bring in a bumper crop off the fields, he could whip up the most delicious meal for us over the campfire as a reward. Give him a guitar or a flute or a drum, and he'd produce a song. Even though he didn't work the fields, if the need arose, he was capable of going into the grove and harvesting bunches with surprising efficiency. His machete's blade would sing through the air. And his speed created a competition among the other men, who would hasten their pace to keep up with him. Rarely did anyone harvest more bunches in an hour than Antônio.

"Learn how dogs think and you will rule men." He told this wisdom to me one evening after leading an informal competition in the banana fields. "Be the top dog. The junior dogs will leap to claim your attention. When they hunt in packs, the young ones run ahead while the old dogs hang back. When a young *Fila* presents the swamp deer with its neck snapped, the top dog sniffs at the accomplishment and struts away unimpressed. It only makes the young ones work harder next time. This is how you will learn to manage other men, Rodrigo. I have watched you these months. You are a different breed than the others. You will become the top dog after I move on from Far Oaks. The junior dogs will do all the work for you."

I came to befriend the dogs in the Harris kennel, even earning the difficult respect of Augustus, a crusty dog set in his ways and vicious in temper. Antônio expressed his admiration at the speed I was able to begin feeding Augustus from my hand. Martin Harris, the Major's only son, used a stick across Augustus' hackles when ordering him around. Augustus simpered and slouched his shoulders in obeisance every time. Antônio confided Martin Harris was unnecessarily cruel to his dogs. "But they're his dogs to do with as he wishes."

Antônio was schooled. He could lecture about bananas as well as he could harvest them. He knew of the international market for them in São Paulo. He spoke of university men studying the banana to improve yield and make the plant resistant to disease. Antônio could repair a wagon axle. He managed the plantation finances, I learned later, although he was not trusted to manage the Harris household money. No matter; he was indispensable to Far Oaks.

From all I've told you about the plantation, it should not surprise you when I say the Harris family did not treat him well. The lesson he'd taught me about top dogs and young whelps, well, he forgot it when it came to his own relationship with Maj. Harris. Antônio labored to prove himself to Maj. Harris, and the Major merely sniffed at the hard work and scolded Antônio for not exerting himself a bit more. Antônio worked that much harder to prove himself the next time.

*

As I worked the dog pen filling feed bowls and checking paws and pupils, a young bespectacled man in formal attire arrived by carriage. His dark suit was clean and pressed, and his hat was crisp and new. He walked gingerly across the muddy drive to meet Maj. Harris, who remained dry under the eaves of the double-door entrance.

"Who is he?" I asked Antônio.

"A businessman with a proposition. The Major is exploring other sources of income."

I wanted to be in that pressed suit. I wanted a crisp hat and a leather valise tucked under my arm. This was a man who carried cards announcing his arrival. I wanted a card of my own, *Sir Rodger of Baskerville* embossed in silver script.

"Not any kind of businessman," Antônio said. "A speculator of some kind."

"Speculator?"

"A fancy name for a gambler." He added softly, "I wonder if he knows who he's gambling against."

It was my first indication of his fear for the Major, and my first inkling that I should fear him too.

*

One night a few weeks later, with a spectacular storm battering Far Oaks, Antônio burst into the bunkhouse. We were settled around a pot-bellied stove keeping warm and playing cards. A bottle of rum was being passed around. Mrs. Harris disapproved, and it was quickly secreted under a pillow.

Antônio was not going to report anyone to Maj. Harris that night, however. "Rodrigo," he called to me. "Get dressed. No time for questions."

Before we left, he barked to the other men: "Do not stray out tonight. Everyone remains in his bunk. Hear me?"

As we scampered through the rain toward the mansion, I witnessed through the drawing room windows what I can only describe to be a scene drawn from a dream—a morbid, profane dream. Martin Harris was posing a man against the window as though preparing to take his photograph, but no camera was assembled in the drawing room. When the subject turned his head, I saw it was the bespectacled man I'd asked Antônio about.

The speculator cooperated with Martin's every request, nodding in agreement and stepping to his left and right as directed. After fussing around, Martin took him by the shoulders and directed him aside the windows, so his back was to a drawing room wall. This, I realized later, was so the bullet would not break the window glass.

On the other side of the room, easily visible through the windows, stood Maj. Harris at the fireplace hearth. He held in one hand a Colt Navy Revolver with brass fittings. He rammed a rod down the barrel to pack the ball tight against the powder and paper. Before my foot reached the servants' entrance, Maj. Harris straightened his arm, steadied his aim, and fired. The report rattled the windows and echoed across the yard.

Inside, we found Martin Harris' young wife lying across a couch in a dark room off the main hall. Rain dripped down the windows behind her. The flame of a kerosene lantern flickered from the center table casting shadows all directions.

"It's over," she called out. "The man was breaking apart our family. It had to be done."

We hurried to the drawing room. It was my first time in the house. Antônio knew his way through the place. He later told me, Maj. Harris had never so much as offered him a chair over the countless times he was inside reporting to him.

Maj. Harris and his son Martin stood at a table beside the fireplace murmuring between themselves. A pistol case lay open before them with a walnut exterior polished to a sheen. Its inner green velvet molding was for the specimen in Maj. Harris' hands. As they spoke, Martin tenderly disassembled the pistol and replaced each piece in its proper fitting.

"Right over there," Martin told us, as though we somehow might have missed the body sprawled on the floor.

The two had evidently prepared for this, as several old sheets had been laid down to catch whatever blood the speculator may have spilled. There was remarkably little, though. And, to my surprise, the man was not dead. At least, not yet.

The ball had penetrated his forehead, creating a deep finger-width hole in the front of his skull. Perhaps the heat of the blast cauterized the wound. Perhaps the ball struck with so much force, the pressure staunched the blood. In any case, the man was conscious. He bore a frightened but accepting expression.

"A confidence man." Maj. Harris shut the pistol case with a resounding *clop*. "If we'd not stopped him, he would have taken Far Oaks from us."

Antônio later explained fragments of the situation to me. The speculator had approached Maj. Harris to survey Far Oaks for evidence of oil deposits. Unlike the generational family farms and plantations along the Amazon River, the *Confederados* had cleared and improved the land outside Santarém only within the last two decades. As no other landholders had claimed the parcels surrounding Far Oaks, Maj. Harris was in a position to increase his holdings on the cheap if a reservoir of the crude was detected.

The peculiarities of Brazil's mineral and oil laws were the rub. To prevent foreign speculation from running rampant, the law required a native Brazilian citizen's name on the deed when filing for mineral rights.

I kneeled beside the speculator. His breath was raspy. "It's understandable," he said in Portuguese. His pupils remained fixed on the ceiling above us, as though blind to my presence. "I overstepped the bounds of propriety. The Harris family is a noble family. It is not my place to profit at nobility's expense."

Up close, I saw the man was unsightly and spindly, with a pronounced Adam's apple. His pasty face was cankered by acne scars and topped with a patch of weedy hair. He bore an elongated neck with a bend in it, like a dog's hind leg. His spectacles were missing. Later, I would learn he had pocketed them in preparation for his execution.

His thick, oafish lips were dry, and his voice sticky. "May I have water?"

Without hesitation, Antônio poured him a small glass from a pitcher on the sideboard. When he turned to carry the glass to the speculator, Martin Harris struck him across the face.

"Are you mad?"

With grim and undeterred resolve, Antônio brought me the glass. I put my hand under the speculator's neck to lift his lips. Most of the water ran out the corners of his mouth. He sputtered up the rest onto me.

"I apologize," he said, not to me, but to the Major and his son. "I do not know what came over me." And he expired.

Martin rebuked Antônio a second time. "Never do anything within this house without our permission."

"Yes, sir," Antônio said.

Across the main table were charts and a raft of paperwork. A surveyor's map of Far Oaks was marked with oblong outlines of suspected oil reserves. They bounded almost all of the property and extended out beyond its demarcations to the adjoining unimproved jungle.

With the surveyor's map and his accompanying report was the modified deed to Far Oaks. João Abreu de Sousa was recorded on the property deed before Maj. Harris' name. Next to the Anglo-Saxon name, the speculator's name appeared exotic. The deed, however, was written entirely in Portuguese. It was Maj. Harris' name that was alien, as alien as the chess pie the Harris family served every Sunday in the heart of the Amazon jungle.

It mattered not—Abreu de Sousa was dead, and the Harris family remained standing.

Today, I cannot help but consider that they were angry this ugly clod of a man—who appeared as intelligent as the Neolithic man who once resided in the very tor I'm writing within—that *this* man would lay claim to a fraction of their wealth. On the Great Chain of Being the Harris family measured themselves against, Abreu de Sousa stood several links beneath them.

More astonishingly, they had somehow convinced him of this as well, for he posed against the wall as though being honored with a portrait.

Maj. Harris folded the surveyor's report and deed and hid them in a kangaroo-sized pocket of his officer's uniform. Martin Harris hurriedly rolled up the surveyor's map and put it away.

"We will wait four months," Maj. Harris announced. "When Abreu de Sousa cannot be located, we'll claim in court he's either left the country, drowned on a ship voyage, or has simply gone missing in the jungle, as many such surveyors due. Once we can legally strike him from the deed, we begin drilling. Just so his family doesn't get any ideas once the oil starts a-flowin'." He patted his pocket where the reports lay hidden. "These valuables I will store under lock and key."

Martin lit a cigar using one of the oil lamps on the mantel. "Your work tonight is to get this trash off Far Oaks. Find a location well away from the plantation."

And so Antônio and I were tasked with hauling a corpse loosely mummified in Mrs. Harris' old bed sheets out to the wagon. The Amazon would claim Abreu de Sousa, just as Grimpen Mire claimed the hunter. From the earth we come, to the earth we return.

Ten

Rain continued to pelt us as we hauled Abreu de Sousa's corpse through the jungle. I swore I could see another horse-drawn wagon behind us in the distance. It was a miserable night and not one I would expect to see many travelers cutting ruts into the muddy narrow road winding through the Amazon.

"You see these European Portuguese and you think they are like you and me," Antônio said, meaning Abreu de Sousa. "They are from a different world, Rodrigo. Titles and nobility are credentials unparalleled to them. Pedigree is more important than any doctorate or baccalaureate. Have you read *Hamlet*?"

"With my father. We read scenes together." He let me read the Danish prince while he played Polonius or Claudius.

"What is the problem paramount to the Danish prince?"

"Revenge in the name of his father."

"No. The play is about restoring order. The murder of the king upset the great balance of the Universe. Hamlet's uncle has profaned the throne. The prince must restore the crown to a monarch so designated by God."

Again, I faintly made out the wet glimmer of a wagon a half-mile or more behind us. I wondered if the moon was playing tricks with my mind. I had seen and heard much that night, more than some men see in a lifetime.

"Abreu De Sousa willingly gave up his life because the Major and his son convinced him they descend from English nobility. The Major claims the Harris name is recorded before the Battle of Hastings. He believes his family is listed in the Domesday Book. He would have us all call him 'Sir Maj. Harris,' but such European affectations offend his American sensibilities."

"But is he of nobility?"

"The Major was a dental surgeon in the United States. In Mississippi, he was Dr. Harris of Greensville. Here in Brazil, he is Maj. Harris of Far Oaks."

"But I don't understand. Why did he shoot the man?"

"Far Oaks stands on shaky finances. The Major is desperate for a new source of income. When Abreu de Sousa went and found oil—" Antônio whistled. "The arithmetic changed. They weren't about to share a dime with him. And with his name on the deed, they suspected he might litigate to take possession of the plantation."

"He did not strike me as that sort of man."

"Nor I, but we are not the head of the Harris family. They are the outsiders here. It only inflames their already-suspicious minds."

"I cannot believe he stood there and let them shoot him dead."

"He upset the great balance of the Universe," Antônio said. "Order had to be restored." He added, "That is why I am always suspicious of European title and pomp. It's a fever in their minds that never cools."

The rain eased. Over the sound of our horses clopping through the rainforest mud, thick as wet cement, I strained to hear similar sounds in the distance behind us. With only the moon for illumination, I could not ascertain if another wagon trailed us.

Antônio brought our wagon to a halt. "We carry him a hundred yards through the trees that way. There we will throw him off a cliff into a ravine. No one will find him."

If we hauled the corpse through the dark jungle without aid, we would certainly have become lost within minutes. Antônio knew this area for some reason, but even he could not navigate it on the light of the moon alone. Cunningly, he had come prepared.

As we progressed through the thick undergrowth carrying our load, Antônio would halt every thirty or forty feet and produce a tin from his pocket. In it contained a grease of his own concoction, its primary ingredient being a fungus called *flor-de-coco* by the locals. This agaric grows at the base of decaying palm trees. During daylight hours, it appears to the uneducated eye a variety of oyster mushroom. At night, however, this wondrous mushroom emits a steady faerie-green luminescence.

"It will glow for hours in this form," he told me. "I make small batches and keep a tin of it handy." He handed me a spare tin of the stuff.

With the luminescent blue-green grease smeared on the trunk of a tree, we pressed on into the jungle with our weighty assignment. With each trunk marked, our trail back to the wagon was apparent.

At the ravine came a sharp gust that put a chill through me. On the count of three, we swung Abreu de Sousa's body over the cliff's edge. His corpse plunged through the tops of trees growing at the base of the ravine. A succession of wood cracks and crashes sounded as he fell until, gratefully, all was silent once more.

"If it's not the snakes, a jaguar will get us," Antônio said. "*Vamos.*"

If only our greatest menace that night were the jungle's natural predators. As we followed the trail of *flor-de-coco* grease back to our wagon, we sensed a presence on the road. Ahead, a lantern sparked and warmed.

Antônio halted me with a raised hand. He did not need to silence me.

A low growling sawed through the still nighttime air. Three sharp barks went up. Men murmured among themselves. There came a rattling of cages and chains.

"Is that Augustus?" Antônio whispered to me.

"That was my very thought," I whispered in return.

Caged in this other wagon was Maj. Harris' prize *Fila*, a colossal Brazilian Mastiff with silky musculature, a clamp-like jaw capable of crushing a whole coconut, and a hair-trigger temper. His cage was too small for him, and yet he still paced it as though memorizing its dimensions. *Fila* are ferocious in loyalty and in service. They are *onceiro*, that is, jaguar hunters. I know of no other domesticated beast capable of tracking down and killing the great jungle cats. *Fila*, they thirst for the chance.

A human whistle went up from the road. A second whistle was sounded in return. From the darkness came a rapid metallic clanking.

"They're setting Augustus loose," Antônio hissed. "We're done for!"

In the blind terror of the moment, we scattered opposite directions into the jungle. I knew better than to run back toward the ravine. In the dim light, we barely noticed the cliff's edge until we were upon it. In my terror, I would certainly have ended my young life hundreds of feet below, somewhere near Abreu de Sousa's wrapped corpse.

As I scrambled through the jungle, flailing the hanging vines and branches aside with both arms, I finally made out in full the second wagon. One man stood beside it while the other was in the bed crouched over the cage holding Augustus. Unthinking, they'd brought a lantern with them to aid their work, which only night-blinded them. They could hear us rustling through the jungle, but they could not see us clearly. I exited the overgrowth and circled around down the road from the wagon. From there, I watched their machinations without making a sound of my own. More importantly, I was downwind. I kept my bluish-green glowing hands deep in my pockets for fear of giving myself away.

Now I saw all. At the side of the wagon was Martin Harris, the Major's son. In the flatbed, crouched beside Augustus' cage, was a *Confederado* named Duffy. He was a Harris cousin whose family owned a land grant, another ersatz Southern plantation named *Esperança Branca*.

Duffy opened the cage and led Augustus off the wagon. Martin jammed a handful of cloth into the great hound's face. He was giving Augustus a deep whiff of my work shirt from the bunkhouse. Martin riled up Augustus by cinching the chain around his neck tight and taking him by the scruff of his neck and yanking hard. He whipped the striking stick across the *Fila*'s snout, an act of domination with no promise of reward. In no time, Augustus saw only blood.

"Get 'em now—go get 'em!"

Augustus bounded snarling into the jungle. In no time, he would pick up my scent and circle around to me.

Duffy produced a shotgun from the wagon. Martin cocked the hammer of his American revolver. I was trapped.

Augustus was upon me with little warning. He knocked me back and pinned my shoulders down. With one arm across my neck to prevent him from worrying at my throat, I grappled with his jowls and jaws using my only free hand. I managed to repeat his name in soothing tones, just as I did at his kennel every morning and evening when I fed and brushed him. His powerful teeth scraped at my forearm, but I held it in place, resolute and fearful of him wrapping his mandibles around my jugular. With all courage I could muster, I continued to wrestle with him and gain his recognition.

After a harrowing length of time on my back, he did recognize me. His growls quieted and his teeth quit scraping at my arm. His sensitive nose began snuffling my face and chest. I dared to hold his head with both hands. His massive glistening snout covered my face with little wet kisses. His wet eyes, shining in the light of the lantern up the road, confessed to the presence of an old weary soul. If your religion does not recognize the essential truth of dogs' humility and generosity, then your god is not my god.

"Did you get 'em?" the lantern-blind Martin called out to Augustus. "Where are you, boy?"

In our grappling, I had covered Augustus' head and neck with Antônio's luminescent grease. Savage bluish-green faerie-fire outlined his eyes and snout. His copious saliva thinned the grease and sent it dripping from his jowls like spectral hellfire.

Down the road, without warning, Antônio burst from the jungle and charged Duffy. They struggled, and the shotgun erupted into the night air. Martin charged around the wagon with his revolver up. He cried out Antônio's full name in warning and made a bead on his head. His hesitation was due to the two men locked in struggle, and his inability in the dim light to get off a clean shot.

With two urgent words from me—"Go, now!"—Augustus leapt with a throaty growl and charged the men. I honestly did not know whom he intended to maul.

He selected Martin Harris.

I enjoy imagining Martin's final moments. A massive hound leaping upon him with a snarl, a beast larger than the jungle cats that roam the Amazon at night, its eyes and snout outlined in a ghastly glow and its jowls dripping liquid flame. His screams ceased almost as soon as they began, as Augustus lunged for his throat and worried at it until it was incapable of voicing any sound at all. With an efficiency that still gives me pause, Augustus deprived Martin Harris of his soul within seconds.

If Martin had spent more time tending to the animals he sold off to the neighboring farms, he might have survived the night. To Augustus, Martin was merely a cruel authority, one scent of many in his personal catalog. Each morning, Martin Harris emerged from the mansion thick with the Parisian *eau de cologne* he used. If I could smell it, Augustus would have been overpowered by it, and he would have been offended by it. Every encounter Augustus had with Martin Harris was accompanied by strikes from a stick, the only tool he had any expertise with when it came to communicating with the dogs in his kennel.

Having made quick work of Martin Harris, Augustus considered his next prey. The two men's struggle had paused as they witnessed this terrible virescent hellhound rip the life from Martin's throat. Antônio stumbled backwards, unsure whom he needed to defend himself from now. Duffy fumbled futilely to yank back the hammer of the shotgun and get a bead on the glowing Mastiff charging him. Duffy's shrieks cut through the air for but a moment. Then he too was dead.

Augustus was painted for war, and now the war was over. He strode between the two sprawled bodies sniffing for evidence of remaining life. Satisfied, he trotted back to me dripping hellfire from his snout. He rested on his haunches and panted. With a green, greasy hand, I stroked his head. His tail thumped against the muddy road.

Antônio rose, gathered himself, and carefully approached Martin Harris' cooling body. He spat on him and swore, "*Monte de merda!*" He retrieved Duffy's shotgun. "The fool I was to come out here without a sidearm!"

I was already admiring Harris' Colt revolver in my hand, nickel-plated with a black walnut grip and scrollwork engraved down the barrel. "Why do you think—?"

"They sent us out here to dispose of their garbage, and they followed us to finish the job. Dead men tell no tales. I never thought I would be a man to say, 'Leave them where they died,' but I will not bury these *cabrãos*."

After a long rest, I said what needed to be said: "We cannot return to Far Oaks. We have to get as far away from here as possible."

He considered it. "There may be a way. We return in the wagon and say we did exactly as the Major ordered. There will be confusion, but they will not accuse us of murder. How could they explain sending two men after us without appearing guilty? When Martin and Duffy fail to return, they will investigate and discover the two dead. We then feign innocence.

They will believe Martin and Duffy lost control of Augustus and the dog killed them both. Which it did."

Up until that moment, I trusted Antônio as an expert on all matters. He was a man who'd earned every *real* paid to him. He enjoyed the cadences of the Catholic life—the regularity of the Catholic calendar, the festivals and holidays and baptisms and marriages. He was my senior in the ways of the world, save for the hearts of corrupt men.

"Returning to Far Oaks is a death sentence," I said. "They will not listen to our excuses. When the Major finds his son dead, he will kill us out of simple rage. We must flee. Once this scene is discovered, there will be notices at all ports and train stations. There will be a price on our heads." I pled with him. "We must make for Panama tonight."

Antônio refused. He began constructing other alibis we might use, each flimsier than its predecessor.

"The Major will set a steep reward for the murders of his only son and his brother's eldest," I said. "The longer we spend here arguing, the greater the chance we are caught."

On the wagon, Antônio groaned. "The weight of these murders will hang about our necks for the rest of our lives."

"We murdered no one. Augustus did all the killing."

Antônio's peered at me with long, wet eyes. "When Kingdom comes, I do not believe our Creator will grant your defense any weight."

Tuesday, the Twenty-third of October, Eighteen hundred and eighty-eight

Eleven

The time has passed for cowering in this tor like a beaten dog. The men of Dartmoor know of my presence in Grimpen Mire. So intent on my destruction, they've demonstrated their resolve in braving the bog's dangers. I'm a better man than any one of them, but I am cognizant of the long odds I play against. One day soon, they will come again to kill me.

Today will not be that day.

More than survival, time in the mire has afforded me time to consider, imagine, and plan. It's not enough to survive. A grandmaster knows victory is not achieved by preserving material and groveling among the rear squares of the board. Victories come from decisive attacks, even if they are executed via cunning rather than brute force or with advantageous numbers.

Numbers: Whom may I count with me? According to Barrymore, Antônio remains in the village of Grimpen, confined to Merripit House where we made a home. In the New World, he and I lived, and quite nearly perished, side-by-side. Certainly I may scrawl his name on the sheet under the heading *Allies*.

My precious Beryl, I am less certain of. Certainly my love for her remains steadfast. Yes, yes, she forced me to bind her up our last night together. What of it? I did no harm to her. I did not strike her, nor did I hold a blade to her throat. Calmly, I reasoned with her: If my plan failed, then being discovered bound and gagged provided her an air-clad alibi. She could claim complete innocence in my plots. No constable or magistrate would question her explanation.

Nevertheless, in my list of allies, I must place a solid question mark beside Beryl's name.

Nero is dead. I still grieve for him. Like myself, he survived a long journey across the Atlantic to this gloomy island, spent a fair amount of time in gloomier Grimpen Mire, and was cut down by Sherlock Holmes and his prattling, loosely woven chains of so-called deduction.

Nero I honor by listing as a friend, but I must strike through his name with a thick line.

Agrippina is the final ally I may claim. If Barrymore and the men of Dartmoor are to be trusted—questionable! questionable!—Nero's mother

Agrippina lives at Merripit House in the cellar of the old stable. Agrippina was my unwavering ally in all of this. Through her, I trained her son Nero. Agrippina's love for me scorched the green fire of jealousy in her son's heart and made him pliable to my wishes. It is as Antônio instructed me years before in the banana fields of Brazil: Through Agrippina, I claimed the mantle of top dog, and all Nero could do was strive to prove himself to me, and therefore her.

On the next page, I list my enemies.

Uncle Charles is dead. His shaky heart and backwards beliefs in a superstitious tale of hellhounds and witch curses snuffed out his soul. He forsook my father, cut off my family from support we desperately required, and denied me as a member of the Baskerville family. My actions are defended thusly.

Cousin Henry lives, but solely due to the prying of Sherlock Holmes. And the prying of Dr. Watson, I must include. I must also append to my list of enemies Dr. James Mortimer (my Uncle Charles' physician and friend), as it was his undertaking to travel to London and enlist the detective and his biographer.

Down the *Enemies* list I add Barrymore—dead, by George!—Mrs. Barrymore, Laura Lyons, the men of Dartmoor…their number grows depressingly lopsided against my list of allies. The question mark beside Beryl's name smolders on the page.

Perhaps my current situation is due to a failure to appreciate the range of forces arrayed against me. To make sense of it all, I will attempt to diagram connections between the individuals.

All lines intersect at Holmes' name.

Can I muster the wit and steel to kill one more? Shall I dream of escape from this mire and freedom on the other side? I admit the long odds of success. Odds perhaps even longer than surviving in Grimpen Mire for another week.

Punishing Sherlock Holmes is about the only satisfying outcome I'm capable of imagining. Even if I'm caught and capitally punished, surely no one will forget the name of the man who destroyed him. Wherever the name "Sherlock Holmes" goes, my name will follow.

*

I spent the early morning plumbing the frigid depths of the mine shaft. I am desperate to recover the shotgun Barrymore kicked into the grim darkness. After hours of search, I emerged shivering uncontrollably and with rope-burned hands, cursing my luck and cursing Barrymore to Hell. With my belt of gold coins sunk at the bottom of the mire, that was two ways he'd hobbled me. Although I acquired Uncle Charles' beautiful nickel-plated hunting rifle from Barrymore, the butler only carried three rounds for it, one of which I used to put him down. Mark that as a third way he hobbled me.

Back at the tor, I reduced my meager possessions to travel essentials. An old black wig and beard, the same I'd used when following Holmes and Watson around London. Spirit gum for application thereof. A tin of the luminescent grease Antônio taught me to make from the palm tree fungus. A purse of pounds sterling I'd fortuitously stashed in the tin mine separate from the money belt of gold coins. A skinning knife. My Colt and spare ammunition. An old wool overcoat effectively concealed the holstered pistol.

And, of course, this journal, so I may continue recording my plea to all readers.

So equipped, I made my way out of the mire and toward Princetown. I traveled under the cover of a stiff fog coasting apparition-like across the moor. No one engaged me until I reached an inn near the Princetown train station, where I secured a room for the night.

The bookseller on Tavistock Road offered a slim selection of Bibles. Conscious of my limited funds, I selected the cheapest Authorized Version on the shelf. The bookseller commended my choice with a trace of sarcasm. He was more agreeable when I produced a five-pound note and held it before his liver-spotted face.

"It is vital this Bible reaches a man in the village of Grimpen. Can you ensure delivery before sundown?"

His spectacles outlined twin dull-brown pupils. They considered my offer with the hesitation of a man who needs to be convinced he is not accepting a bribe before he will accept it.

"Sundown? To the village? Best I can offer is delivery tomorrow after morning tea."

"I am in the area soliciting for a children's fund. The people of Dartmoor have been most generous. Unfortunately, in my haste to reach the station platform, I realized my manners had failed me and I'd not left a gift for one of our benefactors there. It's a most embarrassing situation."

"Certainly a reasonable man would understand if your gift reached him a day later."

The five-pound note did not salivate him. Perhaps I was pushing too hard and giving his greed a reason to stand on its guard.

"Considering the other benefactors in Dartmoor all received a consideration from our charity before I departed, I am concerned word might—" I offered the bookseller a sheepish smile. "Well, villages in the country are infamous for loose tongues wagging at public houses."

"They are indeed." My candor softened him up. "I suppose

considering your unusual circumstances—" He moved a hand of ink-stained fingers toward my proffered banknote. "I could arrange a delivery this evening."

"As soon as possible. If this is not sufficient for your attention, I will locate a delivery boy and acquire speedy service myself." And I made as though preparing to exit.

He relieved me of the note. "I will arrange it immediately."

"Wrapped, please," I said of the Bible. "To be delivered to Merripit House. I require a moment to prepare a card to accompany it."

At the inn, I requested a hot meal be sent to my room. The peasant food was divinity itself. Any other day, I would strenuously argue English cuisine is, by any measure, the worst fare in the world. To be raised on the lively Brazilian diet is to expect a sensuousness at the table. Since my arrival on this island, I've been subjugated to England's bland, greasy meals, where each dish on the plate mingles and congeals with the others to form a bath of oil the same color as Grimpen Mire's murky pools.

But after subsisting on canteen water, hardtack, and salted pork, a hot meat pie with peas and mash washed down with a glass of the local bitters…kingly.

With precious time evaporating, I worried my exercise with the bookseller was an expensive and futile mistake. Hours passed. I whittled away my freedom before the room's fireplace, smoking and reading the paper. Each train whistle from the station sounded like clock chimes—Death's knocking.

My anxiousness was quelled when I spotted from my window an older man in a fine black suit idling at the newsstand below. Between checking his pocket watch and tipping his derby for passing ladies, he craned his neck to study the upper floors of the inn I resided in. With some haste, I assembled my disguise, armed myself, and hurried down the stairs.

When Antônio recognized me, he lit up with a great smile. I worried of a trap, of Sherlock Holmes and Scotland Yard appearing from doorways and shadows to shackle me. Or gun me down.

"It's only me." Antônio, beaming, took my forearms and shook sense into me. "I am alone."

In the privacy of my room, we embraced. Once rid of the disguise, we arranged chairs to face one other and share news. The conversation slipped between Portuguese and Spanish, as is our wont. Antônio's fresh tobacco was most welcome as well.

"The men from London believe you are dead," he told me. "The locals around Dartmoor have kept the secret well. They want you quite dead. I told you before, the folk in these parts were loyal to Sir Charles, and they are warming to Sir Henry. But if they keep losing men to the bog, I am certain they will have no choice but to reach out to Scotland Yard for assistance."

"What say you? 'Losing' men to the bog?"

"The hunter they hired, the bog claimed him. And Barrymore's wife is inconsolable. First her brother, and now her husband. She's convinced he entered the mire seeking you out—"

"He did. And I killed him, just as I killed their hired assassin."

"*You* did? That is not what they told the others in town."

"Of course not. There were eight or ten of them there, not counting their useless dogs. Dogs they cannot control, mind you. These English fools believe you can just let the dog go and it will return with your quarry. They have no sense of managing their hounds."

"Did you have to kill Barrymore, though? He and his wife are humble stock."

"He came for my money belt."

"His wife claims he wanted revenge for what you did to Selden."

"He said as much to me as well. Tell me: Did he strike you as the sort of man to brave the mire's bog-traps for revenge? Retribution for an in-law, and a vicious escaped convict at that?"

Antônio admitted Barrymore did not seem such a man. "So you killed him over a money belt?"

"I killed him because he dared push a rifle barrel to my nose. If you were there, you would back my fury."

Antônio recoiled. My firebrand did not invigorate him. The man sitting before me was a husk of the bullwhip I knew in Brazil.

"Tell me," I said, lightening. "How is Merripit House?"

"Standing. Scotland Yard turned over the household thoroughly. They've placed me under house confinement until they decide what to do with me. They still believe I am Anthony of York, a one-time teacher at St. Oliver. Once they realize I am not of this country, I expect to be deported."

"Yet you escaped your confinement to make it here?"

"More than a teacher, or a domestic at Merripit House, they see me as an old doddering fool incapable of mischief." He clutched his thin head of pepper-gray hair. "Our time together has aged me prematurely. Instead of a man facing his fortieth year in this world, they see a man well beyond his prime." He smirked. "My feigned hard-of-hearing clinched their assessment. 'What's that you say? Eh? Speak up?'" He leaned back and roared.

"So you were not followed—?"

"Confinement is not the word for my situation," Antônio said, sobering up. "They check in on me twice a day to tell me I should shave more often. As long as I'm back before tomorrow morning, they won't notice my absence."

"And Beryl?"

"We share Merripit House as well as the confinement within it."

"So you see her every day."

Antônio folded his hands over his sternum. "We do not speak. It is a quiet house now. Beryl offered Scotland Yard much contrition for Sir Charles' death and for the attack on Sir Henry. She even claims she attempted to prevent the latter. I believe they will treat her with compassion."

"She's a master of the convincing tale," I said.

"She is truly sorry for what happened, Rodrigo."

"She thirsted for the Baskerville fortune and title." Beryl had stood to gain from Henry everything she had relinquished in Costa Rica: An estate, servants, high society, and a complete detachment from the earthly requirement of earning your daily bread. "Uncle Charles' death was good fortune for her."

"You read her heart as colder than it really is. She misses Sir Charles."

"A common rearrangement of priorities when one is facing the gallows."

"And you? What did you thirst for?"

I admit, I brooded for a moment, and demurred.

"The title, yes?" he said. "Sir Rodger of Baskerville? Standing and respect, that is what you crave. The estate could be in financial tatters, it would be no matter to you. You want your portrait in the family gallery. You want your name listed in *Atherton's Peerage* beside the families of barons and dukes and lords—"

"*Enough.*" His fine, keen eye had overlooked a more obvious motivation. "My uncle and cousin are corrupt, merciless people. There is not a single redeeming quality between the two of them. With my *Fila*, I planned on ending the Baskerville line. Snuffing it out—call it annihilation, if you will. If my uncle can erase me from the family tree, then I will erase the family tree entirely. Is that so difficult to understand?"

"It's difficult to believe. With Henry dead, you would stand to inherit the family fortune—"

"And how would I claim it? I had firmly established myself in Dartmoor as Jack Stapleton. After Henry's death, how exactly could I announce I am Rodger Baskerville and claim the family fortune uncontested? I was not merely disinherited by my Uncle Charles. He erased me in favor of Henry. No, my only desire in all of this was to erase the Baskervilles in turn. The money, the estate—you do me a grave injustice, judging me so motivated by material wealth." My heart beat in my neck, and my head was flushed with blood. "They stripped me of my name, and with it, they stripped me of my dignity. Even with Beryl on my arm, the most beautiful woman in all of Creation, I could never stand straight. I was always beneath her and the Garcias. My family's rejection only proved it."

The argument reached a standstill. We implicitly agreed to change the subject.

"So. Tell me. My little coded message. How did you fare?"

Antônio chuckled. "Delivering your message in a Bible was sound. The men of Dartmoor inspect all post arriving at Merripit House. But what proper Englishman would deny a guilty man the Word of God? And one with such a lovely card included inside?"

He produced the card I'd penned at the bookseller. "'With condolences for your recent loss, the Christian Wellbeing Fund of East Yorkshire offer you salvation. Matthew 16:18. Yours in God, Mr. Perry Span II.'"

"And?"

"Well, I knew it was you right off. Mentioning East Yorkshire only confirmed it. Span the Second alludes to Two Bridges, the locale outside of Princetown. Perry, I take it, is your little wordplay for *perro*—"

Dog in Spanish.

"And the verse you listed, I knew it—how do you say it in English? All in memory?"

"You knew the verse by heart."

In Portuguese, he recited, *On this rock I will build my church.* "It regards *São Pedro*. St. Peter Inn."

"Not the most secure coded message history has known. The best I could muster in a moment's notice standing in a bookseller's shop wearing a theater beard."

Antônio thought hard for a moment. "Where will you go now?"

"London."

"London! Are you mad? Plymouth is a mere fifteen miles from here. You could book passage for the New World and put all this behind you."

"I have unfinished business."

"What business? Do not pine for Beryl. Her heart is no longer reserved for you."

"You underestimate her. She is playing a convincing role for Scotland Yard to secure her freedom."

"She fell in love with Sir Henry—"

"An infatuation. Sturdy frontiersman from abroad, newly come into a great inheritance and a title. Any young woman's heart would go wobbly. Besides, Cousin Henry no longer has feelings for her. She's associated with

Uncle Charles' death. She played the role of an unmarried woman while he wooed her. He'll never allow such a woman to set foot in Baskerville Hall."

"That does not mean she'll return to your arms."

I tossed my cigarette into the fireplace with a *bah!* A soft rain began to spatter lines down the room window.

"Tell me of Agrippina. Have they harmed her?"

"Another secret the men of Dartmoor have successfully kept from Holmes and Scotland Yard. The police turned over Merripit House searching for clues of your history, but they failed to discover the cellar beneath the stable. Someone in the village knew of it, though."

"Caring for her, yes? Do not tell me they're abusing her."

"I do not think she is fattening on their scraps. She is berserk the moment they open the cellar doors. They are unable to control her. She will surely tear out their throats at her first chance. They throw food to her and use an old boating oar to taunt her and beat her back. It's the second oar they've used. She broke the oar's mate into splinters between her jaws." He added, "She lives in her own filth down there. I believe they will put her down soon."

I thrust up from my seat and paced about the room. "This is intolerable! I must return to Merripit House immediately."

"A notion even worse than traveling to London. She is done for, Rodrigo. You must put her behind you, as you must with Beryl." He let out a great sigh of air. "And you must leave me behind as well."

"What's this? Join me! Together we travel to London, tonight, on the final express."

"Look at me." Once more, he clutched his graying hair. "I've followed you from the jungles of Brazil into this bog—" He made a dismissive wave in the direction of Grimpen Mire. "A different sort of jungle. Every stop along the way, we have announced our arrival in the bold light of day, and we slunk away in the dead quiet of night. You have made me an old man, Rodrigo. I am exhausted. The Empire of Brazil has been crumbling while we were gone. They say it will soon be a republic, but does that make a difference to men like you and me? No. We are subjects without a king. Citizens without a country. Men without a cause."

From his pocket, he produced a folded packet of banknotes. He took my hand, slapped it into my palm, and closed my fingers about it.

"*Vá com Deus.* I wish you the best, but I wish it from afar."

Tough words to hear from Antônio. "We achieved what other men don't dare to dream of. We didn't merely live like aristocracy. The aristocrats bent on knee before us."

With much sorrow in his eyes, he said, "An empty achievement,

Rodrigo."

I held up the banknotes. "I will put this to good use. Soon you will read of my exploits in all the world's newspapers. London. New York. Paris. São Paulo."

"*Aniquilação,*" he spoke under his breath: *Annihilation.* "If you assassinate Sherlock Holmes in London, you will be killed in a rain of gunfire. These British will go all Wild West hunting you down."

"An eye for an eye—"

"—and soon the world is filled with blind men." He coughed a mocking laugh and tossed his cigarette into the fireplace. "Why do I bother. You will not listen. *Aniquilação* is what you want, and you will have it."

Twelve

Traveling up the isthmus, Antônio and I found we were unable to secure employment beyond the most menial of labor. Word of "The Tragedy at Far Oaks" spread ahead of us. In village after village, we found circulars posted with our names and likenesses, our crimes listed in Spanish and Portuguese, and Maj. Harris' reward, *DEAD or alive.*

I dismissed Antônio's suggestion for us to join his relatives in Colombia, as I knew Maj. Harris would send agents there to watch for our arrival. Early on, Antônio remained confident he would one day return to Brazil and rejoin his family. Maj. Harris' reward only grew over time, and the news we picked up in work camps and saloons led us to realize returning was suicide. That first year in Panama was the most straining on him. He developed a morose nature exacerbated by alcohol or fatigue. If he'd been married or had children, I do believe he would have returned to Santarém and faced the consequences, if only to be buried beside his grandparents.

We dug ditches and shoveled sewers. We toiled in fields of sugar beets, backbreaking labor. We joined jungle work camps building roads and dams, easily the least rewarding job I have ever undertaken, and one of the lowest paying. We trawled rafts across swamps, the foul water up to our chests, hauling lumber, nails, and tools into the jungle. You learn quickly how to dig your feet into the swamp's soft mud floor, and to slap the surface repeatedly with sticks while pulling those rafts, in the name of warning back the reptiles and carnivorous fish that make their home there.

Another young man might have conceded such was his lot in life and dismissed any notion of bettering his place in the world. My father's admonitions never vacated my mind, not even when I was bent at the waist shoveling human excrement from a sewer. It is a crime of nature for a man of aristocracy to waste his life via physical exertion when any number of lesser men could fill his position. That was the nonsense I told myself back then. It fueled me through those difficult times, however, I will give it that.

Antônio came from a family of manual laborers. He was proud of elevating himself to the rank of foreman at Far Oaks. He'd had some education, and had largely avoided the kind of unforgiving, backbreaking work we now found ourselves forced to accept. Between his desperation and my stubborn beliefs, we devised a way out of the sewers and oil fields.

The inspiration came on a street in Colón, when a European in a tailored white suit and Panama hat directed a cutting remark toward me. Antônio tried to hold me back, but I broke free and bearded the man then and there. From his stammering, I determined him capable of only the worst broken Spanish, and was in fact British. In my father's tongue, I administered a lashing I dare not repeat here.

"My apologies," he faltered. "From your mien, I assumed you to be—"

"I am a Baskerville, heir to the baronetcy."

As I was dressed in denim and linen, with sun-browned skin and wearing the soil of the fields, I could not have surprised him further.

He required a moment to compose himself. "You are from Devon, then? Taunton, perhaps?"

We wound up conversing for twenty minutes on the street. When we separated, he believed me to be British, an adventurous young man far from Devon sleeping rough and living the authentic life. He encouraged me to look him up when I returned to England, and left me his card.

"Let's put that silver tongue of yours to use," Antônio told me later. "Let's profit from all that Tennyson you can quote so lovingly."

"What are you imagining?"

"We clean ourselves up. We will say you are a wealthy Britisher visiting Panama, and I am your translator."

"My aide-de-camp."

"Whatever sounds good."

"And I'm not merely wealthy. I am an aristocrat. After all, I *am* an aristocrat. Heir to the Baskerville baronetcy."

How dandified I must have sounded at that moment, standing ankle-deep in mud thinned to a black sludge by the nightly rains.

Under his breath, to avoid being heard by the work boss, he said, "We collect our pay this afternoon. It will be the last *centavo* we take from these slave-driving dogs." He meant the company clearing the road through the Panamanian jungle. "We must procure a good suit and shoes for each of us. We will have our hair cut and our beards shaved. Then we must find some way to perfume ourselves as the gentry in London and Paris do."

A crisp shave and haircut for Antônio softened his craggy face. His gentleman's suit made him as beautiful as a black *touro* with wildflowers and roses woven between his horns. As for myself, my purloined suit, while on the shabby side, was smartened up by the private school accent my father had instilled in me. Like a gull, I had spoken Spanish to the Panamanians since arriving in their country; they tossed me a shovel and ordered me to work. When I began speaking proper English—they stopped and listened.

Early on, I attempted to trade on my family name, only to discover the upper classes of Panama had never heard the name Baskerville, and possessed little curiosity about the finer points of the English baronetcy. Antônio convinced me to use a name and title more familiar to the region. I adopted the pseudonym Vandeleur, a surname of Dutch origin found in the northern counties of Ireland. The Baskervilles had campaigned in Ulster under King Charles I, and my father had told me stories of a valiant cavalier named Vandeleur fighting alongside my ancestor Hugo Baskerville in the name of the crown. I also claimed for Vandeleur the title of baron, a nice upgrade from baronet, which also elevated me into the British peerage.

This tidy scheme of ours was, as they say, hit-or-miss. We found ourselves dining at some of the finest establishments in Panama's cities, but twice as often, we were forced to scurry out of town in the dead of night with unpaid bills behind us and outraged fathers in pursuit. We always escaped with the fine clothes on our backs, my travel case of butterflies I'd begun collecting, and the Colt pistol I'd inherited from Martin Harris upon his demise. Our purses filled—gradually— but opportunities in Panama dwindled.

When Antônio and I arrived at Puerto Limón one bright hot morning, we found it to be a simple city of refreshing vitality. Its embarcadero was lined with open-air markets of colorful fruit, barrels of coffee and chocolate beans, and bolts of bright cloth, all traded in a brotherly manner. In the coastal air wafted the aroma of fried meat, warm tortillas, and sugar-dusted pastries. Screeching cockatiels and stolid toucans were sold from cages swinging on lines overhead. This was our introduction to Costa Rica, and immediately, we decided to make a play here.

At the Hotel San José, Antônio revealed my title to the front desk—as though by accident, of course—and arranged for a suite overlooking the harbor. The desk clerk, ever the model of indiscretion, never pried Antônio with the uncomfortable question of payment. The unspoken assurance was that those matters would be settled later. We left the desk in charge of our trunks—weighed down with driftwood—and made our way to the dining room. The goal was not nourishment, but to set in motion Act Two of our little performance.

False starts and botched playacting up the isthmus had provided us with an invaluable education in the ways of the upper classes. Early on, I'd assumed the persona of the fussy Englishman never satisfied. Oh, the nuisances I endured. The dining room was horridly decorated. The food smelled unappealing and was horribly presented. The wait to be served was interminable. And so on.

It is the mistake of a novitiate. Only after we'd been thrown out of some of the finest establishments in Central America did we come around.

Too often, people focus on *rich* when speaking of the idle rich. *Idle* is the key term. It's not that money is plentiful when you're wealthy. Money is an abstraction. Consider the time in Colón I reached for my pocket when the bill arrived. A nobleman does not carry money. He is the poorest man in the dining room, for he has on him not *un peso* nor farthing. It is the burden of his secretary to dirty his hands with the foul Mammon. And so, from that embarrassment forward, Antônio was tasked with carrying what little money we'd accumulated, but flaunting it in such a manner to foster the illusion of endless wealth.

We were seated at a table on the veranda with a sweeping view of the bay and port. Without a glance at the *vin de carte*, I ordered in English a bottle of Italian white wine, leaving Antônio to translate. With the wine poured, Antônio peppered me with questions about itineraries and schedules. I answered all noncommittally while admiring the Atlantic Ocean stretching to the horizon.

"Lord Vandeleur," he implored me, "we cannot stay more than one night in Puerto Limón. We are expected in San José to meet with the president of the university."

"Send a telegram. Explain I find this port town charming and would like to acquaint myself with it for at least one more day."

"The endowment, my Lord, and the reception afterward—"

"I will not hear more of it. Telegram my regrets."

Our little stage play attracted the attention of the occupants of a table near us. Once certain we were captivating them, I feigned mild embarrassment at their attentions.

"Apologies. My secretary takes his duties quite seriously."

"That is a good quality in a secretary," said the patriarch at the table.

His English was tinted with a fine, refined Spanish accent. His wife at his side was a lovely older woman in a floral-pattern dress.

"How long have you been in Puerto Limón?" he asked.

"This is our first day in your fine city. Our first day in Costa Rica, in fact."

"If I may be forward, may I ask what brings you to our great country?"

"I am an aurelian, that is, an admirer and studier of butterflies and moths."

"Most impressive, Lord…?"

Antônio rose. "May I present Vandeleur of Brixcombe." Antônio thought it sounded very British-like.

The patriarch stood and made a slight bow. "The honor is mine."

I rose from my chair with a mild expression of resigned

embarrassment. This too came from some experimentation in Panama.

"Please." I motioned for him and his wife to *sit, sit, please sit*. She was preparing to curtsy, which only made my feigned embarrassment tangible.

"I am Ramon Luis Garcia," he said, twirling his R's with every opportunity his name afforded him. "I confess I have never met royalty before."

"You still have not," I said.

"Lord Vandeleur is a *peer*," Antônio rushed to explain. "The family title reaches back before the Restoration of the English crown."

Garcia and his wife remained standing in awe. "My apologies—this is my wife, Anita Conchita Lopez."

"*Enchante.*" I took her extended hand delicately in mine. Every stage actor knows it is not the mimicry of realism you are awarded for, but the provision of a reality your audience craves.

"If I may be so bold," Garcia said with much haste. "It would be an honor if you were to dine with my family this afternoon. My daughter and her fiancé will be joining us shortly."

On cue, Antônio refused with strict explanations of schedule and obligations. Like a fisherman allowing the line on the reel run out, I let Antônio explain and apologize until it was time for me step in, dismiss his concerns, and accept their offer. I assured Garcia we'd be grateful for the opportunity to dine with a citizen of this charming and beautiful fishing village.

"Compared to your London, I imagine Puerto Limón does appear a fishing village," Garcia said after the table had been rearranged and all were seated. "If you extend your stay and acquaint yourself with our little city, you will discover Limón has much to offer. It is the second-largest city in Costa Rica. We enjoy a vibrant trade with foreign markets both in the New and Old Worlds."

"And what is your trade?"

"I am a city father. I oversee town planning and finances, as well as solicit the establishment of new industry by local and foreign investment. Garcias have flourished in Puerto Limón since before its founding." He rose from his chair with a warm smile. "My lovely daughter Beryl."

My newfound skill in the theater was tested by the arrival of the young lady. She was, without exaggeration, the most beautiful woman I had ever seen. She glided to the table as though delivered to us upon an Arabian rug woven from airy winds and cottony clouds. She presented herself to us with a delicate neckline holding aloft a confident, almost haughty, expression.

I rose weakly from my chair and made as gracious and noble a bow I could manage. It is rare to meet a woman who can halt a busy dining room by her mere arrival. From the faces around us in that bustling yet refined room, her mere presence focused a spotlight upon our table.

"I present Lord Vandeleur of Brixcombe, England. He has deeply honored our family by joining us."

Beryl was escorted by a man nearer to Antônio's age than my own. I first thought him to be a desk clerk ushering her from the lobby. No, this was her fiancé, an American named John D. Lowell of San Francisco, California.

"Pleasetameetcha." This sludge of purported English slopped from his mouth all at once. He touched the brim of a modest brown bowler crowning an oily mat of dark but flecked hair. "Great to meet someone who speaks the King's English in this country."

"Quite." I introduced Antônio as my aide-de-camp.

"A lawyer, then?" Lowell asked Antônio. "Me too. Mineral rights are my specialty. Yours?"

"English…common law," Antônio fumbled.

"What brings you two to Costa Rica?"

Beryl's fine raven hair framed the creamy skin of her shoulders and face. Beryl, I would come to learn, has the natural skill to peer down on anyone, even a person of higher stature than herself. As I stood towering over her, mute and gifted with Baskervillean height, she performed her trick on me.

"Vandeleur does not sound like much of an English name," she said tartly.

"Beryl!" Garcia reprimanded from across the table.

"My family is of Dutch extraction."

"You are not English, then?"

"The Vandeleur lineage is amply documented," Antônio assured the Garcias.

"Well, I've never heard of a nobleman with such a ridiculous name."

Garcia reprimanded her again. "My Lord, I deeply apologize for—"

"Vandeleur," I told him with a smile I could not refrain from expressing. I pulled out Beryl's chair and dusted it off with my handkerchief. "It is always 'Vandeleur' among friends."

Lowell peeled the bowler off his greased-back hair and pushed it at a hovering waiter. "Let's take a seat and order up."

Wine was poured. A cold *amuse-gueule* of oysters on ice and ceviche was served.

"Señor Lowell has lived in Puerto Limón for, I believe, two years now?"

"Three." He ate with fork and knife as an American would, and I reminded myself I was not to copy his eating manners. It was not difficult.

He was coarse in every respect.

"I represent American business interests in-country." He spoke out the corner of his mouth while chewing. "Mining, primarily. Gold, silver, copper, iron. And oil, of course."

"Oil?" Antônio asked him while glancing at me.

"Healthy amount of oil speculation up and down the isthmus. They're finding it in northern Brazil too. There's a boom coming, I tell you what."

What confounded me was what a proud and exquisite woman such as Beryl could see in this lout. His attention was fixed on the plate he was hunched over. Beryl sat patiently beside him, back erect and hands in her lap, watching us all with a penetrating, judgmental gaze.

The art of conversation is knowing what to listen for and when not to speak. With only a single question from me regarding his lineage, Garcia launched into a long-winded telling of his family line. Like the Harris family, he claimed to be of a direct line from nobility in Madrid extending back to the time of the Moors. However, he admitted the Garcia family could not claim a title.

"That made it easier for me to ask Beryl's hand in marriage," Lowell said with a grating chuckle. "No barons or earls in the Lowell family."

"Where is this place you call 'Brixcombe?'" Beryl asked me. "Is it near London?"

"In the southwest of England," I said. "We are blessed with a beautiful countryside, with rolling green hills and horse stables, and lots of fresh English air."

"So it is not near London, then."

"Devon is home to many of England's oldest families." I said it as much to her as to her father, who was lapping up my every word. "The Baskervilles, for example, have resided on their estate for six hundred years now."

"Another name I have never heard of."

"Beryl!"

"At least it *sounds* English." Mockingly, she pronounced my family name with a thick Valencian accent: *Vath-ker-bille*. "A name most thick. As is your English cuisine."

Before her father could protest, I said, "The letters patent were assigned by Charles II to Hugo Baskerville for demonstrating great courage and mettle in the Great Rebellion. Hugo married a lady from Inverness whose line traces to the Lancasters—"

"How unappealing," Beryl said with exaggerated weariness. "One begins to wonder if the topic is nobility or dog-breeding."

"Perhaps the young lady would prefer to hear of the Vandeleurs," Antônio warned me, "and not this history of the Baskervilles."

She bore a smug smile that detracted from her natural radiance—an irresistible flaw in an otherwise perfect porcelain doll. She had succeeded in scoring a streak of points in this little game of conversational tennis.

"I apologize for my daughter's impertinence," Garcia said across the table.

"I find it refreshing. Such forthright talk is most welcome."

I do not believe any man (father, suitor, or otherwise) had ever spoken to Beryl quite the way I did that afternoon. She began to regard me with a notable seriousness. "I would think barons and earls are...older than you."

"The title does not make the man," I said. "It is deed, not word, which defines me."

When the final course arrived, Antônio made much of being unable to find his purse. He excused himself from the table, muttering he must have left it with our trunks at the desk. Beryl sat upright before her cold lime custard, seemingly unable to locate her appetite.

"I thought you English weren't much for coffee," Lowell said to me.

"When traveling, follow local customs," I said. "And pursue local tastes," I said to Beryl.

"I believe Costa Rica produces the finest beans in the world," Garcia said. "I hope you will agree."

"I'm beginning to see there is much to appreciate about Costa Rica," I said, gazing upon her.

"It would be my pleasure to have a blend formulated for the Vandeleurs by one of our coffee agents. They could ship a bag to your estate in England. At your behest, of course."

"Perhaps I could sample it during my stay."

"Your secretary left me with the impression you would not be in Puerto Limón for more than a day. Blending beans is a high art. I would not want you to be disappointed due to rushed work."

"What if I told you I wanted to extend my stay in Puerto Limón indefinitely?" All around the table were surprised, in particular Beryl. "My visit to Costa Rica is not merely for pleasure. I mentioned I make a private study of butterflies. It is not a passing interest. I have traveled to Costa Rica to propose establishing in your nation's capital a landmark unlike any known to the world. I wish to build a permanent zoological exhibition of all species of butterflies and moths native to the New World. It would be known simply as the Butterfly Pavilion. The Vandeleur family, of course, will be the foremost patron of this pavilion, which shall be dedicated the peoples of Costa Rica, the Americas, and all of the world."

With each utterance from me, the expression on Garcia's grew from surprise and anticipation to sheer delight. "Lord Vandeleur, this is most wonderful news!"

"However, Señor Garcia, your hospitality has led me to reconsider."

Aghast, he wilted into his chair.

Brightly, I told him: "I will establish the Butterfly Pavilion here, in Puerto Limón. The cornerstone will be laid—"

With a poised hand, I indicated a steep flat hill across the inlet bay facing the trade winds coming off the Atlantic.

"There."

"*Monte Concepción,*" Garcia breathed.

"Every ship that sails or steams into Puerto Limón will steer past one of the great wonders of the New World, a grand pavilion dedicated to the natural wonders that have been blessed to the Americas by our Creator above."

Lowell whistled. "Sounds pricey."

"I have read of your British Museum, and the wonders it has collected from across the ancient world," Garcia said. "It is my understanding it holds the largest collection of butterflies known to man. Now, you will bring such fame to the country of my family!"

"Not at all. The British Museum keeps their butterflies dead and pinned in place. The curators of the British Museum are little more than postage stamp collectors. My Butterfly Pavilion will be an open-air habitat of living butterflies and moths. Visitors will not review them under glass in orderly rows and columns. The butterflies will flutter and dance and play in my magnificent greenhouse. Visitors may extend their hand—"

I took Beryl's and extended her delicate fingers. Enchanted by my little tale, she could not resist.

"And a butterfly will perch there and preen itself for their admiration."

And I placed my hand in her palm, allowing hers to close around mine.

"As it should be," she said softly.

Garcia was beside himself. "You humble yourself, Lord Vandeleur. For such a monument to Costa Rica would be the finest gift to our country at this crucial moment in history. Certainly it must be named the Vandeleur Butterfly Pavilion. Especially given that you will be bringing your family fortune to bear upon its completion."

"It would be, you understand, uncouth for me to glorify my family name when the substantial goal is to further the education and appreciation of Costa Rica's natural blessings."

"Lord Vandeleur, I am certain no one would object."

"Your lovely daughter's onomastic insights weigh on my mind." Taking her hand once more, I said, "I would prefer the Pavilion's name to indicate the substantial goodwill between Costa Rica and the people of England. Perhaps a proper Anglo-Saxon name would be more fitting?"

Lowell's attention had detached from his dessert. His jovial and passing interest in my presence in the country had withdrawn. He now regarded my attentions toward Beryl with a cool and muted suspicion.

"Perhaps we should get the check," and he snapped his fingers for the waiter.

"Before departing, I conferred with the Baskervilles in England," I said. "The family has tentatively pledged a substantial donation toward the Pavilion's construction. I am certain that, with some encouragement from myself, they will gladly acquiesce to their family name being attached to the project."

"The Baskerville Butterfly Pavilion it is," Garcia announced.

"A gleaming glass hothouse of flora and flutters overlooking the gorgeous *Bahia de Limon.*"

"Your Spanish is most remarkable, Lord Vandeleur."

It slipped out in my exuberance. "In the spirit of cooperation, I traveled to Costa Rica not merely to supply an endowment and return to my home in England. Rather, I seek to connect with benefactors here who share my vision and will contribute to its construction and operation."

"Of course. Most sensible. We must form a board of trustees and incorporate."

"'We?'"

"You have found your greatest champion," Garcia declared. "I will work tirelessly for the Butterfly Pavilion. As of this moment, I am dedicating myself to your cause. I now insist you stay in my hacienda during your time here in Puerto Limón. No, do not object, it is now demanded of you. You English are unfamiliar with Costa Rican hospitality. You are welcome into our house as though you are family. You are not permitted to refuse."

Antônio met me at the desk, furious. "What took you so long?"

The usual manner of our escape was for him to retreat to the front desk to find his mislaid purse. After a prolonged absence from the table, I would excuse myself under the pretense that there must have been some kind of confusion with the hotel staff.

"This is the haul we've been seeking. Tonight we board at Hacienda Garcia."

"Have you lost your senses? He is a *city father*. This is man who dines with judges and lawmen. We need to be extricating ourselves from him."

"We've made enough distance from Santarém. We've left that behind us."

"You underestimate the Major. When it comes to the death of his son, there is no distance great enough. He will track us all the way to his Mississippi, if he must."

"We have an opportunity here unlike any other. We can establish ourselves in Puerto Limón. Live here. Be respected here." And I explained to him my proposal for the Butterfly Pavilion. "It will be the first of its kind in the world."

Antônio was beside himself. "Where did this come from?"

"My imagination. Garcia stoked the fires of inspiration."

When we returned to the table, Garcia had paid the bill and called for his carriage.

"Here is where I part ways." Lowell extended a hand. "Vanderlay, good meeting you."

"Vandeleur," Antônio corrected him. "It is improper for—"

I planted my hand in his and shook. Lowell made a crushing handshake, did the same with Antônio, and departed without so much as a kiss goodbye on Beryl's cheek.

Beryl and I strode behind the others with her arm through mine. She was not imperious with me now. Tucked inside her magnificent and prideful beauty was a kernel of terror. As we strolled, she glanced up at me with a nervous expression, as though foreseeing the carnage I would wreak. She didn't pull away, though. She pressed close, and I could only grin and lead her onward.

Thirteen

The Garcia family hacienda was built in the traditional manner, that is, a compound of concentric squares atop one of the hills overlooking the bay. Fortified walls around the property surrounded a home of plaster and red clay tiles and brick. The innermost tiled plaza was where most meals were taken, and where the family would consort during the morning and evening hours. A modest pineapple grove behind the compound provided the family with an additional income. The design was utilitarian, but Señora Garcia decorated and furnished the hacienda with soft traditional touches. It was a cool and comfortable retreat from the bustle of commerce at the port and the hard realities of the Limón street.

Our first evening, Garcia invited us to join him in his billiards room. This space was perhaps the only one in the hacienda untouched by a woman's tastes, and the one room where his Anglophilia was most on display. He enjoyed English snooker, which neither of us had ever played, leading to some disappointment as the two of us scrambled to make excuses.

"Snooker is a wagering game," I explained to Garcia. "Unbecoming for a peer of the crown to partake."

"My Lord, forgive me, I did not intend to—"

"No wager was presented," Antônio declared. "No offense is taken."

Garcia poured Scotch and led us on a little tour of his civic awards lining the hardwood walls. They hung in-between dartboards, scorekeeping chalkboards, and daguerreotypes of a rugby exhibition held in Costa Rica's capital. The room was typically British, but the British manner of decor is intended for a colder clime where fireplaces rage day and night. In Costa Rica, it was stuffy and stultifying, like wearing tweed to the beach.

"If I may." Garcia removed a sturdy volume from a case. As he consulted it, Antônio moved to his side and made a subtle glance down at it. Preoccupied with his tome, Garcia failed to register Antônio telegraphing me a look of terror.

"What have you got there, old boy?" I said to Garcia as lackadaisically as I could manage.

He had taken down an edition of *Atherton's Peerage*. "I thought I might look up your family history."

"Please. Time enough for that later."

"I find British aristocratic titles fascinating. The terminology, for someone not fluent in English, I confess they are a bit...*exotic*."

Studying the cherry of my cigar, I said, "It's overly familiar to speak of one's family to a man he met over a meal."

"Oh—but of course..."

"But it's mighty delicious to talk about *another* family," I said with bared teeth. "Why don't you see what it says about the Baskervilles? Awfully happy to chat about old Hugo and his issue."

"Would it be...uncouth?"

"Yes," Antônio said.

"No," I said over him. "The Vandeleurs and the Baskervilles are chummy." I was laying it on pretty thick. "How old is that copy of *Atherton's*, might I ask?"

"The latest edition." He beamed. "I ordered it direct from the London publisher." Garcia located my family's entry in no time. "It appears the title has changed hands, Lord Vandeleur. It says here the baronetcy is now held by one Sir Charles Baskerville. What am I saying? You must certainly know this yourself."

Seeking to dampen my natural surprise, I made a great show of climbing out of the easy chair and meandering to his side with Scotch in hand. "I did not," I murmured. "When did this occur?"

"It appears fourteen months ago. It says Sir Charles returned home from South Africa, fresh from earning a small fortune in gold speculation. Have you met him?"

Uncle Charles? My father spoke little about his brothers, but I did recall mention of a Charles.

"When I return to England, I will have to pay a visit and offer my congratulations."

This was my moment before Antônio. Since Santarém, he had scoffed at my claimed ancestry. For the past year, as we risked blood together running from town to town up the isthmus, Antônio's skepticism hardened with every socialite I attempted to woo who rebuked me, saying, "I never heard of any family named 'Baskerville.'" Now he faced documented proof of my family's existence, and that it holds letters patent to their title.

"I believe his father produced three male issue," I said to Garcia. "Sir Charles and two brothers. Their names escape me..."

Garcia studied the registry for a cold moment. "One brother, Lord Vandeleur. Sir Charles and his brother Henry." He squinted at the fine text. "It appears Henry died some years ago. Sir Charles is the last of the Baskerville line."

Antônio, Scotch glass to his lips, glared at me.

"Should be a Rodger listed there, old boy," I said. "Rodger Baskerville."

Garcia dumbly studied *Atherton's* for another cold moment. "No one named Rodger is listed, Lord Vandeleur."

I set aside the cigar and Scotch and took the volume off the table. In the dim gaslights illuminating the billiards table, I read and reread the entry. The Baskerville title originated with Hugo, a man as wild and lawless as the painted Celtic tribesmen who once ran rough across the damp plains of Devon. Hugo II, Hugo III, and the rest of the family lineage tumbled down the page, name after familiar name. It was all just as my father had recited to me from his chair at the window with his tequila and limes within reach. I had even discreetly consulted *Atherton's Peerage* in Panama City, before we began employing the Lord Vandeleur ruse. I had located a dusty copy in a private club's library we'd wrangled an invitation into. My father was listed in their copy. Now, with this fresh edition in my own hands, I discovered not only was I not listed, my father had been scrubbed as well.

Antônio and I were given adjoining guest rooms. Before retiring, Antônio joined me beside a window overlooking the tiled plaza.

"I never want to hear the name Baskerville spoken by you again."

"I do not deny you your family."

"No one can take a book off a shelf and look up the Melo family history. No one would care to record it. If I know this Garcia—and I think I have a good idea of what makes him tick—he's no doubt consulting that book of his right now for the name 'Vandeleur.' What will you say when he questions you about it?"

"A printing mistake. Editorial oversight."

"I see. Just like your name was not listed among the Baskervilles?" He snorted. "It's an infection with you. Listen: You are not a Baskerville. Understand? You are Rodrigo. We touch Garcia for a few hundred pesos and we make for the next town."

Breaking the nighttime quiet came three soft taps on my bedroom door. Antônio and I went still. Three more taps sounded, as soft as a fingernail on a tabletop.

"Señor Vandeleur?" Beryl whispered through the door. "Are you awake?"

"Go," I whispered to Antônio, and hurried him to the door between our rooms.

"That girl is danger," he whispered. "She will get the noose put around our necks. Do not forget, her fiancé is a lawyer—"

"Oil and mineral rights."

"Lawyers work with other lawyers. He drinks with the prosecutor, he drinks with the judge, and he probably knows names of the hangman's children." She tapped the door once more. "Send her away." And he retreated to his bedroom.

Opening the door revealed Beryl in a loose silk robe over a flimsy dressing gown.

"I have some questions about the British aristocracy."

I ushered her inside and quietly closed the door.

"Your father may not appreciate my lesson at this time of night. Perhaps in the morning, I can go over the finer points."

She circled my room. The ends of her robe's sash dragged on the floor behind her.

"Your accommodations? They are acceptable?"

"Your mother keeps a fine home."

"And the meal?"

"Most delicious."

"'Delicious?' That is the only word you have? I thought the English language was rich and varied."

"Scrumptious," I offered.

She drew close. "English is so harsh. It expresses itself like a dog worrying a bone."

"You are the loveliest woman in all of Creation," I said in Spanish.

Her eyes flamed up. "Lord Vandeleur. You are…surprising."

"I would climb the highest mountain to peer upon your face."

Delighted, she said, "So says a man of deed, not word."

"Upon this bed I will spread a blanket of rose petals for you—"

With her pressed up against me, I wove my hands into her robe. I held her by the small of her back.

She whispered into my ear, "You are a man of many secrets."

"Your father keeps you under glass like a butterfly. Be with me, and I will set you free upon the world, so all can admire your beauty."

I clutched her tight and kissed her. For a fiery, drawn-out moment, we were as one.

Then it was over. She withdrew to the bedroom door, backing away from me with meager, hesitant steps.

"I will keep your secrets," she told me.

"Will you trust me with yours?"

"I have secrets?"

"You've told me at least one. I believe I could guess two more without much trouble."

"Keep them, then. They're yours." She cautiously opened the door and peered down the dark hallway.

"Will I see you tomorrow night?"

"That is my secret," she said. "For now." And she slipped away.

Fourteen

Before joining the others for breakfast, Antônio and I ornamented the plan I'd improvised at the hotel veranda. Ever optimistic, Garcia happily obliged us with a list of the best architects in Puerto Limón. With his introduction in hand, we convinced the first on the list to produce mocked sketches of a Victorian glass-house pavilion atop the hill overlooking the bay. At the second architect, Antônio negotiated for a rough blueprint of the pavilion itself, paid upon delivery. Garcia also asked Beryl's fiancé to draw up *pro bono* letters of incorporation. Antônio told Lowell we did not require the letters to be signed, notarized, or filed quite yet, but we did hold on to the papers for our own purposes.

We developed a simple methodology. At Garcia's behest, and bearing letters of introduction, Antônio approached wealthy society members in Puerto Limón and San José. Antônio initially met them alone, using the sketches, blueprints, and letters of incorporation as evidence of our sincerity and progress. If unimpressed, Antônio would provoke their curiosity by mentioning the backing of a mysterious and unnamed English baron.

"I quit trying to explain a baron is not a member of the royal family," he told me once. "Let these yokels believe what they want."

Only after their requests turned to insistence—or even pleas—did I accompany Antônio to their private residence, never a place of business or trade. Introductions were short and terse. Antônio brought with us my travel case of captured butterflies and moths. On the harder sells, I would capture a live specimen near Hacienda Garcia and produce it from my cloak before the benefactor-to-be, like a parlor magician drawing a starling from a lady's bouffant. It never failed to delight.

Then Antônio would cut the conclave short and whisk me away, almost always with bank paper in hand. Converting the transferred money into ready cash merely required Antônio make a pretense to Garcia of "expenses" and needing "demonstration money," as he had opened the Pavilion's bank account and oversaw all its transactions.

"It's one thing for our playacting to provide us fine meals and French wine," Antônio told me one evening. "We're engaged in larceny."

"A little walking around money won't be missed."

"I was not raised this way. The shame would stop my mother's heart."

"Once the Pavilion is built—"

"There will be no Pavilion! Are you daft, man?" He steadied himself, and lowered his voice. "Tomorrow we go to the bank and withdraw as much as we can without attracting attention. There is an express north. We set out for Nicaragua, and we do not look back. We can make it to San Juan del Norte before dawn."

"Antônio," I said with a shake of my head. "We are not leaving Costa Rica."

"We cannot maintain this ruse for much longer. When Garcia and his friends catch on we've made fools of them, they will let every city, town, and village in Costa Rica know of our embezzlement. They will come for our heads."

"It's only embezzlement if we don't build the Pavilion. Do you not see the genius? We build it. We will be in charge of it. I as Pavilion Director will draw a sizable salary for my work, and you as Assistant Director will draw one as well."

"They will want to know when the Vandeleur money will be donated. All of these donations are contingent on the Vandeleur family in England providing the bulk of the funding." He slapped his forehead. "And the Baskervilles as well. We've peddled so many falsehoods to so many people, I cannot keep track of them all..."

"My suggestion to name it after the Baskervilles was a miscalculation on my part. If my family in Devon were to hear of it, they most certainly would inquire—"

"They will learn you are impersonating an English title. Knowing the British, they will treat that as a capital offense."

"They don't behead the aristocracy."

"They'll behead two Brazilians without a twinge of guilt."

With our room and board provided for, and the newfound luxury of a full bank account, I pursued my interest in butterflies and moths unfettered by worldly obligations. I purchased butterfly nets and gear, and set out to search among the overgrowth on the outskirts of town. Within weeks, I'd fortified my growing collection of specimens, mostly common species but also a smattering of rarities. They went into the portable display case I brought to benefactors when closing the deal, "a sampling of Lord Vandeleur's personal collection," as Antônio liked to introduce it.

The longwing; the pink-spotted cattle heart; glasswings as intricate as the stained windows of Europe's grandest cathedrals; monarchs; white-angled sulphurs mimicking leaves so perfectly, a hundred of them can make a dead tree appear verdant and thriving. And, the crown jewel of the Vandeleur collection, a giant blue morpho with deep azure wings and a wingspan as large as a dog's heart.

When I caught the morpho, I held it much as the fieldworker held the tiger-striped butterfly at Far Oaks. Spread across my two hands, its body twisted and its antennae squirmed for its freedom. Before, I would have set the butterfly free. My early interest in them had been moments of passing connection with these exquisite creatures. I was like a man of humble means shuffling between the framed masters on the walls of a museum, admiring each one in turn, never for a moment engaging in the fantasy of possessing any. With the Pavilion at stake, my interest in these creatures intensified. After admiring the blue morpho, I gently set it in the killing jar, sealed the lid, and started the hike back to Hacienda Garcia with my prize.

Thrice more Beryl visited my bedroom at midnight, and with each visit, she would break away at an inconvenient moment in our intimacies. I never complained nor protested. Yes, she was toying with me as a cat would bat around a mouse, but this mouse knew as long as I entertained her whims, I remained in play. My desire for her attentions was such that I debated what I feared most: Her revealing my deception to her father, or her growing fatigued with me and ceasing our little game.

During her fourth visit, we lay in bed caressing each other, inhaling each other's scent and tasting each other's flesh. We were young. We thought we were privy to all the secrets of the world. In fact, we'd yet to be introduced to most of them.

"Will you take me away from here?"

"To where?"

"Away from my father. Away from John D. Lowell." She pronounced each syllable of the Anglo name with biting sarcasm.

"Your father arranged the marriage. Ask him to send Lowell away."

She pushed away from me with a piercing glare. "Who told you?"

"One of your secrets I guessed at."

"You guessed well," she said after a moment. "I despise Señor Lowell. He is vulgar and low. He plays cards for money and drinks his whiskey on Sunday." She inched her face toward me again. "He is not like you." She pressed her nose into the cup of my sternum. "But I also know one of your secrets."

I stroked the back of her head. "Which is?"

"My father could not find your family in his book of English nobility." She twirled my chest hair around her finger—and tugged hard. "You are not who you say you are."

I clenched her hand and yanked it away. "What does your father say about me?"

"You are hurting me—There are two Vandeleur families with titles. *Release me.* One in England, another in Scotland. Neither are barons. *Let me go*. And he cannot find any such Brixcombe on his map of your island. He blames the English and their uneven spelling."

"We saw your father in town yesterday leaving the telegram office."

"He believes there is some defect with the book he purchased on British titles. He wired the university in San José to deliver an older edition, to see if his is a bad printing."

I had weeks to devise an explanation for this eventuality. Enjoying our newfound luxuries, and eager to see the Butterfly Pavilion come to fruition, I simply had not taken the time to fabricate one.

"I will speak to him tomorrow of it. I will set his mind at ease." I released her hand.

"And what will you tell him? You do not know yet, do you? You must invent a tale, yes? For that is what you do. You spin stories for people. You tell the stories your audience wants to hear."

"You said you would keep my secrets." I took her by the back of her neck. "Will you still?"

She swallowed, glaring at me. Gently, she tilted up her chin and exposed more of her delicate neck. Her gaze dared me to pull harder on her hair, and I did, firmly.

"Answer me."

"What is another secret of mine you guessed?" A look of terror made her eyes flare.

"That your father and Lowell beat you."

"How do you know that?"

"Because you are proud. Your father does not possess the imagination required to tame you without using a stick or his hands."

Almost crying, she said, "Señor Lowell does not beat me yet. But when we are married, I know he will take up where my father leaves off."

With her hair wrapped through my fist, I brought my lips to her ear and whispered,

"I will not beat you. I do not have to. You've already decided you will do everything I ask of you."

"You are wrong," she whispered. "Do you want to know why?"

"Tell me."

"Because you are poor. It is apparent. And you are learning here in Limón that money is not enough. You desire respect. That is what you take from my father's friends. Not their money. Their respect."

Her words had bite. "Is that so?"

"I cannot respect a man who is so empty of it."

I released her. "Then leave me."

She massaged her neck and checked her chin. She eased ever so gently back to me.

"I cannot."

With a low moan, she leapt on me like an animal uncaged. We wrestled and pawed at each other in a twist of sheets and blankets. Only when we were spent did we separate into sweaty, heaving heaps.

"Take me away from here," she finally said.

"Patience now," I told her, sweaty and dazed.

"I have no patience."

Gazing up at the ceiling, imagination running, I said, "What if John D. Lowell was to disappear. Would your father consider another suitor?"

Quietly, her voice sounding quite distant, she asked, "Why do you ask?"

"Patience now," I said.

Fifteen

Antônio woke me with a hiss to remain quiet. He threw clothes at me.

"They've come for us. We must leave."

Beryl rose from the bed with the blanket wrapped about her. Furious, Antônio took her by the arm.

"And you keep quiet as well. I have half a mind this is your fault—"

"Take me," Beryl pleaded.

"What is it?" I demanded from him.

"Voices. Horses. Men at the front gate, too many to count. They're using our names—our *real* names."

"She's coming with us. Turn your back so she may dress."

"I have only my bed clothes!" she said.

I told her to make do with a pair of my trousers and one of my shirts.

Antônio and I argued over Beryl in hissed whispers until he relented. "You are not thinking with your head, but so be it."

I strapped on my money belt, which I'd been filling with the gold coins we'd collected from Garcia's friends, and tucked my pistol beneath it. The walnut case of my best butterfly specimens was the only other possession I gathered.

We crossed the courtyard under the cover of night. Only then did I hear the men at the front gate of the Garcia compound. They were boisterous voices, and many spoke with the Scotch-Irish drawl of the *Confederados*.

Beryl led us to the rear gate intended for tradesmen and deliveries.

"Last chance," I whispered to Beryl. "Pass through this gate and you are with me for good."

"Forever," she whispered in the dark.

We scurried hand-in-hand ahead of Antônio. Before the side road curved to meet the frontage, Beryl led us to the mouth of a pitch-dark alley sparsely bounded by wood shacks. They housed the handful of workers who tended the Garcia pineapple grove.

Behind us came the clatter of men regrouping and scuffling about. The clopping of horses suggested they were attempting to route around us and cut off our escape. Beryl led us to the precipice of a narrow flight of stairs cut into the hillside. Shanties lined both sides of the flight.

The three of us scampered down them single-file. The flight was steep and ran the length of four city blocks. Only halfway down did it dawn on me that we may have trapped ourselves, but there was no option other than pressing on.

Antônio reached the base of the stairway first. In a panic, he turned about and rushed back up flailing his arms in warning. Gunshots cracked. Chips of brick and wood sprayed up behind him.

"Three or four of them," Antônio told us. "Our guide has led us into a pretty little trap."

"I am doing my best," Beryl snapped back at him.

I removed Martin Harris' Colt from my weighty belt. Antônio drew his own weapon, a nickel and brass Smith & Wesson he kept in his vest pocket: a gentleman's pistol. He purchased it after a night much as this one in Panama City, where we fled to avoid a growing number of creditors impatient with our promises.

Flickering lights danced like fireflies at the head of the steep flight of stairs. With the lights came a smattering of men's voices.

"Rodrigo," Antônio said. "To give ourselves up to the law is to live another day."

Beneath us, near the shanty at the base of the stairs, a man called out in an American drawl: "Come out showin' some empty hands!"

I cocked my pistol. "This is not the law." With a dry throat, my body shaking, I called down in English: "On what authority—"

"The authority of the honorable Maj. Leland Claude Harris!" came back. "We have come for the cold-blooded butchers of his only son Martin Donald Harris and his brother-in-law's eldest, Jimboy Duffy! Clan Harris and Clan Duffy have traveled five hundred miles for you. God have mercy on your souls, for you will get none from us tonight!"

Antônio swore in Portuguese, and not for Beryl's sake. With palsied hands, he prepared his revolver.

"Stay down and steel yourself," he told Beryl. "When we are dead, call out your family name and make it known you are unarmed. These men are animals, but they would not dare dishonor a woman or a reputable family." He placed a trembling hand on my shoulder. It worsened my own jangling nerves. "It has been a good run, my friend."

Voice dry and unsteady, I said with as much confidence as I could muster, "I will not give the Harris family the satisfaction."

To whoever lived in the wood shanty beside the base of those stairs in Puerto Limón, I offer a humble and heartfelt apology. To place you and your family in harm's way is unforgiveable. I beg you understand I only did so to preserve my life, the life of my partner Antônio, and the life of my love, Beryl Garcia.

Antônio and Beryl helped me shimmy up and through a blanket-covered hole cut in the side of the shanty. The family of six or seven occupying the hovel had gathered to hide behind an upturned bed. I raised a palm as request for their silence. With soft steps, I crept to the door. Through its thin wood, I overheard four men whispering among themselves. They weighed whether to rush the stairs and take a chance on catching us unawares, or waiting for us to surrender, where they could kill us with our hands raised in the air.

I settled the argument for them. I flung open the door, stepped onto the dirt road, and let loose the hellfire stored within the Colt.

Two of the men died with stunned expressions. My surprise gave them not a moment to level their weapons at me. A third scrambled away hunched over. One more bullet from my pistol caught him in the midsection and he tumbled to the road.

I swiveled for the fourth man, who was leveling his sidearm at me. Antônio came through. The man, a Harris or a Duffy, I know not which, he had backed up to make distance and train his sight on me. Thoughtlessly, he stepped into view of Antônio, who blasted him through the neck. He spun about spraying blood before he collapsed.

The noise at the top of the stairs changed tone. Men bearing shotguns and pistols and lanterns flowed down the stairs like raising a sluice gate during a storm.

We sprinted from the scene with Beryl again in the lead. If Antônio had any further complaints to lodge, the sickening rush of taking a man's life point-blank had chilled his vocal cords. A chaos of voices and cries of revenge trailed us. Brass whistles cut banshee shrieks through the night air as watchmen let it be known of violence erupting across the town. We ran without stopping to the base of the hill, pursued relentlessly by Clan Harris and Clan Duffy.

"No train until dawn," I said out of breath.

"They would only arrest us at the next stop," Antônio said.

"My father does business with a man who operates a horse stable—"

"Your father will not help us out of this," Antônio snapped at her. "We were fools to remain in Puerto Limón for so long!"

"By ship, then," Beryl offered.

Antônio and I pondered it for a moment. "It will have to make port far away from here," I said. Those words stabbed at Antônio's soul. I believe it was only at that moment he realized he would never see his family again.

At the docks, with the eastern sky toasting orange from the impending sunrise, Antônio made quiet inquiries. After some negotiations and introductions, he brought us to a Portuguese captain steaming for

Plymouth in four hours.

"England?" I said to Antônio.

"All other ships are bound for Panama and Brazil."

"In Brazil, there is warm air and beautiful beaches," Beryl said.

"Den of the lions," Antônio muttered.

"Do you trust this captain?"

"Not especially. I do not see any alternative."

The fare for booking passage was every *peso* of Antônio's walking-around money from the Butterfly Pavilion bank account sweetened with one of my California gold coins. It was a tidy bit of cash if one wished to live large in Puerto Limón. Now the sum was merely sufficient to survive another day, and only just.

There is one final detail I must account for. While Beryl remained hidden at the docks, and Antônio made quiet inquiries in search of passage out of Costa Rica, I slipped off into the night. At the end of the embarcadero was the foreign quarter. In particular, I sought out the residence of John D. Lowell of San Francisco.

He relaxed on the veranda of his abode holding a glass of fruit juice and bearing a mild, smug smile. His cigar smoldered in the cool ocean air coming off the coast. I don't know what he was thinking at the moment, but I would wager hard money he was enjoying the police whistles and cries in the streets as we were hunted down like dogs.

It made the stunned expression on his face all the more pleasurable when I emerged from the hedge surrounding his property, leveled the Colt, and put one square into his right eye.

Sixteen

So far, my disguise has drawn little attention. I am emboldened by its effectiveness. The line stopped in Reading, where I alighted for an hour to exercise my legs and take a modest lunch. With a bit of time on hand, I continue my journal with the sustained optimism it will be read in due course by interested parties.

Oh, how the simple comforts of the British railway system beats tumbling about in the hold of that creaky Portuguese steamer bound for Plymouth. The three of us lived a cramped existence among crates of coffee beans, salted game, and green dessert bananas. They fumed their gas as they ripened, and made the hold aromatic with their pasty and sickly odor.

The Anglo-Saxons of this hard, wet island find much delight in bananas. They make creams of them, they fry them crisp, they sauté slices of them, they boil them down to syrups, they serve them with Devonshire cream, and they distill them down to liqueurs sold in dainty bottles like French perfume. You will never see me partaking of these delicacies. To live a year on Far Oaks harvesting bananas and making a staple of them, more familiar on our plates than even bread or beans, is not the worst torture imaginable. To live in the hold of that swaying steamer, breathing nothing but banana gas day and night...there are a multitude of Hells, each tailored for the sinner.

Antônio's amiable nature fostered an easy acquaintance with the ship's captain, which gave us more latitude topside. Beryl was popular among the crew for obvious reasons. They treated her presence as a gift of heavenly sunshine breaking through the storm-ridden sea. Notwithstanding the torture of that banana-laden hold, I preferred to remain down there and in seclusion from the crew. My peace was found in the netting of our makeshift hammocks. Beryl brought meals to me from the galley, and related news to me of our journey as I ate.

Our second day at sea, she thrust a crumpled sheet of paper into my hands. "This explains much."

It was a copy of Maj. Harris' wanted poster. The charges against us had swelled, as we were now guilty of rustling and extortion as well as murder. The reward for our capture—or deaths—had swelled as well.

"This was circulated to all ships docked at Limón," she said. "Why did you not tell me?"

"The Major spread the news all the way to Costa Rica. He's a dogged old cur. This seals it. Your fiancé turned us in. Lawyers know everything first."

"I do not believe that," she said.

"This bill would certainly have reached your father's desk. Perhaps he sent word to Maj. Harris and coddled us to keep us from fleeing before Harris's men arrived."

With a stern expression, she retracted from me. "No. It is not possible."

"Why not?" Antônio said from the darkness of the hold. He had returned from topside. Apparently, he lingered in the shadows while we spoke. "Why would your father keep such information to himself? Is your father in the practice of harboring fugitives of the law?"

"My father would have confronted you," she said defiantly. "He would not have looked away while a trap was laid. He trusted you both."

He approached her with thoughtful steps. "And what did your father think of Lord Vandeleur? Señor Garcia holds high esteem for British nobility. What private remarks did he share with his family about lodging a mighty English baron in his hacienda?"

She fumed and shrugged. "He was proud of himself, as you would expect."

"You told us he sent for an earlier edition of his book from San José. Did it arrive?"

"I do not believe so."

"Beryl—please."

"Why do I have to be so honest with you?" she demanded. "Have you been honest with me? Even once?" She snatched the wanted poster from my hands and shook it in my face. "You are Rodrigo. You are a common thief, nothing more. I did not run off with you because I wanted the life of the aristocracy. I am here for *you*."

"I am in line to be the baronet of Baskerville."

With a scoffing laugh, she threw up her hands at our surroundings. "Are baronets always accustomed to traveling in such luxury?"

Antônio drew quite near. "How long have you known he was not a baron?"

"I sensed it the moment we met. The story of butterflies and pavilions, they hypnotized my father and his cigar-smoking friends, but not me." She pressed against me. "I knew you were a man cut from a coarser bolt."

Antônio was seized by a realization. "You told him. You told your father."

"I told him nothing."

"She told him we were wanted in Santarém." Antônio spoke directly to me now. "To force our hand. To force us to flee and take her with us. She's toyed with us since the day we arrived in Puerto Limón, and she continues to toy with us now."

Antônio's counsel was always most valuable to me. He was not a man given to baseless suspicions. The spooks of the mind, we all possess them, the voices in our head of taunting friends and cruel bosses and violent parents. Some men give much weight to these ghouls. In private, some men talk back to them, and some even talk to them in public. Some are overcome by the voices, and treat every person they encounter with unfounded misgivings and skepticisms. Antônio was a man whose mind was remarkably free of these hauntings. His advice to me always emerged from a stream of rational thought flowing through his mind. To ignore him was foolish. But now I wondered if he'd given in to irrationality.

"What say you to this?" I asked Beryl.

"I said nothing to Father. And I do not believe it was he who informed this—" She crumpled the wanted poster a bit more with a delicate hand. "—Maj. Harris, whomever he may be."

"If Maj. Harris was circulating our likenesses all the way to Puerto Limón, we were bound to be discovered," I said.

Antônio remained defiant. "São Paulo, yes, I am certain we are wanted there. Colombia, yes, there too. Maj. Harris is a stubborn and persistent man. I worked for him for over six years. He would send word far and wide to catch us. To see him stretch his search to Panama surprised even me. But Costa Rica? I do not believe he would go to such lengths."

"You said yourself, he would follow us all the way to his old Mississippi."

Antônio spat a *bah!* "She told her father we were fraudulent and he had us looked into."

"We were collecting thousands of *pesos* from his friends," I said. "To quietly investigate our backgrounds would be prudent."

"Then why didn't you want to leave when the leaving was good?"

Beryl reached out to me, and I took her hand. She glared at Antônio with sharp, hating eyes and a severe frown.

"My father is not a coward. You do not have the right to speak of him in such a way."

"Then why do you run from him?" Antônio roared.

I placed myself between them. "It was Lowell," I said to Antônio. "He saw the poster and sent word to Santarém—"

Antônio stabbed a finger at the poster. "That was *nowhere* to be seen in Puerto Limón when we departed! I have not seen a copy circulated since we left Panama."

I gently extracted the poster from her clenched hand.

"You never asked if we are guilty of murder," I said to her. "Did you already decide?"

"I decided nothing," she said defiantly.

"Do you believe me, then?"

"You have told me nothing about this for me to believe."

With both hands, I crushed the stiff poster paper into a tight ball. "The two men who died deserved everything they got."

I peered down on her soft face, hoping she would understand and not carry this further. Seemingly, she heard my thoughts. "I believe you," she said, touching my cheek.

After she left us, Antônio braced me. "You put too much trust in her."

"Let us see if they are waiting for us in Plymouth with shackles and warrants. Only then will we know if our escape was as successful as we believe."

"And if they are waiting? What then?"

From under the pillow in my hammock, I produced my Colt. It was fully loaded when we fled Hacienda Garcia.

"Mine still holds two rounds. Yours?"

Seventeen

The tracks between Reading and London are better maintained than the rails that carried me from Princetown. Hopefully, my penmanship will improve for this stretch of my account.

Beryl accepted my proposal on the third day of our voyage. The unshaven captain married us in his cramped cabin, sealing the sacrament in continental Portuguese, and even made a brief speech about the sea bearing witness to all of mankind's acts, terrible and beautiful. Antônio was my best man. The captain dug out of a trunk a sundress for Beryl. "I do not believe I am the first *señorita* to stow away," Beryl said as she modeled for me.

The three of us held an informal reception in the cargo hold, Antônio and I taking turns dancing with the bride. Beryl and I pretended we were in the ballroom at Baskerville Hall, surrounded by doting lords and ladies and earls and dukes. Antônio slept topside that night, leaving Beryl and me to the banana gas, the rats, and the younger sailors sneaking down to the hold at odd hours while we consummated our betrothal.

I made a singular acquaintance on the voyage across the Atlantic. An Englishman named Fraser had traveled to South America in search of a fresh-air cure for his consumption. He arrived in the New World a man wasted thin by the foul and sulfurous smoke of England's notorious coal-burning factories. He did not find the humid Amazon delta to be his anticipated Eden. His search up the coast for drier and fresher air brought him to Puerto Limón, where some relief was had. Alas, his funds were so depleted by then, he had little choice but to book passage home on a trade ship with a single passenger cabin for let.

My initial encounter with him was a two-hour conversation on the history of schooling in Yorkshire, the adaptive mimicry of Amazonian longwing butterflies, and his observations on the baronets of England. We parted on amicable terms with an agreement to meet the next afternoon for another illuminating conversation.

I gathered Antônio and Beryl in the hold to formulate a new design. My ulterior motive was to force an alliance of necessity between them, a kind of negotiated peace, while also forging a new identity for us in England.

Fraser knew nothing of our fresh marriage, as he mostly delegated himself to his cabin. My design was this: Beryl would be my wife of three months. All our luggage and valuables, right down to our wedding rings, had been stolen during our honeymoon in Puerto Limón, hence our situation on the ship. Antônio would be my manservant and attendant: a gentleman's gentleman. He bristled at the role, but conceded to the logic of the request.

"But no more aristocracy," he demanded. "Sir this, Lord that, no more!" Before I could protest, he added, "The peerage game played well in Panama and Limón. I do not believe it will fare so well in England." He clapped his hands about my face. "You, though, with your cherry-red cheeks and Saxon nose and mannered English...you will camouflage yourself well among their ranks."

And so I would be Vandeleur, nothing more and nothing less. I was forced to keep the name, as the ship's captain had informed Fraser of it before we met.

We disembarked at Plymouth with a kind of jumpy calm that is difficult to express. Down the gangplank of the *Ilhas Canárias* we descended, three bedraggled passengers on a merchant steamer, bearing neither bag nor purse, only in possession of the clothes on our backs and the pistols concealed under our coats.

Thankfully, there was no constabulary waiting for us at Plymouth that morning, no exchange of gunfire, only the welcome relief of walking upon steady ground in a banana-free land.

The emaciated Fraser deserves only the briefest of descriptions for the purposes of this journal. A man slight in every way, from frame to personality, he hid in plain view behind a pair of spectacles oversized for the dimensions of his face. He was a tutor, never a teacher, a profession I surmised he aspired toward. He had neither the constitution nor the head for the life of an academic. He had lived with his mother until she died the year prior. His inheritance afforded him a measure of freedom to travel abroad. Without him admitting as much, I gathered he traveled to South America in search of a nurturing soul mate of Latin extraction, as well as a respite for his bronchial troubles.

Most notably, his ability to hold a conversation faltered when Beryl entered the room. It was through her I found my lever.

Fraser needed little coaxing from Beryl to purchase passage for us to London. Onboard the express, we found a compartment for four, but Antônio successfully boxed him out with the apology that Beryl needed space for a nap. With him out of our presence, Antônio latched the door, and we had our privacy once more.

"He has family in London he must attend to," I told them. "After three nights, we all continue on to Yorkshire. In Limón, he learned of a unique opportunity there. A private boarding school has been closed for a decade and failed to find new owners. It was slated to be condemned by the city. Fraser offered to acquire the deed, attract instructors, and return the school to its former glory. He has staked his inheritance and pledged to raise the remaining capital himself."

Antônio patiently waited for me to reach the conclusion of my explanation. "A *school*?"

"We will accept only children of gentry, nobility, and good breeding. And we will only employ the finest teachers in Northern England."

Antônio flung up his hands. "You are *louco*. Surely you do not expect to fulfill this dream of yours. Tell him," he said to Beryl. "This is as empty as his Butterfly Pavilion."

"My sweet," Beryl said to me in elegant Spanish. "This will not succeed."

I told them, "We are not in the New World! These English, do you believe they will receive us with great delight when they learn of our history? Think back on the station platform in Plymouth. Did you see a solitary person pleased at our appearance? This is a place most unwelcoming to strangers."

"You mean they will send us back?" Beryl asked.

"Not at all. They are more than happy to put us to work. You think only Panama has need for strong backs to shovel shit and mud? We can certainly find employment here in England. We can wait on them hand and foot. We can hoe and water their lovely gardens. We could enlist in their army and go fight their battles in Africa and India. Why, we could even sleep with their pigs and slaughter their hogs when they're fat."

"You have made your point, Rodrigo."

"If I can make a name for myself in Yorkshire, I can rejoin my family in Devon with my head held high. As the headmaster of a prestigious boarding school in Yorkshire, the Baskervilles will surely welcome me to the fold."

"As a Vandeleur?" Antônio asked. "Or a Baskerville?"

"I will handle the transition when the time comes." I took Beryl's hand. "We are young. One day, I promise you, the baronetcy will be granted to me. I will be Sir Rodger."

She put her pert nose in the air. "Lady Rodger. It suits me."

"Antônio, you will be my counsel and secretary. We will all live at Baskerville Hall in the style and manner which we deserve."

Antônio fumed and argued for many miles. Finally, he acquiesced to my vision with a *Bah, have it your way*.

Beryl curled next to me. The door to the car offered auditory privacy, but anyone passing could look inside and see us plainly. I told her not to sit so close, and to mind herself in public. No throwing her arms around me, no hands held in public.

"The English look down upon such displays. If we are to put on the pretense of English husband and wife, we must be mindful of English customs."

"Where I am from—"

"We are no longer where you are from," Antônio said. "Do as he says."

Outside the window, the English countryside flew past. The rolling green hills had been tilled into orderly squares and cleanly demarcated property lines. It was just as the British had laid down their gridded railway lines and systematic laws in every country they conquered. Nothing is so orderly in the Amazon, where the jungle grows in all directions at once, or in Grimpen Mire, where any building left untended will be consumed by the bog.

"So gray here. So cold and wet." Beryl sounded disappointed. "When will we see the beautiful English springtime you have told me about?"

"This is springtime," Antônio said without averting his gaze from the window.

Eventually, Beryl asked me, "What is a baronet?"

Antônio groaned and stood. "I will see if there is a bar car." And he left us.

"A title bestowed upon my family hundreds of years ago by the English king," I explained. "My forefather Hugo fought for preservation of the crown."

"So you are noble?"

"No. I am a member of the aristocracy."

"What is the difference?"

"What's important is, my family is recognized across the land. When I become the baronet, we will lead the Baskerville family line into the twentieth century." I stroked her chin.

In London, Fraser once again came through with eight five-pound notes for us to use during our stay. He was buying our companionship, and at that moment, we were selling it. Then he was off to Kensington to visit extended relatives.

The first order of business was to secure lodgings within our means. Beryl complained we would have enjoyed comfortable and warm board with Fraser's relatives in Kensington. She was more aggrieved when I mentioned it was a tony district, as I recalled from my father's recollections of life in England. Antônio, a human bloodhound if there was one, managed to locate rather cheap lodgings near the station. The landlady demanded we take two rooms, as my story of being robbed of our wedding bands held no water with her.

While negotiating the charges, Antônio overheard the distinct chatter of Brazilian Portuguese outside the door. Asking for a moment from the landlady, he discovered in a side-alley a pair of dun-haired men arguing over a debt. Antônio intervened and I joined him. Soon we learned of a cafe in London run by Brazilian expatriates. The two men warmly invited us to join them that evening for supper and revelry.

When we returned to the diminutive landlady, she stood with the room keys clutched in one hand and her arms folded stoutly. "We don't take kindly to foreigners around here."

In my highest accent, I said, "Madam, my considerable business dealings with São Paulo traders has left me with a command of the country's native tongue. I assure you, I am of hearty English stock—"

"Well, you certainly don't speak like the sort of man who needs lodgings in these parts!"

"As I explained: We are low on funds due to a brazen act of theft." A crisp five-pound note settled the issue.

Eighteen

I retread today the London roads I first traversed those many years ago. Antônio found England an alien and gray world; Beryl, a cold place inhabited by cold people. London invigorated me then, and it invigorates me today. Its liveliness and multiplicities outshine any city I have visited. Puerto Limón's vibrant embarcadero would be one marketplace of many in a London square, and London's outdoor stalls outshine Limón's exotic offerings ten-to-one. All the world stands on London's doorstep with its goods in a seller's case, and London looks over their wares with its infamous stiff upper-lip.

Crossing Vauxhall Bridge today recalls the first time Antônio, Beryl, and I crossed it. Standing over the Thames, we watched the flat-bottomed boats skating over the river to taxi their fares from shore to shore. On the south bank, we followed our new Brazilian friends' muddled directions. We soon found ourselves lost among the warehouses and machine shops, all closed due to the lateness of the hour. It was Beryl's fine ear that saved us. She led us to the source of the guitar and maracas, an underground late-night cafe at the bottom of a stubby flight of stairs.

Café *Dona Isabel* was steamy inside from the hot cooking and the innumerable Brazilians crammed inside the narrow room. Compatriots from our homeland occupied elbow-to-elbow long tables draped in motley cloths. Antônio and I recognized the dialects peppering the raucous air, mostly from Rio de Janeiro, but truly a sampling of all of Brazil.

The guitarist in the far corner ended abruptly upon my entrance, terminating with a jerk the dancing and the rattle of the maracas. Dozens of faces, all so familiar to me, yet all strangers, glared back from their tables and chairs.

Antônio said to the silence in Portuguese: "We are friends."

An overweight man in a sauce-stained apron with a thick brambly beard stood at the kitchen. He raised a wooden ladle toward me. "And him?"

In Portuguese, I said, "I was told the best *feijoada* outside of Brazil could be found here."

Someone laughed, and the laughter spread to a few more gentle souls. Gradually, the din of conversation returned, as did the music and dancing.

Two expatriates made room for us at one of the tables running the length of the room. Within minutes, plates of *feijoada* and bottles of English beer were before us. A basket of stale bread, all crust, joined our plates.

My ravenousness stunned me. I heaped spoonful after spoonful of beans and meat into my mouth. With the simple food came a sense of helplessness, a moment when you have no one around you to thank, but you feel you must thank someone, and exuberantly. So starved for the soul-nourishing pleasures only *feijoada* can offer, I found myself bent over the meal like a dog before his only bowl of the day. When I stopped for air, I peered at Antônio across the table. He was mirroring my single-mindedness over his own bowl of the stew. Breathing through our noses, mouths full of beans and sauce, we nodded at one another with expressions of such surprise, they might have been mistaken for horror. We returned to our noisy but wordless meal.

"Good food, eh?" It was Jorge, one of the men we'd met outside the rooming house. He dropped into the bench between Beryl and myself without warning. "Tell me of news from home."

"We would ask you the same," Antônio said warily. "We come by way of Costa Rica."

"Is that where you found this beauty?" He was a rough man, and unshaven, and he eyed Beryl up and down as though valuing a cut of veal. "There is news, and there is no news. The Empire of Brazil lives another day, although I wonder if the end-times are near." His grave suggestion was broken with a great smile and a clap across my back. "Do not worry! No spies here. Tell me—" His businesslike demeanor returned with such suddenness. "We are small in number here in London, but we are a tight people. We have to be. This city would divide us, if we allowed it. It makes us compete for the same jobs, and we scrabble among ourselves for the same boarding. So we stay together, and we spread the word to keep us bonded."

"We know no one here," Antônio said. "We followed no one. I am the first of my family and friends, I am sure."

"I am Costa Rican," Beryl said softly. "Just as you said."

"No Costa Ricans in London, I am afraid." Jorge clapped my shoulder a second time. "And you, my friend?"

Well aware Antônio would smolder if I broached the subject, I stood upon my dignity and declared: "I am a Baskerville. My family lives in Devon, although I was born outside of São Paulo."

Jorge pursed his lips and murmured to himself, *Baskerville, Baskerville, Baskerville.* Whereas Beryl's mock Valencian accent at the Hotel San José reduced my family's name with a pronounced lisp, Jorge spoke it in earnest Portuguese, with the twin *elles* at the finale sustaining rather than coming to a drowsy stop.

"Francisca Baskerville?" he asked me with a confused expression.

"That is my mother's name. How did you come to know this?"

"She is in London," he said excitedly. "Not far from here."

He raised himself from the bench with as much force as he'd used to pry himself between Beryl and me. "My friend, you must go to her now. She is not long for England."

"How do you know—?"

"I told you, we are a tight people here. I make it my business to know all Brazilians who come and go from this city."

He practically lifted me from the bench. He fetched my hat and coat from the peg I'd hung it on. He clapped my hat on my head and put me into my coat.

"Your friend and beautiful gal, they will be waiting for you here. I will keep them company until you return." Forcing me to the door, he explained in brisk Portuguese where to find her. "She lodges with a woman from Fortaleza. Hurry. Your mother, I believe she leaves in the early morning. You must see her, go now."

Pushed out into the brisk night air, I climbed the stairs two loping steps at a time. Peering down at the golden light and joyous music spilling out the open cafe door, I pondered for a moment if there was tomfoolery afoot—that I would return in an hour to find my wife and friend robbed, or worse. We were new in London, and our naive wonder at its splendors and scope were exploitable. For all his rapid shifts of emotional emphasis, and his rush in hustling me outside, Jorge did seem the only person we could count on in this city. *We don't take kindly to foreigners around here.* What's more, against striking odds, he knew my mother's given name. That is a quite a parlor trick, if it was one.

The directions he fed to me in the clamorous cafe were of the same high caliber as the directions offered to us outside the rooming house. Making my way through the dark streets of the Vauxhall district, I found myself nearly lost once more. Thankfully, I located the address, a lonely residence with a tin roof and a dark red door among the warehouses. Lights from within told me I was not too late.

"Yes? Yes?" answered a woman. I told her in Portuguese I was there to see Francisca Baskerville. I remained suspicious Jorge was guilty of some manner of ruse. The woman, however, answered in return, "Who is calling?"

"Tell her Rodger Baskerville, her son."

Startled, she permitted me inside. She showed me to a sitting room of kerosene lamps, English doilies, sepia portraits of Brazilian ancestors, and hard chairs and old sofas. I remained standing with my hat in my hands, fingers nibbling at the brim.

When my mother entered, she gasped and slumped at the sight of me. We helped her to a chair. As I patted her hand, the door to the room creaked closed. I peered up in time to see our host's grave face before she shut it.

"Mother—" I went to the basin and drew a glass of water for her. "How did you come to be here?"

"You ask me such a question? Are the charges I have seen you accused of accurate?"

"Absolutely not." Martin Harris and Jimboy Duffy riled Augustus to violence, and he came back at them as a lion might a circus trainer. "The Americans blindly rage over their dead sons, and we Brazilians are their scapegoats."

"So you fled to England. The land of your forefathers. The dream of your father."

"Where is he?" I made a motion for the door leading to the inner part of the house. "Can I speak to him?"

"Your father is dead."

The word *morto* smoldered between us, just as the flame in the kerosene lamp did.

"His heart gave out. His heart gave out thirty years ago, I should say. It took me far too long to realize it. I mistook his frailty for an uncommon gentleness. And his English, aristocratic ways, I mistook them for actual gentility. When we married, I believed he would love me as much as I loved him."

"Didn't he?"

"Did he love any of us? Sitting in that chair night after night, pining for England? Well, he finally has returned. With every bit of money I could scrape up, I brought him home."

"In Devon? Buried at Baskerville Hall?"

"No, here, in London! A pauper's grave."

"We should go together to Uncle Charles—"

"I leave this godforsaken place in the morning. I charred for three months to earn my return fare to São Paulo. I wash my hands of the Baskervilles once and for all."

"I will have him disinterred. He has every right to be buried at Baskerville Hall."

My mother sat still for a long while beside the lamp. Inky shadows darted across the side of her face and her bun of hair. In the years since last seeing her, she'd aged twice as much. Her tired eyes and puckered mouth told me of a weariness I'd only faintly detected living with her in that plank board house. Every evening, she set our dinner on the table with a weary thud of the bowls, and she washed our clothes with a weary frown and lifeless eyes. That night, she spoke of my father as bad luck being shaken off at last.

"Why do you respect him so?" she asked.

"He was a great man. He was subject to a misfortune."

"He married me thinking a woman would save him from his past. How could I? What could I possibly do, when his problems arose here, thousands of miles from our home? And you—he wanted you brought into this world to carry on his name. But what name did he have to carry? He has only saddled you with his curse."

"I do not view my family name as a curse."

"It's a curse all the same, and you will never be free of it." She turned away from me, as though in disgust. "I should never have come to England."

It was poison she was pouring into my ear. It made me sick and left me feeling vile. She was cold to me as a child. Perhaps I looked too much like my father. Certainly I looked nothing like her or her brothers, whom I have met only once. In my last years at our home, she treated me and my father like weary obligations. Writing this now, I cannot say I blame her.

When I was four, I told her to stop calling me "Rodje," her term of affection for me. "My name is Rodger now," I informed her. And when she forbade me from leaving home at age seventeen, I told her without a twinge of remorse: "You care for my father. I will care for myself." And I left.

I dropped to one knee before her. When I took the hands in her lap and held them, she shook me off much as I shook her off years before.

"I see the weight you carried," I said. "Father was never going to support us. You did. I see that now."

She refused to look at me. She dug the heels of her palms into the chair's arms, to push away from me.

"I am your son. I deserve your—"

"You deserve nothing." The way it's pronounced in Portuguese, it sounds taunting to the English ear, and not the flat dismissal she intended. "You left me alone with him for the most miserable years of his wasted life."

"He was a hurt man—"

"Who refused my love, who refused your admiration, who rejected us out of hand. Every evening, to see you on the rug before him lapping up his stories about this land. You wanted Camelot. Look—look outside!"

Though the lace curtains were closed, I could make out the flames erupting from the factory stacks at Battersea. They bellowed coal soot all hours of the day.

"Your father's family never answered my requests to bury their son at their estate. I forget how many letters I sent, and they answered not one. Behold your inheritance, Rodger. There is nothing for you in England."

I stood before the cold fireplace for a long while. The flame of the lamp darted and made dancing shadows, and the wick sizzled.

"My inheritance is my responsibility," I told her. "But I want from you one parting memento."

"Your father left nothing behind."

"Every night in that chair, he told me of the grand institution his father boarded him in as a child. I have forgotten its name."

She spoke the English words thickly: "Downey School. In a place called Bristol."

"And the teachers. The ones who hurt him."

"Your father rarely spoke of his time there. I only know the name because—"

"He spoke of them when he drank himself into a stupor. He told me their names, but I do not recall them."

She shook her head and murmured an old Portuguese saying about children who don't listen. "Your father's curse, you wear it like a badge of pride."

"It is my inheritance."

She said something under her breath, and it sounded like a hex being cast upon me. "The teachers, he called them Lawson, Carrington, and Dell. That is all I remember."

From my purse, I extracted one of Fraser's five-pound notes. With a grim sneer, she wrapped her bony hand around it and crumpled it into a pocket of her dress.

"You think you've cared for me now?" she called at me.

As I stood at the open front door, a hearty blast of frigid air coming off the Thames chilled me to the core. The lamp's flame almost died.

"What do those names mean to you?" my mother called out. Her tone had an edge of apprehension to it. "What will you do with them?"

"Return to Brazil," I said. "Never concern yourself with the Baskervilles again."

Nineteen

With the money Antônio lent me in Princetown, I paid for a room in full and retired for a few hours of rest. Afterwards, I spread a map of the city across the room's table. I pored over the warren of faint lines marking London's countless roads and alleys. My goal was to acquaint myself with a minimum of three escape routes from 221B Baker Street should I be forced to flee with time against me. Only when I was satisfied with my plans did I administer my disguise, check my pistol, and set out from my lodgings.

On Baker Street, I located a bench and hired a bootblack to make them shine like sterling. Half an eye on the house entrance, half an eye on the boy at work before me, I couldn't help but reminiscence over Antônio finding me so many years ago on the streets of Santarém. This London scamp on hand and knee scarcely glanced me in the face, and not once in the eye. Once finished, he efficiently swallowed my tendered coin with one hand, closed up his kit, and set on his way to locate his next pair of boots.

Soon an older lady emerged from the Baker Street entrance bundled up and with scarf around her head, evidently departing for the evening. From her attire, I expected her to be the landlady, or perhaps a house cook. Half an hour passed with no indication of life within the residence. Dr. Watson's writings—yes, I read them in the papers, just as every other English-speaking person in the world has—informed me Holmes' residence was on the first floor overlooking Baker Street, where he could stand at the curtains like a hawk and observe London street life. No stirrings for a great deal of time, and no illumination from within. If he'd addled his mind with cocaine, as he apparently is wont to do, he might still be in the apartment in a stupor. To be so brazen about one's addictions! To have your so-called friend publicize them worldwide, and approve of these personal revelations to his eager readership!

I located a brief alley behind Baker Street referred to as March's Way on the map, although the Way went nowhere. The stubby dead-end was narrow and lined with refuse cans and rubbish. It terminated at a brick wall several stories high. Mentally, I calculated which set of windows along the alley's south face belonged to 221B Baker Street. Once assured no one approached on the street, and that no one was peering down on me from above, I screwed up a sizable amount of courage and set about with what could have been my final labor in this world.

I stripped off my overcoat: There was no way to continue wearing it. In the dim evening light, I started my careful climb up the back of the house. The ground floor windows were barred and locked. I continued up the wall using the bars of the windows as hand- and footholds. With considerable exertion, I pulled myself to the first-floor windows. The initial one resisted, evidently locked, or perhaps stuck, as wood-frame windows are wont to warp in the damp English clime. Careful to avoid scuffing the wall and alerting any inhabitants inside, I made my way horizontally to a narrow window farther down the alley.

Below me sounded the telltale clopping of men's boots and the clicking of women's shoes. I pressed myself against the side of the house and held my breath.

The evidently inebriated couple made merry at the mouth of the alley. He tugged at her arm to coax her into the dark recesses of March's Way. She laughingly resisted and smacked at his arms. Their merriment included some choice banter I shall not record here. Each dropped their fair share of aitches while exchanging their crude double entendres.

After an excruciating period of time—three minutes? five?—the couple stumbled along. I only relaxed when I could no longer hear their slurred voices and uneven steps. My arms shook so, I thought they would buckle and I would fall to the street.

Hanging now from the windowsill, I made a final exertive effort to bring my eyes up over it and peer inside. It was dark inside, no evidence at all of a soul within. Emboldened by this welcome news, I clamored to lift myself and force the window open. It rose with some effort. Scrambling now, I heaved myself through it and rolled on the floor, heaving hard and arms trembling from exertion.

I lay in a hallway at the head of the entry stairs. A washroom to one side offered a place for guests to freshen themselves.

Heart thumping in my neck, I crept to the only other door the hallway presented. It was deceptively narrow, as though for a utility closet. I surmised it led to the inner sanctum: Sherlock Holmes' apartment and residence. Inside would be his sitting chair, his violin, his laboratory, his pipes and tobacco, and piles and piles of books and newspapers. I laid a gentle hand on the knob and twisted ever so softly. It did not give.

From the floor below came the unmistakable sound of a door unlocking. Streetlamp light and the din of Baker Street's evening traffic threw themselves up the stairwell. Reasoning it was the landlady returning home, and further reasoning she resided on the ground floor, I remained still at in the upper hallway believing I might still avoid discovery.

Voices came up the stairwell. Not one voice, but two, and both men's. The pitch and timbre of Holmes' voice is unmistakable. The other may or may not have been Dr. Watson's, but at that moment, his identity seemed irrelevant.

Climbing out the window from which I entered was foolhardy. The men would discover my exit, and in my haste, I would risk injury or death.

The safest option, but one with its own risks, was to step gingerly for the narrow washroom, close the door, and wait inside. Colt up and ready, I waited in the powdered darkness.

The men climbed the stairs with some noisiness. Holmes spoke with the flourishes his biographer loves to emphasize in his writings:

"So, Inspector, you've traveled across the city to inform me the business in Devon has concluded to your satisfaction? Hmm? Yes?"

The other man's voice did not fill the house the way Holmes' did:

"Indeed I am satisfied, Mr. Holmes. Your work in Devon was exemplary."

"What, then? Pray, what preys on your mind this evening, Lestrade? The warm comfort of hearth and family awaits. Certainly your doubts can wait until morning. Never overlook the benefits of a good night's sleep when organizing one's thoughts."

Lestrade—a Scotland Yard inspector. I have read of him in Watson's accounts.

"The missus sends you her regards," Lestrade offered weakly.

"I return my compliments as well."

They passed before the washroom door. The clomping of Holmes' feet down the hallway was as much a signature as his voice. To face the man, as I have, is to face a man most peculiar. He can stand in sheer stillness before you, his thin pink lips moving minutely as he utters the harshest condemnations of your actions or inactions. Then, like a jackrabbit, he bolts off in a flurry, announcing up to the air his grand intentions and schemes, with men like Dr. Watson and Lestrade chasing him in a wake of dust and pronouncements swirling behind him.

"You are not here to exchange pleasantries."

"No, I am not," Lestrade said. "I am satisfied with the outcome of the business in Dartmoor, but even you must recognize there remain unanswered questions."

"'Even I?'"

Lestrade cleared his throat. "Especially you, Mr. Holmes."

A scratching came from the end of the hall, Holmes unlocking the door to his flat.

"After some rumination, I enumerate, hmm...*six* unanswered questions in the matter of the Baskervilles, Lestrade. How many do you number?"

"Well, I confess I've not taken the time to tally them."

"Precision, Lestrade! All matters of deduction are founded on precision of detail. Lacking such precision muddies the clarity required to progress toward a solution."

Their voices muted at that moment, followed by the sound of a door easing shut.

Heart galloping, I ventured out to the hallway. Holmes had lit the gas lamps up the stairs. They remained burning. Without the cover of darkness, I suffered a further disadvantage. Still, to be so close to my revenge—although I never considered I might have to kill Holmes in the presence of a Scotland Yard inspector. In Grimpen Mire, I calculated my odds of survival as five-to-one against; in Princetown, I reckoned ten-to-one; here in the hallway, I realized there was no ratio capable of expressing the futility of my plan.

But I would see this through. Holmes has destroyed my life. My prospects for happiness with my love Beryl and my best friend Antônio—wrecked upon the shoals of Holmes' damnable deductive reasoning.

Holmes' bold voice carried through the door's wood panel, and so it was not difficult to eavesdrop on their conversation. Lestrade was forced to speak over him at times in order to be heard above his declarations.

"Tobacco?" Holmes offered.

"I carry my own."

"An inferior blend. Perhaps you're aware of my monograph on tobacco ash. In the course of my study, I detail twenty-two species of tobacco plants native to the Southeastern United States and Mexico, and the varieties cultivated in Africa and Southeast Asia."

"Returning to the matter of Dartmoor and the Baskerville estate—"

"Yes, the six unanswered questions of the great crimes perpetrated there. Unless," Holmes added slyly, "you care to pool your observations with mine, and we discover together the set forms a number greater than six."

"I would greatly appreciate such a cooperation!"

Around the doors cracks wafted the odor of a fine tobacco redolent of chocolate and walnuts. Cushion springs eased and creaked on the other side of the door.

"Begin," Holmes murmured.

"First, there's the history of Jack Stapleton, alias for Rodger Baskerville the Second—"

"One of many aliases, Lestrade. My investigation into his background has led me to a boarding school in Yorkshire which failed under suspicious circumstances."

"Yorkshire? You don't say."

"He let slip to Watson he was a headmaster there. Thanks to my contacts, I learned more of his enterprise. From this information, as well as my brief discussions with Sir Henry, I have traced Rodger's history all the way back to Costa Rica. I believe with further investigation we will discover him to be a national of Panama or the Empire of Brazil."

A low whistle cut through the air. "A foreigner, eh?" Lestrade said. "He certainly looked English to me. Dr. Watson told me his diction and manner were impeccable."

"Impeccable because it is quite authentic. I believe Rodger was closely raised by his father, who took it upon himself to train the boy in the minutiae and peculiarities of our language and culture. Not only is he fluent in our English, we can also assume fluency in the Spanish of the New World and perhaps even the dialect of Portuguese particular to Brazil."

"Well, this information supersedes my investigation into his background."

"Indeed. Your second question?"

"His motivations. He lived an extended amount of time in Dartmoor under an assumed name while pretending to be an entomologist. It is your claim that he assassinated Sir Charles so he could ascend to the head of Baskerville Hall."

"Wrong on both counts." Holmes spoke clipped tones. "Rodger Baskerville did not assassinate Sir Charles."

"Certainly you are not going to blame his wrongdoing on that fiend dog you and the doctor shot up on the moor."

"Obviously, I do not assign human agency to a canine. I do, however, point out that the hound did not even touch Sir Charles. It was merely the sight of such a ferocious beast charging him in the nighttime, compounded by his obsession with the family curse, that caused his heart to fail. Do not object, Lestrade! Ordering an assassination is as criminal an offense and as morally bankrupt as performing the deed one self. Precision, I remind you! Precision in detail is the only sure-footing in matters this complex."

After a lull, which I believe Lestrade used to gather his thoughts, he said, "You declared I was wrong on two counts."

"I never claimed Rodger intended to become the head of Baskerville Hall."

"Well, what then?"

"Being so well known to the residents of Dartmoor, I see no way for Rodger Baskerville to shed his identity as Jack Stapleton and claim the estate in the flesh. Three possibilities exist. One is that he planned to return to Central or South America and claim his inheritance from afar. Presumably he would sell off his family's hard properties and have the liquidity transferred abroad."

"That would be most unfortunate, to have the good name and legacy of the Baskervilles eliminated in such a manner."

"Second, he may have planned to develop a disguise and claim the estate, either in Devon or here in London."

"That seems more reasonable. Although—"

"Yes?"

Lestrade spoke hesitatingly. "He would have to maintain such a disguise continually while in Devon. Or perhaps in all of England! If even one person were to recognize him from his past life, well, the entire charade would collapse." After a moment of silence, he said, "Mr. Holmes?"

"I am considering your suggestion. It is backed by considerable insight. I am unwilling to give up on the possibility. Do not underestimate the man! He masqueraded about the streets of London when I first became involved in this business, and no less than Jack Stapleton's good friend Dr. Mortimer failed to recognize him."

"And your third possibility?"

"That he planned to employ an accomplice as a puppet to claim the fortune, ensuring this prop was fronted by impeccable credentials."

"Also seems unlikely, Mr. Holmes. This is not the matter of claiming a hundred pounds for a widow who passed away. This puppet would be claiming a title extending back to the time before the Great Rebellion. His petition would be vetted by observers of the peerage. Even the slightest of suspicion would be cause for delay and questions."

"I reluctantly agree with you, Lestrade, but your reasoning does not eliminate the possibility. That exhausts my list of his possible motivations. What others can you name?"

Lestrade audibly squirmed. "As a man born on foreign soil, perhaps he is an agent of the Empire of Brazil."

"And what possible design could the Emperor there have against a mere baronet whose estate sits in the bog-mire of southwestern England? Sir Charles made his fortune in South Africa, not South America. We know of no dealings or enemies he may have made in Brazil, or indeed the continent it lies upon."

After a pause, and with a considerable amount of pipe smoke filtering into the hall, Lestrade spoke up as though struck with a sudden possibility. "Perhaps he wished to extinguish the Baskerville line?"

I sucked in a sharp breath.

"That strikes me as specious," Holmes said carefully. "He would gain nothing and lose a great deal."

"With Sir Charles dead, the only remaining claimants are Sir Henry and himself. If he succeeded in killing Sir Henry, the Baskerville line would be perilously close to extinguishment."

"True, although my investigations uncovered a relation named Desmond as a viable heir to the Baskerville estate, if not the baronetcy. Perhaps this escaped your attention?"

"I had one of my men visit him yesterday. Mr. James Desmond of Newquay is infirm and bedridden. His mind is such that he fails even to recognize his nurse, who tends to him in his waning days. In private confidence with my man, she admitted he is not long for this world. His children perished in a fire some years ago." Lestrade cleared his throat. "Regardless, I maintain Stapleton's plan could have been the extinguishment of the family line. The Baskerville family line hangs by a thread of gossamer."

Lestrade's revelation hung in the air for a considerable amount of time. The inspector had uncovered much the same information as I did some months back when I too looked into the matter of James Desmond's claim to my family's estate.

"We will continue this line of inquiry later," Holmes said darkly. "Your third point, please."

"Yes, Mr. Holmes. What is your information on Stapleton's father? I believe the Baskervilles made some effort to cover up Sir Charles' brother's existence years ago. It was related to a matter of some delicacy they did not wish circulated."

"While in school, Sir Charles' brother engaged in…improper conduct, I am told."

"Improper? Or criminal?"

"Now, Inspector, let's not start a new investigation while still concluding the matters of the current one, yes?"

"I ask because we often discover these so-called embarrassing boarding school situations involve the faculty. Were any mentioned in your inquiries?"

"Sir Henry specifically requested I limit questions regarding family matters."

"That's…to be expected," Lestrade said.

Another pause. More curls of pipe smoke escaping under the door.

"Perhaps my reasoning is flawed," Lestrade admitted. "I have been discussing Rodger as an Englishman of good stock and good breeding. He is not. He comes from a place whose values do not comport to our own."

"Yes," Holmes said.

"It is unthinkable for a proper Englishman to wish such…*annihilation* upon his own family and his lineage. The Baskervilles are an esteemed family. Even with the carnage wrought upon them these past weeks by their own issue, their reputation remains unblemished. To destroy all that in a fit of chaotic madness is unthinkable."

"Unthinkable to us, yes. 'Tis agreed then: We will not permit this foreign fellow's indiscriminate violence to smear the Baskerville name. We must consider Sir Henry's reputation. He is young and fit, newly flush with title and treasure. Certainly a healthy and bountiful life awaits him." The vitality in Holmes' voice, which had diminished with Lestrade's speculations, began to return. "I will speak with the good doctor about this issue. In his reports for the newspapers, he will ensure Sir Henry's family name remains unblemished in his account of the hound upon the moors."

"Perhaps he can make much of Rodger's foreignness."

"Nay, Lestrade. I will ask Watson to write him out of the tale."

"But Rodger's culpability!"

"Oh, we will preserve his guilt in the telling. But with my encouragement, Watson will simply—" Holmes clapped his hands. "Reduce him."

"I've never read a criminal account, true or otherwise, that failed to spend an appropriate amount of time detailing the criminal himself."

"Watson's power of storytelling is such, he can focus his readers' attentions on the other mysterious details and push our foreigner into the shadows. There's the matter of the escaped convict, the hound and the curse, and the mysterious nighttime activities of Mr. and Mrs. Barrymore. No, our criminal element will remain in the shadows, sidelined to the role of the bumbling butterfly-chaser until the final unraveling of his plan by myself and the doctor."

"The doctor's readership will demand *some* explanation of Rodger's motivations."

"And they will have it, but obliquely. We will strive to distance this violent man from his family. So much so, readers of Watson's tale will barely know his true name. To them, he will be Jack Stapleton and little more. His relation to the Baskervilles will seem almost incidental."

I cannot describe the rage that began percolating within me at this moment. Gun in hand, door unlocked, the temptation to barge inside and let loose cannot have been greater. I never truly considered the mighty power of the pen and press until that moment. To cravenly conspire and agree to this decision over pipe smoke continues to appall me.

"Let us move on to the fourth point," Lestrade said. "It is the matter of his co-conspirators. His man Anthony, well, we've questioned him and learned almost nothing. He is as tight-lipped as they come."

"I believe you will find him also of South American extraction," Holmes said. "His age is deceptive. You noted he's going gray, but he possesses a fine, full head of hair and no indications of developing baldness.

My studies and the work of Mssrs. Balloc and Devereaux on the continent have demonstrated the ease of developing gray across the head and beard due to sudden fright. No doubt this Anthony fellow has shared in many criminal close calls with Rodger, which has led to his appearance as a man in his late fifties. I estimate him to be forty or forty-one."

"Well-observed, Mr. Holmes. He's currently under watch in Dartmoor. We plan on questioning him once more before releasing him."

"Certainly with all the evidence I've provided, and the heinous natures of the crimes in Dartmoor, you could hold him for longer."

"Sir Henry has requested the matter be brought to an end as expeditiously as possible."

"Of course. I trust his judgment implicitly. And yours as well, Inspector."

"That leaves the matter of his wife," Lestrade said.

"A beauty as hers is not to be found among the lower classes," Holmes observed. "You must certainly have noted her slight lisp and the softness of her vowels. It indicates a native speaker of the Romance languages. I believe we will learn she comes from a respected family in Costa Rica or Panama. You will note her manners and courtesies are not as thoughtful as the young women prepared by our country's finer finishing schools. I suspect we will learn she fled from a strict family with rigid designs upon her future. The peoples of the Americas, they view their continents as remaining untamed and unexplored, even though their lands have been successfully mapped down to the smallest wellsprings and tributaries. This thinking infected her with fanciful notions of an outlaw life, and she followed Stapleton across the Atlantic seeking excitement."

Lestrade broke in. "Well, she's been far more cooperative with us than this Anthony fellow. Once we've extracted a complete story from her, we will send her home. I will communicate with the appropriate governments of Rodger's crimes. If he attempts to flee, we should be able to convince them to extradite rather than risk tension with the Empire."

Holmes harrumphed. "That, Inspector, is most unnecessary."

"I know your thoughts on this matter, Mr. Holmes, but you must admit, that is the fifth unanswered question in this ghastly business of the Dartmoor hound."

"He is dead, swallowed up by Grimpen Mire. His corpse lies at the bottom of the bog. It is at this moment being consumed by the roiling sulfurous mud."

"And yet, a corpse is what we need. Without one, we cannot be sure the man is dead."

After a long silence, a mumbling came through the panel of the door.

"What's that?" Lestrade said.

"He *must* be dead," Holmes stated emphatically. "Watson and I searched the moor most thoroughly."

"That moor is treacherous. You can't be certain you looked under every rock and behind every tree."

"The townspeople would certainly have reported him by now!" Holmes declared. "A wild man on the moor pilfering victuals and looting wells for fresh water."

"You told me yourself he was a man of considerable resourcefulness. Perhaps he cached supplies in the bog-mire for such eventualities."

"We searched the tin mine. Empty, save for the kennel he kept there to hold his dog."

"That's another point," Lestrade announced with some pride. "You said you found *two* cages there?"

"What of it?"

"Call it unanswered question number six."

"Six? I question the premise that a spare kennel deserves a whole number to itself."

"Why two cages when there was only one dog on the moor?"

Rustling and footsteps sounded inside. The tapping of wood upon hollow brass came from the door, and a clearing of the throat. A pronounced noise followed, a crisp *schick*, the unmistakable sound of a struck match. Soon, the spicy aromatics of fresh tobacco wafted out the edges of the door.

I waited with Colt in hand for the door to be flung open. Holmes' powers of observations are so legendary, I could not tame the suspicion he was aware of my presence in the hallway. This conversation is a theatrical ruse, I told myself. Any moment he will open the door and cuff my wrists with a great exclamation. If he does, I told myself, I will open fire. My arrest will be the final act of Sherlock Holmes, if I have any say in the matter.

Soon came the sour raspy notes of a bow being drawn across the strings of a violin. After a few scattered measures of a piece I did not recognize, Holmes said:

"The hound was most ferocious. In the course of training the dog, Rodger would have need to move it from one kennel to the other, for purposes of cleaning and supplying the animal with food and fresh water. That is all there is to that matter."

"You don't believe it possible he had two dogs out there?"

"And where, pray tell, is the second hound? Watson and I killed the dog on the moor." The violin began playing again and stopped just as abruptly. "What possible need would he have for a second hound? The one he set upon Sir Charles and Sir Henry was amply ferocious."

"Maybe it was a secondary, in case the first was incapacitated."

"This is not a game of cricket where one has bowlers waiting in relief! Now, Lestrade, I believe our business has concluded. There was one dog, and that dog is dead! Rodger Baskerville planned and executed this entire affair, and he is dead! Really, you tax my patience with your insinuations."

"If I could return to the fifth point—"

"Blast the fifth point. Blast your sixth point with it, the mystery of the second dog you've concocted from vapor. The case is settled. Rodger Baskerville was lost to Grimpen Mire, and the hound of the Baskervilles was shot dead on the moor."

Lestrade cleared his throat. "Of course, Mr. Holmes."

After a long passage of screechy violin notes, Lestrade dared speak again. "If I may, I would like to turn to the rippings in Whitechapel. The business in Dartmoor interrupted our investigations into the murders, and the public continues to demand answers."

"Hold, Inspector. The doctor has arrived on the street below. Allow him to join us before we continue this fresh subject."

With Dr. Watson now approaching the front door downstairs, my time had expired. While the opportunity was as great as my desire, to kill Sherlock Holmes before an armed Scotland Yard inspector and his doctor-friend blocking my escape route required more nerve than I could muster. With the reedy sound of his violin covering my sounds, I trod to the window, eased it open, and hoisted myself outside. When I reached the ground, I hastened into the cool, damp London twilight with my hands deep in my coat pockets. I was not finished with Holmes, but the time simply was not right.

Wednesday, the Twenty-fourth of October, Eighteen hundred and eighty-eight

Twenty

A few days after leaving my mother and the warm reminders of Brazil at Café *Dona Isabel*, we accompanied the consumptive Fraser to Yorkshire. Further conversations with the emaciated tutor revealed he was not quite as thinly strung financially as I'd read him to be on the trade ship. He'd depleted his funds in the New World, but plenty more waited for him at home in York. Enough, it turned out, to put a deposit on the abandoned boarding school on the edge of the city, a place where the urban life dwindled off and the countryside started to blossom. Fraser had used our sojourn in London to make a preliminary offer on the school's deed and charter. The property was on the verge of being condemned by the city so the land may be put to more productive uses. Fraser's lump deposit gave him a grace period of three months to set the school's finances in order and to begin attracting students.

Fraser was slight and insignificant in every way, with an imagination wont to inflate every detail. The facility was far more modest than he'd described to me. The structures would house a mere twenty students, with three cramped classrooms and a drafty dining hall. As we toured the facility with him, he would leap upon any supposed opportunity that could be squeezed from the dry, cobwebbed hulk once known as a school of moral and intellectual instruction.

"The kitchen comes stocked," he said, showing us with some excitement.

"There's not enough equipment here to cook for six mouths, let alone twenty plus faculty," Antônio pointed out.

"We'll require sixty students for profitability," I said. "Three boys bunking in each sleeping quarter. At least the bedrooms are spacious, I'll give it that. Eight instructors at least, twelve if possible. We'll partition the classrooms in half if we have to, and use the dining hall for ad hoc lecturing."

"Surely the instructors will not live at the school," Fraser said.

"The married ones, no. But we will be expected to offer housing for the bachelors. They will have to make do with what we can offer. Except for you, of course," I said to him as graciously as I could manage. "As our premier instructor, I expect you will wish to continue living in town. But I, as headmaster, should live here under the same roof as the students."

"Yes, of course." With a warm smile he reserved for Beryl, he said to her, "But is your lovely wife amenable to such an arrangement? Such a musty and dank place. If you would prefer more comfortable lodgings in York proper, dear, I could procure them." He took her hand and soothed it between his palms.

"My husband should reside here with the students, and I with him."

Fraser took his leave. Our first night in Yorkshire, Antônio, Beryl, and I found ourselves sleeping in the derelict school. We would not see Fraser for several days, giving us time to wander the derelict property and inventory our situation.

So began the arduous task of creating a private boarding school, step-by-step.

An early task was convincing Antônio, in no uncertain terms, this was not a charade to relieve Fraser of his inheritance.

"We will build a world-class institution here," I told him. "Our students will leave here with the benefit of a top-notch education."

"What do we know of education? A year ago, we were harvesting bananas!"

I recited a stanza of Gray with the proper accent, just as my father had taught me. "We will blend a classical education with injected with perspectives from the New World." And I recited a sonnet of Peixoto's, and a bit of Basílio da Gama's *O Uraguai.*

"I do not believe the English will cotton to their children reciting Peixoto when they return home for Christ's Mass."

In a large shed outside, we discovered old bedframes and rusty bed springs stacked in a disorderly heap. From the dining hall, we salvaged wood chairs and serviceable student desks. Fraser had thoughtfully supplied us blankets, pillows, and kerosene lamps. Antônio and I hastily assembled our living quarters before the sun set, while Beryl walked to town for food.

Antônio's initial estimation of the kitchen's inadequacy was off. A fuller inspection revealed three areas for food preparation, plenty of knives and plates and utensils, and a rather spacious oven. Antônio guessed the school's earlier management fed their students big meals so the boys would report home they were eating well, if not learning well.

Our alien Spanish and Portuguese revelries echoed from the kitchen rafters as we cooked, danced, and celebrated. It was not gracious living, but it was *ours*. Beryl did not cozy to her parents' demands for social graces, but she had learned from her mother how to prepare traditional Costa Rican fare. The raw ingredients for such could not be found in Yorkshire, of course, but her skills, and Antônio's long history of cooking grub over campfires, brought together our first home-cooked meal since the three of us came together.

We ate standing up in the kitchen. We laughed and joked, and grew quiet when mention was made of the places or people we'd left behind in the New World. Beryl heated water on the stove for washing the dishes and pots. While Antônio went off to check on the locks throughout the school, Beryl and I washed and dried.

"Regrets?" I asked her in Spanish.

"None."

She extended her arms and twirled about, her drying rag trailing her like a streamer.

"Look at us now," she said. "We have this old, forgotten school all to ourselves. No one telling us what to do. No one ordering me to pinch my cheeks and perfume myself, for my father's business partners are coming for supper."

She took me by the back of the neck and kissed me passionately. Her hair, wild and loose, fell about my face.

"With you, I never know what the next day will bring. I only know you will find a way." She ran a sour, soapy finger across my bottom lip. The lye made my nostrils flare. "But this Fraser and his eyes on me—I do not like it. Only you may look at me that way. And his touch—it is cold."

"Fraser will harden on us. Once he sees that running a boarding school is difficult work, and the social rewards are slim, his purse will close. It will be your job to soften his heart and keep him involved in the school's business."

"How involved?"

"Just enough for him to think he's respected around here. Fraser is not merely a source of money. He is on good terms with the Yorkshire council. He comes from a respectable family, and that will shield us from scrutiny." I seized her sour, lye-ridden finger before she ran it across my gums. "Soon *I* will hold the school's purse, and *I* will have the respectability."

"And me?"

"And you as well, Mrs. Vandeleur."

*

We faced two immediate obstacles. The first was to attract students. Enrollment meant deposit money from parents and benefactors. Deposits meant pound sterling to renovate the school and create an air of propriety and sophistication. As our reputation grew, we could use the names of those planning to send their children as leverage against other well-to-do families, who dared not fall behind in the game of appearances.

This job lay in Antônio's hands. His English was more than passable.

If asked about his accent, he claimed he'd been raised in Portugal before returning home to England, which usually satisfied. As he'd demonstrated in Panama, his power of influence was subtle but profound. If a father were, as they say, "on the fence," I would join Antônio on a subsequent visit, much as my presence in Puerto Limón sealed benefactors for the Butterfly Pavilion. As in the Americas, my accent contributed significant credibility to our enterprise. In Central America, I was a baron. In Yorkshire, I was an Oxford graduate.

We also had to attract instructors. Once we inked agreements of employment from them, even if only tentative, this documentation was leveraged for procuring enrollments. Locating instructors fell upon my shoulders. I demanded this task over Antônio's objections. He argued such a task should go to Fraser who, as a tutor, was more familiar with instructors living in and around Yorkshire. No, I demanded: I will locate our teachers.

A third task remained, one I did not take up with the rest. I contacted a Yorkshire dog trainer with a modest kennel. He sold his canines to the neighboring farmers and warehouses and factories. After some examination of his offerings, and the usual haggling the merchant class so enjoys, I purchased a great brindle Bullmastiff. His coat was bristly, like an enlisted man's haircut, and faintly striped with fawn markings. The trainer was not an amateur by any means, but the dog had not been acclimated to humans. When I first approached, the Bullmastiff reared on its hind legs and snapped at my face and throat, restricted only by his collar and chain.

"This is the one," I told the astonished trainer, who was trying to sell me a Boxer. I named him Aurelius, both after the philosopher-emperor of repute, and as a nod to my pursuit of butterflies and moths. I returned from York with the Bullmastiff, as well as an inexpensive but serviceable hunting shotgun and two boxes of cartridges.

Antônio traveled the countryside seeking parents with children in need of moral instruction. Fraser vetted teaching candidates for me to interview. Beryl prepared the facilities for the inevitable tours we would soon offer. Meanwhile, I started my training of Aurelius.

Breaking his ferocious nature toward me took a matter of days, and was a straightforward matter. After that, my training style was, I dare say, untraditional. On some days, I would give Aurelius the love every dog seeks from their master. I would brush his fur, feed him well, scratch him behind his ears and rub his belly while he murmured a throaty approval. Other days, I would punish him for the slightest mistake or wrongdoing, allow him to go hungry, and tighten the chain about his collar at the slightest complaint from him. I giveth and I taketh away. I was his alpha and his omega.

To the southwest of the school's grounds stood broad groves of aspen and maple among the bald rolling hills. Early mornings and late evenings, I explored the groves to fortify my collection of butterflies and moths. The countryside of York, I discovered to my delight, is a cornucopia of *Nymphalidae*, *Hesperiidae*, and the regal *A. iris*, the sight of which makes me nostalgic for the *D. agathina* of my beloved Brazil. The portable case I'd brought from Costa Rica could no longer hold them all. My collection grew to occupy a utility room in the boarding school, a half-dozen trays of specimens. Beryl found my passion puzzling, but she remained supportive. Antônio declared it a maddening waste of time.

With Aurelius, I began a new morning ritual. Shotgun broken open and Aurelius striding alongside, we entered the groves in search of prey. Those first forays, I would have to bag a jackrabbit myself. Aurelius ran to the felled animal without my permission, and when I caught up, I discovered him tearing apart the rabbit.

Soon, I had trained him to fetch the rabbit and return with it intact. He would present the offering to me and sit on his haunches waiting my next command. After a minute of staring at one another, I would give him permission to tear the dead animal apart.

With more training and patience, I had Aurelius going into the bush and scaring out the animal from its burrow. With great yelps, he alerted me to his discovery. He instinctively knew to drive the jackrabbit into the open, and then to pull back to allow me to finish the coney off with the rifle. Often my shot was glancing, and Aurelius would return with the twitching animal clutching to life itself. We would go through our ritual of him offering me the kill, and me granting him the final death blow.

After a month, I no longer had to carry the shotgun into the groves and thickets. Aurelius would tramp alongside me until he caught the rabbit's scent in the air. He growled and waited for my grant to launch the chase. So given, off he sprung, bounding through the undergrowth and scaring the rabbit out of its hiding place. As fast as the rabbit could sprint, Aurelius was speedier on the turns, prophesying the creature's movements through the brush. He would catch the hare by the neck and give it a great shake. He returned it to me and, panting and faithful, awaited my permission to rip it to pieces, bloody fur billowing into the air.

I was not finished, though. Next was to unwind all the training I'd administered. I granted Aurelius standing permission to bolt the moment he smelled the fear of the rabbit in the air. Later, I granted permission to destroy the jackrabbit the moment he captured it. In time, I only had to offer a low whistle to set the entire orgiastic sequence into motion. So well trained, he didn't even expect a reward or treat from me. The killing was the reward, and his quivering eagerness to destroy was palpable.

Twenty-one

The boarding school, known as Shroudsbury before it closed, had failed miserably for several tedious reasons, all related to financial mismanagement. It was this reputation that lay upon the school like a dogged curse. Antônio's strenuous assertions of the new school's potential and financial stability found no truck with the local gentry. We agreed he would travel further afield. Six weeks after we'd settled into the abandoned buildings, he returned waving a banker's check like a victory flag. It was our first deposit toward enrollment.

"The Pendletons of Sherburn in Elmet," he announced. "They recommended two other families in the area with boys of age I should call upon."

Fraser's vetting of candidates also began to bear fruit. With some coaxing, and invigorated by the Pendleton family's deposit, I secured a signed agreement from two instructors seeking employ in the instruction of Euclidean geometry and ancient philosophy. With their names under our belts, Antônio used them to secure additional deposits from families locked out of other boarding schools, due either to financial considerations or a lack of proper references. From this virtuous cycle, we gradually built a roster of students and a healthy bank account. It was all new money, successful merchants eager to climb to the higher limbs on the tree of English society.

"Three names are key," I pressed Fraser. "Lawson, Carrington, and Dell."

"I've searched the usual registries. They are common names. Why are they important to you?"

"They would have taught at an Anglican boarding school in Bristol."

He coughed phlegmatically. "You mean Downey?"

"Start there."

"You do not know their given names, yet you wish to employ them?"

He excused himself to clear his throat and lungs. Fraser's consumption had noticeably worsened since his return to England and its thick, soot-laden air. Out of earshot, I pulled aside Beryl and asked for her help once more.

"Take him for a walk," I whispered. "Bolster his spirits."

"I do not like it. It is not nice to do this to him."

"There is no discussion. You will do this."

"Please, my love, it is difficult." She fretted over Fraser from afar. "He is a gentle soul. Do you know he lived with his mother his entire life? He nursed her in her old age, and even comforted her at her deathbed. I do not like toying with him so…"

"He is our investor, and he brings an air of respectability to this endeavor. Darling—" I smoothed down the hem of her collar and straightened the peridot pendant dangling from the center of her choker. "When the school is up and running, *we* will be the respectable ones. And then we can leave poor Fraser to his schoolchildren and his aunts' tea parties."

"Promise me we will not hurt him."

I laughed and squeezed her wrists. "He is our ticket to independence. Why would I do anything to harm him?"

And Beryl led him on a walk of the school's grounds, her arm through his, where he recounted for her once more the great busyness that was made there before his beloved Shroudsbury was shuttered.

*

Although our school remained devoid of students or instructors, Antônio still found it necessary to lead me to a quiet room to secure our privacy. It was what was once a small and cozy library, now a barren room of dusty shelves waiting for the remaindered books we'd purchased from a local dealer.

"Why did you send me to Dartmoor?" he demanded. "You told me the mansion there was occupied by a wealthy tin merchant. It was Baskerville, and you knew it."

"Did you speak with him? Uncle Charles?"

"I spoke briefly with *Sir* Charles, yes. He's past my father's age. He complained about his heart twice during our meeting."

"Friendly?"

"Amiable enough. I do not believe he entertains many visitors out there on the moor. Lives with two sturdy servants who have been with the family their entire lives. A husband and wife named Barrymore."

"Any sons?"

"No. He's childless."

I clapped my hands. "Look at me with a twinkle of respect in the eye, old friend. I am next in line for the Baskerville estate. I am the next baronet of Baskerville."

"You wish to see Sir Charles dead? He is your family."

"He's a frail old man with a bad heart. Time is our ally, my friend. We bide here. We establish ourselves as a proper school of instruction for young men. When Uncle Charles dies, which he will in due course, I travel to Dartmoor and claim my inheritance and the title."

"As Headmaster Vandeleur?"

"The distance between York and Baskerville Hall will provide sufficient cover. When I arrive there, I will arrive as Rodger."

"And this place?"

Peering out the window, I waved him off. "We will unload it on Fraser."

Beryl and the consumptive tutor trudged slowly through what was once a vegetable garden tended by the students. Fraser patted her hand as they strode.

"The three of us will live well at Baskerville Hall." I swung back to him with a bright grin. "Tell me of it."

"You've never seen the estate?"

"Not even sketches. My father described it to me countless times. Describe it to me, in your words."

"First, tell me about these three teachers you're so desperate to hire. Lawson, Carrington, and Dell."

"It's a trifle. An impulse. Tell me about the Hall."

He let out a low, disapproving groan. "No," he said with a shake of his head. "Fraser bends to your will. And if he balks, he will bend to Beryl's entreaties. And Beryl will do whatever you ask of her. I see it in her eyes. You have smitten her, although you never quite give her all that she wants of you."

"What of it?"

"Give some love. Withhold some love. Give some reward. Withhold some reward. I taught you that. But it was to raise the Major's *Fila* at Far Oaks. It's not how you treat a woman. Especially as fine a lady as Beryl."

I sized him up. "And you? Do you bend to my will?"

"Not I. Oh, yes, here in Yorkshire, I'm your faithful man, your assistant. Beyond this county, I'm an able representative of this school. But within these walls, I am the man who scraped you off the streets of Santarém and gave you a life worth living. You will not forget that, or I will abandon you."

He fumed across the room, seething. I relinquished.

"Those three names are the men who damaged my father. While at boarding school in Bristol, they conspired to take advantage of him as a young man."

He paled. "That is a grave accusation. Are you certain—?"

"All my young life, my father sat peering out his window and drinking from a bottle and telling me stories. His stories of England and Baskerville

Hall, well, they got better with each telling. This is the one story he never wavered on. The details were always the same, and he was a wreck when he finished telling it. My family in Dartmoor, they sent him to Brazil rather than have the scandal breach the doors of Baskerville Hall."

Antônio spent a deal of time in deep thought. He emerged from his ruminations with the steady voice of earnest counsel.

"My friend, this path is destruction. What you are planning will only bring hearings, and charges, and investigations. There will be statements and testimony. Newspapers will come from London and Dublin. What we've built here is fragile. Your actions will shine so much light upon us, it will destroy all that we've worked toward."

He quietly approached me.

"Rodrigo, we are foreigners. Your family name does not erase that. If the English do not throw us in their prisons, they will ship us back to South America. Do not forget, at home, there are several clans of *Confederados* eager for our blood."

"We are not returning to Brazil. Our life is now here!"

"Of course, a great success we have achieved." He flung a loose hand at the musty, empty bookshelves and the dingy windows. "This plan of yours, starting a school, I never believed it. But I always believed in *you*. Where you lead, gold always seems to be found. I told myself, 'This plan is insane, but it is more achievable than a pavilion for butterflies. Maybe there is merit to it.'"

Antônio put heavy hands on my shoulders, the lead weights of honesty and plain talking. "Will you forget about these three teachers?"

I said, "Never."

He pushed away from me. "What will you do when you find these men?"

I composed myself, smoothed back my hair, and straightened my shirt and tie.

"You are traveling tomorrow?" he asked.

"Yes. I have an appointment in Leicester."

"I will travel with you," he said.

"No. You have your schedule. With only two more enrollments, we will be able to open the school and begin instruction."

"Beryl can travel with you, then."

"I do not want either of you near Leicester tomorrow."

"Why?"

With the heel of my palm, I wiped clear a circle of caked dirt from the glass. "I meet Carrington and Dell in the midday. I will interview them for positions on our faculty."

Antônio emitted a deep, regretful sigh. "Rodrigo—"

"Tell me, did you bring any of your luminescent grease across the ocean?"

"No. I did not have the chance to obtain any of the fungus after we reached Puerto Limón. Why do you ask?"

"Shame."

He waited for more. "What will you do after the interview?"

I said, "I will take the two men on a long walk in the woods."

Twenty-two

I rented a cottage in the country outside of Leicester for the interview with Carrington and Dell. A widower living three towns away owned it. He was content to take my money and hand over the key without question.

Both teachers were pleased to hear that their tenure at Downey's in Bristol had left them with a fine reputation. The interview was friendly and perfunctory.

"If I may," Carrington said, "would it not have been more appropriate to hold the interview at the school itself?"

"For this initial interview, I thought it convenient to meet you halfway," I told them. "If things go well here, and I must say, I am impressed, then we will hold a second round of interviews at the school grounds."

"And where is it located?" Dell asked. "Your telegram was not specific." He made a nervous laugh toward Carrington. "The 'north of England' could be just about anywhere."

"But the telegram was quite specific about the money," Carrington said. "The figure is quite generous."

"I will get to your questions in a moment. I was told of the fine instruction one of your colleagues offered in Bristol. A man named Lawson?"

"Yes," Carrington said, almost too quickly. "Music. He taught music."

Carrington was a towering, stately man with a face cut from granite and eyes of the same color. He wore an over-starched collared shirt about his thin neck, cinched tight with a club tie.

"We could not locate him. Perhaps you remain in touch with him yourselves?"

"Lawson met with an untimely fate," Dell said. He was most unlike Carrington, squat and rotund. His pink cheeks and chin shined, as though waxed like a grocer's apple. "It was most unfortunate."

"I'm shocked. What happened?"

The two men had arrived in the same cab. From their familiarity with each other, I knew this interview was not a long-overdue reunion, but rather that they had remained in touch since their days teaching in Bristol.

"He was murdered," Carrington said dispassionately. "In a most heinous way."

"I prefer not to discuss it," Dell added.

Maintaining an act of piqued curiosity, I pressed. "It's unseemly to pry, but hearing of such a foul demise after words of high praise from my contacts..."

"He emerged from a pub one evening and was attacked," Carrington said in his brisk, clipped voice. "It happened in Bristol, in fact. His attacker savaged him until he was dead. He had no time to mount a defense or an opportunity to flee."

"Poor, poor, man," Dell added.

"Did they catch the fiend?"

"They did," Dell said, warming up to the topic. "His attacker didn't flee. He didn't even resist arrest."

"What, the attacker didn't do it for gain? Was it over a woman, perhaps?"

Carrington and Dell glanced at one another in a knowing fashion.

"It was one of his students." Carrington announced it as though performing an act of bravery. "Twelve or thirteen years after leaving Downey's, he returned to Bristol, located Lawson, and jumped him. A young man named Terry Douglass."

"No!" I exclaimed.

"His family hailed from Essex," Dell said. "Of Scottish descent, I believe."

"But why the attack?"

"Psychosis," Carrington said.

"We all knew the young Terry," Dell said. "We all had instructed him at some point during his time at Downey's."

"Perhaps we can change the subject," Carrington interrupted.

"Most shocking," I murmured as I peered down at their *curriculum vitae* once more. "Such savagery. Abroad, yes, I would expect no less. But here in England!"

"Mental illness," Carrington said. When he spoke, his graven lips practically buttoned up between sentences. "Voices in his mind directing him to violence."

"He was a beautiful boy," Dell said.

Acknowledging the interview had turned a morbid direction, I suggested a walk to stretch the legs and take in some fresh air. At the rear of the cottage, I introduced them to Aurelius.

With wide eyes, Dell said of him: "A rather enormous hound!"

"I never travel alone," I said. "We are as one."

"A sound measure, being out here alone," Carrington said. Leicester city center was several miles away, the cottage standing alone on a rolling dirt road. "You never know what miscreant might mistake this place as abandoned and attempt to break in. Such a beast would give any lawbreaker second thoughts."

With Aurelius leashed and leading us, we ventured into the grove behind the cottage. The sun was low in the sky, and the men appeared reticent to venture far into the woods.

"Not dressed for this," Carrington murmured.

I urged them on. Past the trees bordering the grove, I led them by narrow footpaths to a clearing. Tall grass and prickly weeds grew thick there. Moths fluttered about us, beating their glorious translucent wings in their nightly fluttery prayer not to become a meal for an owl or sparrow.

"It's so serene," Dell said, although the quivering in his voice spoke otherwise.

"Might I offer—?" I produced two clean and pressed white handkerchiefs. They gratefully accepted them and dabbed off the sheen of perspiration across their faces and necks.

"This student that killed Lawson," I said. "How well did you know him?"

"Not well," Carrington said, returning the handkerchief.

"He was a fine boy," Dell added, returning his as well. "But he was severely deranged at the end of his life."

"End?"

"He was hanged for his crime." Carrington peered at me dimly. "Why are you so persistent on him? Do you believe it bears on our qualifications in some manner?"

"Do you recall another of your students? A Rodger Baskerville, nephew of a baronet in Devon?"

Carrington and Dell exchanged another glance reminiscent of their silent exchanges in the cottage.

"Perhaps," Carrington demurred. "We taught in Bristol many years ago."

"So many faces and names. A river of memories," poetry teacher Dell added.

"You remember this Terry Douglass well enough. Certainly a young man in line for a baronetcy would leave some lasting impression in your sticky little minds."

Those last words came out a bit brutishly. Good-natured Dell did not seem to notice, but they stirred immediate suspicion within Carrington.

"How do you know of Rodger Baskerville?" he asked. "Are you in contact with his family?"

I released Aurelius from the leash. He had been champing to be free of it. With two soft whistles, I sent him into the undergrowth. He barked reports as he chased to and fro for his prey. Although the sun had not set, it was low in the sky. A smoky fog was creeping across the ground.

"What else did you teach in Bristol?" I asked them both.

"Poetry and the classics," Dell said.

"This is ridiculous," Carrington said. "You've read our *curriculum vitae* and you've interviewed us all afternoon. Certainly we don't need to—"

"What extracurricular lessons did you feel entitled to teach your charges?"

"I say." Carrington stiffened. "I'm tiring of your tone."

"We taught Western values," Dell said, playing the peacemaker. "It was a proper British education, through and through."

"Did your instruction ever take place outside of the classroom?"

Dell, confused, smiled ignorantly. "We lived on the grounds. We were charged with leading by example every hour of the day. We were young men at the time, not the graying souls standing before you now. If you're suggesting we were too strict—"

"I'm speaking of what you did to my father."

Carrington had backed away a pace or two. Dell stared up at me with an incredulous mouth hanging open.

"Did you invade his sleeping quarters in the dead of night? Or did you arrange to meet him elsewhere, where you could control the privacy?"

"Who *are* you?" Dell asked.

"A man named Baskerville."

Aurelius' cries and yelps informed me he had captured his prey. With two more whistles, I called him back to my side. He arrived with a bloody jackrabbit hanging limply from his mouth. Its comically long ears and feet dragged on the ground.

"He won't let it go." I tugged on the rabbit by its hind legs. The Bullmastiff's jaws remained locked about the lifeless animal. "A dog has a single-mindedness, a sense of obligation second to no creature." With a low whistle sounded, his jaw relaxed and the jackrabbit fell to the dirt. "And a sense of utter loyalty."

"We did nothing untoward to Rodger," Dell said, wary of the bloody-mouthed Bullmastiff panting before him.

"That's not what my father told me."

"We cared for him," Dell said. "He was a beautiful boy."

"Quiet!" Carrington snapped.

"I'll give you to the count of three to admit your crimes," I said.

"Admit to what?" Carrington said.

"Otherwise, you'll wind up like this pitiful creature here."

"You wouldn't," Carrington said.

"One."

Dell stepped backward and stumbled. Arms out, he swiveled about searching for an exit from the grove. A cry launched from his mouth.

I pushed the handkerchief Dell had used into Aurelius' snout. It was quite damp with the poetry teacher's copious perspiration. Aurelius' nose snuffled at the new scent, and he began growling.

"You have the wrong men," Carrington said, eyeing my actions. "Your father has told you dire lies—"

"Two."

With the handkerchief covering Aurelius' nose, I grabbed him by the collar and began working him into a froth.

"Terry Douglass was a torched soul," Carrington said rapidly. "Perhaps your father also succumbed to a disease of the mind—"

"Three," I called to Dell, who was now running as fast as his short, round body could carry him. And I whistled twice.

Aurelius launched after Dell like a snare trap snapping shut. Even with the generous lead I granted him, Aurelius was on Dell in moments. The teacher fell to the grass with a scream that ripped through the damp evening air. Another shrill whistle from me gave Aurelius permission to worry the poetry teacher's throat and snap his neck.

While the carnage ensued, I said to the shocked Carrington, "I'm giving you until the count of three to confess."

The stolid, granite-like Carrington now leaked forth a diarrhea of words. "I'm telling you, we are innocent of the crime you are suggesting. We would never do anything to hurt the boys in our charge. To do such a thing to the children would be illegal and unethical—"

"You're speaking of ethics?"

"I have over thirty years' experience in instruction. You have seen my credentials and references, they are impeccable!"

His task complete, Aurelius trotted to my side. The blood about his snout and jaw was rich and dark red. A bubbly pink froth coated his mouth and jaw. It dripped as thin strings to the ground.

"I never hurt your father," Carrington implored me.

"One."

"Dear God, man! I am innocent!"

I stuffed the handkerchief he had dampened into Aurelius' face. The dog activated again, growling and snarling. I held his collar tight to restrain him. I worked up a second rage in him.

"Terry Douglass," I prompted over the dog's growls.

"Terry—he was a strange lad, a quiet soul who preferred the company of one rather than twenty—"

"Two," I said, barely able to hold Aurelius down.

Carrington sprinted. His long legs carried him further and faster than

Dell could achieve.

"Three!"

When Aurelius was right upon him, Carrington produced a sap from his pocket. He lived in the City of London. He must have armed himself out of necessity, a cheap and effective deterrent against cutpurses and ruffians. Perhaps Lawson's fate had put a fear of retribution into his head, and he'd equipped himself to avoid a similar death at the hands of one of his ex-students.

He managed to cuff Aurelius' throat, and then placed the sap across the dog's eyes. The Bullmastiff yelped and fell to the ground. Carrington rained blow after blow across his head, and all he could manage was a pathetic paw up to defend himself. By the time I reached them, Carrington had knocked Aurelius unconscious. The pathetic thing lay on its side, its head open and bleeding profusely.

Carrington bared his teeth. His trim and oiled hair was frazzled. Aurelius had succeeded in tearing a chunk of flesh from his left arm, and his pressed crisp suit was nothing more than wrinkled laundry now.

"What say you now, now that your advantage has been taken away?" He stepped forward menacingly with the sap in hand.

"What did you three do to Terry Douglass?" With every step he took, I retreated in stride.

"I taught him how to be a man," the manic Carrington shouted at me. "They taught him tenderness and gentleness. Dell and Lawson were soft. I made Terry complete."

"He was eleven or twelve," I said, still in retreat. "Just like my father."

Carrington took a practice swipe at me. The sap whistled through the still air.

"Rodger Baskerville was the best of them all," Carrington said through a boastful smile. "The other two, Lawson and—Dell!" He spat in the direction of the corpse fifty feet from us. "The first time they had their chance with Rodger, they were…relieved? He was a wild, proud pony, and they were salivating at the prospect of having him. A baronet's son! A Baskerville, one of England's most storied families! To them, having Rodger was like having a prince. He walked through the halls as though the Baskervilles owned the school." He thumped his sternum twice. "I tamed your father. When I was through with him, I'd broken his spirit. I put him in his place."

"He told me he accused you—"

Carrington coughed a bitter laugh. "Yes, dammit all, yes! Your father thought he could point the finger at us. A student accusing his teachers—what neck he had! Why, he even had the gall to organize his school chums to speak against us."

"Including Terry Douglass?"

He sliced the sap through the air, forcing me back against the dense ring of aspens about the clearing.

"Aye, includin' good ol' Terry!" he said with an affected Northern accent. "But Rodger's school chums, they spoke out against *him.* We let them know the deep shame that would fall upon their families if they stood with Rodger. When the inquest finished, the only pederast at Downey was Rodger Hugo Baskerville. And with that—" He made a motion with his free hand, like a magician's smoke rising to the rafters. "They sent little tattletale Rodger away."

There were only a few feet between the trees and me. He swung the sap once more, keeping me on my toes.

"Once I've broken you, that'll be two Baskervilles I've put down. Graeme Carrington, son and grandson of Northumberland coal miners, a better man than any the Baskervilles managed to produce."

With that, I produced the Colt I'd kept under my coat.

Carrington went down with a great groan I somehow managed to hear over the din of two bullets going into his chest. He was still breathing when I knelt before him. I thought he might give a valediction. Up from the bloody bubbles on his lips, he mumbled before expiring: *Baskerville.*

Twenty-three

Over the duration of the train ride south, Beryl cried over the damage we'd done to Fraser and his dream of opening a school of moral and intellectual instruction. I assured her we had not touched any of Fraser's inheritance. I concede that was far from the case. Money is liquid, and he had poured a substantial amount of his personal funds into running the school.

"He all but proposed marriage to me this morning," she told me. "It broke my heart to say goodbye."

"The truth is an antiseptic. Stings, but necessary all the same."

"The England air is eating him alive, from the inside to the outside." She took my hand. "His skin, it is frigid, and I can feel the bones in his hands. If I did not know we were leaving Yorkshire, I would have offered to become his nurse. I would tell him: 'You stay home and rest. I will be responsible for your health.' But no. We abandon him with the school and all its bills."

"And a plague of yellow fever," Antônio said. We shared a private compartment on the train. "What did you tell the authorities to keep us out of quarantine?"

I ignored him for the moment. When Beryl left us, I explained it to him:

"I convinced Fraser not to tell the doctors we traveled from Costa Rica with him—that it would cast suspicion upon Beryl as a foreigner. When he explained he had traveled alone along the isthmus, they assumed he alone carried it back." Fraser and three sick students were immediately quarantined, while the rest of us in the school were cautioned to remain on the grounds. A caution we ignored, obviously.

We were not sick, and indeed, none of us developed the symptoms of the deadly fever. Perhaps growing up on the continent gave us a kind of immunity, albeit a weak one. Sickly Fraser, already a walking corpse when he arrived in Brazil for his extended holiday, must have been a welcoming carrier of the disease.

Another motivation urged me leave Yorkshire: Scotland Yard had been canvassing schools up through England, and they finally reached ours. Yes, I told them, as we have been interviewing educators for positions. No, I told them after reviewing our records, we never interviewed anyone named Carrington or Dell, nor would any of my staff have met them in Leicester to do so.

I patted the pocket where I kept my billfold. "Our future is bright."

Antônio murmured an entreaty to God. "Now we are robbing children."

"No, the children's parents. Very rich parents, do not forget. None of those boys we left behind will go hungry."

"And Fraser?"

In truth, I felt sorry for the weak, dawdling man who dreamed of nothing more than running a respectable school. From his state when I last saw him, it was apparent he was done for.

We did run a good school. At some point, Antônio conceded my intentions were being fulfilled. Our school housed forty-four young minds, all from reputable families. We exposed them to fresh ideas, teachings they simply could not find anywhere else in England. Twice weekly, I led my class out to the grove behind the school to search for butterflies and moths. Back in the classroom, we spent hours discussing and categorizing our finds. Most went into my burgeoning collection, which I'd managed to pack in two trunks and load onto the train. Antônio argued vehemently against the extra weight, and even Beryl quietly suggested we leave them at the school, but I refused. Everyone has a lifelong pursuit, whether it's books or raising respectable children or world travel. Mine lives in felt-lined cases, pinned down by their wings and organized by species and genus.

After Beryl returned, Antônio said, "Once we reach the port, we should board the first ship to the continent. We could be in France in two days' time. Even earlier, if we move with determination."

"Paris!" Beryl limped across the bench and into my arms. "Let us live there!"

"Our destination is Devon," I told them. "The village of Dartmoor."

Antônio groaned. Beryl, confused, asked me what I hoped to achieve there.

"Your family will not be proud of you," she said. "We do not leave Yorkshire with our heads up high. You will not find approval at your family estate."

"Which is why we should flee for the continent," Antônio said. "It is the height of foolishness to remain on this island a moment longer than we need to."

"We have money," she said. "Enough to live well in a Paris apartment. We can walk along the Seine and drink wine in the cafes."

"In due time, my love. Due time!" I said to Antônio, "When we arrive at Birmingham, purchase three tickets to Devon. We travel in a luxury car!"

For the first time since we had joined, they hesitated together. Their glances signaled an alliance I had not seen before.

"I am not traveling to Dartmoor as a Baskerville," I told them. "We will have to leave the Vandeleur mask in Yorkshire. I will devise new aliases and biographies during our journey to Devon—now, Antônio, hear me out before speaking. We will establish ourselves in Dartmoor. There I will meet my Uncle Charles and insinuate myself into his personal affairs. I will," I grinned wide, "*dazzle* him with my rakish charm."

"To what ends?"

"He sits fat atop a great sum of money. His landholdings alone must be worth a royal ransom. To tear off even a chunk of the Baskerville estate would make what we left Yorkshire with seem a pittance."

"You want to steal from your uncle?" Beryl asked. "This I do not like."

"He will give it to me in a quite legal fashion. He will add me to his will. Old men like Uncle Charles, with no children and few relatives, they are ceaseless in their search for ways to seal their legacy. And men with great wealth have little imagination. Why work for a legacy, when one can merely buy it? He wants his name engraved on buildings and monuments. He wants newspapers announcing charitable endowments he's made."

"The Butterfly Pavilion," Antônio said, thinking ahead of me.

"In Devonshire itself, and named for him. It will be the first of its kind in Europe. The first in the world! All we have to do is butter him up, propose the Pavilion to him, and ensure he makes me a beneficiary in his will as its Director." Then, I did not say aloud, we wait for the final stirrings of his feeble heart.

In silence, we sat in the train compartment as the locomotive rumbled past factories coughing soot into the air.

"I want to see Paris," Beryl pled with me.

"The way we left Yorkshire, we are not innocent in the eyes of the law," Antônio said.

"The way forward is to leverage past success. When we met in Brazil, my friend, we were working in Amazonian rainstorms and shoveling manure from stables. Look at us now! My love in fur and mink gloves! My best friend in a Savile Row suit and bowler! We are on the brink. However—" I took Beryl's hands in mine and clamped them tight. "We cannot live in Dartmoor as husband and wife."

"What? No!"

"In private, we are betrothed. In public, we will be brother and sister."

"Why?"

Seeing Beryl's effects on Fraser, it had occurred to me many times how much more potent her effect would have been if he believed her to be unwed.

"Trust me," is all I told her. "I do this for all of us."

She pouted. "How long?"

"Six months, darling. Once we have the money, we will decamp for Paris and live the rich life. Antônio met my uncle. He appeared about done for. Yes?"

With a deep breath, Antônio nodded an admission. "It is true. He is a cheery fellow, and he welcomed me into his magnificent home, but it was apparent to my eye that he has only a short wick of life remaining. A local friend of his was there, a country doctor named Mortimer, who is apparently looking after his health. While we chatted in the library, Mortimer made some idle talk about a curse upon the family, which visibly agitated the old man."

"A curse?" Beryl glanced between us. "What is this curse you speak of?"

"Some curse laid upon the family hundreds of years ago. From what I gathered, Sir Charles was terror-stricken by it. It caused his frail heart to…Rodrigo?"

My plotting brain had spun up like a dynamo. I was deep in thought, desperate to recall one of the many stories my tequila-soaked father burbled to me as he sat beside that window overlooking the Atlantic.

"A curse laid upon my ancestor, Hugo Baskerville." The memory unspooled in fits and starts from the deepest reaches of my mind. "It was laid upon him for kidnapping a young woman. A fiery hellhound chased my ancestor across the moors of Devon. It delivered retribution by tearing out his throat."

"This is horrible!" Beryl said.

"Apparently, Sir Charles believes the curse rests upon him as well," Antônio said.

"Because the curse was laid upon all Baskervilles to come. Oh, come now, Beryl. It is a peasant's tale, a story to scare children and keep them in line. No one in this day and age would believe it."

"Your Uncle Charles certainly does."

Laughing, I rose. Antônio sat with a brooding, sour expression. I coaxed him to his feet. Finally, a smile managed to break across his face. We clasped and embraced, a display common in Brazil but inexcusably uncouth in dour England. Beryl rose, blushing, and embraced me as well.

"We finish this, and then off to Paris," Antônio said.

"Agreed," I said.

"Your uncle sounds like a gentle soul," she said. "Please tell me you will not hurt him."

"Ours is a game of patience," I assured her. "I will not lift a hand against Uncle Charles."

Antônio began chuckling and shaking his head. Puzzled, I asked him to share the joke.

"What will I do in Paris? I have been a ranch hand my entire life. At least in Dartmoor, I can enjoy the fresh country air."

"We will find you a fat country woman in France," Beryl said.

"You will raise goats with her in the provinces," I added. "You will grow fat with her, eating her cheese and drinking burgundy."

Spirits lightened considerably. That evening, we partook a fine meal of squab, buttered and glazed carrots, and white wine imported from the continent. As they relaxed and enjoyed the countryside moving past, my plotting mind continued to develop our aliases and our backgrounds. The spectral hellhound savaging the Baskervilles had churned up long-compacted topsoil. My family's hoary curse now suggested to me another course of action in Dartmoor.

Twenty-four

The six months I forecasted we would spend in Dartmoor drew out to two years' time. The urgency of life in London and Yorkshire was absent in the countryside. Arrangements are made at a leisurely pace, and fulfilled just as lethargically.

It's remarkable how the British make no bones about class and education. When I first met Dr. Mortimer, he enthusiastically shook my hand and proclaimed relief that another educated person had joined him in Dartmoor. "It is only myself and Sir Charles out here," he said. "And you make three."

Where he saw three, I saw panoply. The grocer, the postman and his wife, the pub regulars, a seamstress and a charwoman—all invisible in his calculations. Mortimer is a high-strung yet amiable fellow, easily induced to agree with suggestions if made forcefully enough, but as a practitioner of medicine, he left much to be desired. To tend to the villagers of Dartmoor as a veterinarian would treat livestock is the key to understanding Dr. Mortimer's character.

And for a man of such supposed education, he held an uncomfortable fascination with craniology. The duration of my initial visit to his practice was spent studying my skull, its lobe sizes and cranial bumps and so forth, each detail fodder for his rather unscientific deductions of my intelligence and mien. I fed him a manufactured biography of my higher education, as well as my father and grandfather's fictional academic achievements. Lo, he discovered it all mapped out across my skull, just as a general's breast medals tell a story of his victories on the field.

The doctor, however, was the village's linchpin. He was one of the few people in Dartmoor who spoke to everyone on a regular basis. He was also one of the few men on cordial relations with Uncle Charles, whereas I, a newcomer, could hardly approach the baronet without seeming toady. In my first visit to Mortimer's office, I pondered aloud how a man such as myself could ever earn an audience with an esteemed gentleman such as Sir Charles Baskerville. Dr. Mortimer suggested he could arrange such a meeting, if the occasion were to arise. Over the months, I made several more appointments with the doctor regarding made-up ailments, always insinuating my desire. He readily suggested such a meeting could be arranged, without ever committing to one. Even Beryl's mesmerizing charms affected him none. I bemoaned my chances of ever seeing my uncle.

As months dissolved away, Beryl and Antônio began to bite at my heels. We should abandon the plan and make for the continent, they said. Beryl in particular grew morose. The English weather was always hard on her, but the dampness and thick fog of Dartmoor proved overwhelming. She was a child raised in the sun, running along beaches and diving into the warm, salty ocean without a care. She complained bitterly of the cold in our house, which never could be warded off, even when she was nestled under layers of blankets beside the fire, which Antônio was tasked to keep lit day and night as part of his role as manservant.

"I miss my family," she told me one evening. "I need to see my mother and father."

"Soon," I told her. "When we are finished here, we can arrange for them to take an ocean liner to the continent and meet us in Paris."

"I miss the sun. And the sweet ocean air."

"The south of France is beautiful."

"I want to see Costa Rica once more."

"If we return, they will hang us."

"They will hang *you*." It snapped from her mouth. "I did nothing."

"My love, if you return to Costa Rica, will you come back to me here?"

"Return to this place?" She flung a hand up at the portraits on the furnished home's walls, old gray British men posing before landscapes of the far-flung British Empire, their moustaches as wide as the horizon. "What is here for me?"

After a year in Dartmoor, Antônio came to me with the morning edition.

"The school was razed." The story said Fraser had died not long after the headmaster and his wife emptied the school's bank account and fled.

"Yes, yes, yes." I pushed the paper aside. "Beryl came to me this morning, crying her eyes out." It was the first we learned of Fraser and St. Oliver's fate.

"Why did you make inquiries with the dog seller in London?" We were arguing in Portuguese. "Ross & Mangles of Brompton Cross?"

Beryl was in an adjoining room sleeping. I had given her a glass of brandy with a few drops of laudanum to settle her down.

"Now you're reading my correspondence?"

"You told me to watch Beryl and confirm she did not communicate with anyone. I found a letter addressed to London. I naturally assumed she was attempting to correspond. When I saw 'Ross & Mangles' on the envelope, I suspected she was contacting a law practice."

Stalemate. "You did as I asked," I said. "I cannot be angry. My inquiry was merely asking if they imported dogs from abroad. Nothing more."

The melancholy weighing down the house lifted two weeks later. Dr. Mortimer sent a note inviting me to accompany him to Baskerville Hall for a gentleman's evening of cards, tobacco, and sherry. Beryl delighted in helping me dress for the occasion. Antônio braced me at the door before I stepped outside.

"Remember, you should have Sir Charles think the Butterfly Pavilion is his idea, not yours."

"I will plant the first seed in his mind tonight."

"If the topic doesn't arise, don't force it. There will be other opportunities."

"I fear there may not." Beryl would suffer if I returned without some evidence of progress. It weighed on me.

After a rough and cold ride across the moor in Mortimer's dog-cart, two servants met us in the drive of Baskerville Hall. He was a gaunt silver-haired man of height and stature, and she a stout woman in a pilgrim's collared black dress. These were the Barrymores, whom I had heard of around the village but never met.

Barrymore led us to the entry of a grand library. Shelves ascended thirty feet to the ceiling, each neatly stocked with bound and buckled tomes. The room was carefully appointed with divans and padded chairs. A raging hearth held a fire larger than even the fires we would burn in the jungle from dead banana leaves and dried palm tree wood, and those fires had to keep a dozen men warm and cook their meals.

"Dr. James Mortimer," Barrymore announced. "Mr. Jack Stapleton of Merripit House."

Across the wide carpeted library stood an elderly man in a dark suit and short black tie, wearing a crosshatched vest and ivory spats. He posed with a hand in his vest pocket and a crooked arm on the mantel. A slim pipe stood straight from the corner of his mouth.

"Good evening, Sir Charles," Mortimer said. "Thank you for having us this evening."

Uncle Charles asked me, "You are the naturalist who has joined us way out here on the moor. What is your specialty?"

"Butterflies and moths."

"A lepidopterist, then."

He surprised me. Few people know the term, and even fewer can produce and pronounce it with such ease. I speculate Mortimer had informed him of my fictional profession prior to the engagement. Uncle Charles had prepared himself to create the effect of appearing well educated.

"I prefer the term *aurelian*," I said. "A more ancient term for those who share my passion."

It soured him, if only a tinge. To correct a man like Uncle Charles is to dance on his dignity.

"Well then," he said, a touch disgruntled. "Sherry?"

Although the evening's entertainments were to involve cards and tobacco, Uncle Charles suggested a brief tour of Baskerville Hall before we settled in. Barrymore trailed with a petite silver tray in hand, for us to rest our sherry glasses upon as we traversed the spacious, ancient mansion of black granite and aged oak.

This was the dream of my youth. It was a dream of verdant green lawns and blue skies above, horses prancing and maids a'dancing, with a moat and a drawbridge and knights in plate mail. From the spangled spires of Baskerville Hall, I had dreamed of peering down upon a countryside of commoners frolicking and making merry.

Baskerville Hall was damnably cold, and the roaring hearths did little to warm it. The estate was a monotonous procession of appointed room after appointed room, velvet walls and stamped-tin ceilings and oil portraits of dead men named Hugo, Baskerville, or Hugo Baskerville. The place stunk of must, rot, and corruption. Beryl's mother managed to make Hacienda Garcia warm and inviting to all, and it was not a tenth the size of Baskerville Hall. Mrs. Barrymore might be a fine servant, but she did not bring a woman's touch to that place. She was fighting at every turn quarried rock, hardwood trim, and tradition. It was a granite battlement erected against the march of time and progress.

"Dr. Mortimer told me of your good fortunes in South Africa," I said.

"I did?" Mortimer said.

"Gold speculation, yes," Uncle Charles said. "As a man of science, you must find such pursuits stifling."

"Finance is not my calling, to be sure. How did you find yourself in South Africa?"

"Oh, that's a story I'd prefer not to tell."

I worried I'd stepped on his toes again. Not that I fretted over his feelings—no!—but rather that doing so might impinge upon my personal goal of planting a seed in my uncle's mind.

He continued after hesitating. "You see, my younger brother died many years ago." He was not cross at all, but wistful. "My mother was heartbroken, of course. And it was quite a blow to my father. My brother's death is also how I learned that I was not the favorite in the family."

"Sir Charles—" Mortimer was visibly uncomfortable. "Perhaps we can see the old chapel?" To me, he said, "Baskerville Hall has extraordinary stained glass—"

"It's fine, doctor, it's fine." He confided to me, "My time is near. My heart is weak. What once angered me later embarrassed me. Now, in my old age, I've learned to accept things. My younger brother was gifted with a natural handsomeness and an easy charm. My parents invested a great deal into his future, which they believed was bright. His death broke their hearts. I fled to South Africa to escape their grief." He smiled as though making a deep joke. "It does not work that way, of course. Well, look here."

In a stale, stony hallway, with an upper story looking down upon us from ornate railing, Uncle Charles halted before a great heraldic shield mounted between racks of spears. It was impressively large, so much so it could have been mounted to the nose of a freight train. Uncle Charles interpreted the heraldry for us, the *dexter* and the *bordure* and *inescutcheon*, and, of high importance, the Red Hand of Ulster in *canton* over the saltire. In his telling, the lines and colors and shapes preserved the history of our family: An ancient Baskerville defending England by defending Ireland. I do wonder what the Irish think of all this.

When we arrived at the parlor, he said to me, "My brother enjoyed a bit of fresh air, just as you do, Stapleton." He motioned to the butler. "I had Barrymore bring this out. Call it an heirloom, an oddity in the history of the Baskervilles."

Barrymore brought to a side table a case of tarnished wood with brass hinges and a clasp. Uncle Charles opened it to reveal eight butterflies pinned to the inner felt. Beside each was a handwritten card noting the species and date of capture. It was an amateur and meager collection.

"He found these on the moor?" I asked.

"I'm not certain how far afield he may have traveled to stock his collection."

Bent over the box, I examined each specimen in turn.

"These four are abundant in this part of Devon," I said. "This *Nymphalidae* here is known as a red admirable, not the *V. cardui* he's mistaken it for. It's less common, but by no means rare. Here is a specimen quite uncommon on the moor, *M. galathea*, or the marbled white. I have seen them flourish around the prison in Princetown over the summer months. This one, however," I tapped the glass, "I have not seen in these parts."

"Wonderful!" Uncle Charles exclaimed. "I should have invited you here earlier."

"Moreover," I continued, "these species cards, while undoubtedly made with the best of intentions, are not entirely accurate. It appears your brother has mistaken some of the species for more rare varieties. I would be happy to provide you with corrections."

"With no disrespect to your deceased brother," Mortimer chimed in.

"Your expertise would be invaluable," Uncle Charles said to me. "We will store your emendations with the case. We would not, of course, replace the cards, as they are in my brother's own hand."

"Dr. Mortimer told me you might have a keen interest in my profession. I took the liberty of bringing a sample of my own collection. I left it with the carriage driver—"

As though a soothsayer capable of foreseeing the future, Barrymore entered with my collection case. He placed it on the table beside Uncle Charles' tarnished one. Within moments of opening it, I had Uncle Charles in a trance. I detailed the varieties with some verbal flourishes, much as I did in Puerto Limón when meeting Garcia's contacts. As I went over each butterfly and moth, he listened with an old man's delight at learning there are still an abundance of secrets in this world, and that they are worth learning.

"And this is a mere sampling of your collection?"

"I have an entire room in Merripit House dedicated to my passion. I have specimens from the north of England, and even Central and South America."

"Stapleton, you are most impressive."

"They are…lifelike." Mortimer had blanched during my presentation, perhaps green at the experience of coming so close to the critters that crawl on our skin and tangle in our hair. He was an odd man to select medicine as a profession, far too squeamish a person to be examining blood and pustules and open wounds.

"I am awestruck with your depth of knowledge in the field. James tells me your sister lives with you? How does she feel about your pursuit?"

"Beryl is a great lover of nature. She has a generous heart for all of God's creatures."

"Have you traveled there? To the New World, I mean?"

"Yes, and it was wondrous. The rich variety of life there is truly awe-inspiring. But to house my prodigious collection…well, it's becoming a bit of a burden."

Uncle Charles considered it for a moment. "Have you considered donating it to the British Museum? They have the foremost collection of butterflies and moths in Europe."

He asked this question not knowing I had already donated a moth I found in Yorkshire, a moth now named after my Vandeleur pseudonym. Uncle Charles went to the grave not knowing the Baskervilles are represented in the British Museum.

"Most decidedly, when I pass on, I would be honored if the society there would absorb my modest collection into their own," I said. "But—well—I feel my contribution, although a mere fraction of God's bounty, still has a special significance. Particularly since my collection has been so enriched with varieties local to Devonshire."

"Perhaps you should found your own museum," Mortimer said, a touch sarcastically, it seemed to me.

"If you could find the right backing, that might be a fine goal," Uncle Charles said.

This was the moment I had planned for. Uncle Charles had latched on to the idea, and better yet, it would seem the suggestion came from Dr. Mortimer and not myself. This should have been my moment. Before I could launch into my vision for the Butterfly Pavilion, Uncle Charles made a fateful comment.

"And I would happily donate my only brother's collection here to help you begin," he said, motioning to the tattered case. "It would be a fine tribute to his name."

"Your sole brother?" I asked. "You don't have two?"

"Jack," Mortimer said, warning me.

"No," Uncle Charles said. "My only brother is Henry. As I said, he died many years ago."

Barrymore arrived with the sherry bottle. I waved him away from my glass.

"I do not wish to appear intrusive," I said, "but before arriving, I consulted a copy of *Atherton's Peerage*. It did note you and your two brothers as heirs to the baronetcy."

"It's mistaken." Uncle Charles had grown quite cold. "A misprint. Printer's error."

"I consulted two copies. They both listed three brothers."

"It's now coming to me." He pressed a hand to his forehead as though sensing a headache. "Many years ago, an acquaintance alerted me to an error in *Atherton's*. Once I confirmed their mistake, I sent a personal note to the publisher with a request to amend the entry."

"Undoubtedly you were consulting older editions," Mortimer said to me.

"Undoubtedly." It was all I could manage to bottle up my rage. "You can understand my curiosity. With your brother deceased, I assumed your second brother would be in line for the title. I was hoping to meet him."

"There is no second brother," he said.

"Sir Charles would be most displeased if you were to spread such fictions," Mortimer added.

I took a chance. "Before arriving here in Dartmoor, I lived near a school in the north of England. Two instructors there told me of teaching a Rodger Baskerville in Bristol. I naturally assumed this Rodger Baskerville was the second brother described in *Atherton's*."

Uncle Charles had grown red with fury. "Now see here. If you have told anyone such a tale, Mr. Stapleton, be warned I will seek recourse. I view such nonsense as slander!"

"Perhaps they were recalling another student with a similar name," Mortimer said.

"Perhaps!" Uncle Charles raged.

I refused to let it go. I would not be browbeaten by his title and his wealth. "They were quite certain he was in line for the baronetcy. The school was Downey's, a prestigious institution. They would not have made such a mistake."

Uncle Charles called for Barrymore to bring a glass of water. While the servant made the preparations, Charles set his hand over his sternum. Mortimer approached and laid a hand on Charles' forehead. With the other, he pressed his fingers into Charles' wrist.

"I will be fine." Uncle Charles drank greedily. "I will not raise my bile over this impertinence." His breathing began to return to normal. "Mr. Stapleton, your time in the field searching for insects has left you wanting in the realm of basic etiquette. The hour is waning, as is my patience. Good evening to you both."

Dr. Mortimer was silently furious with me on the ride home. A thick, smoky fog coated the land and slowed our journey. Mortimer finally broke his silence and berated me.

"That was deeply uncalled for. Sir Charles' heart is weak. You repaid his generosity by exercising him over his brother Rodger."

"So there is a brother Rodger? You don't deny it?"

"Of course not! Rodger was the black sheep of the family. His lasciviousness at Downey's led to an immense scandal there. It cast a blemish on the Baskerville name that Sir Charles thought the family might never recover from. That is why he saw fit to remove the name from the registry."

"What if he was to return to England?"

"He's long gone, taken by yellow fever twelve years ago in the South American jungle." Another of my uncle's fabrications from the pasteboard of lies he built up around my father.

"Then why wait to strike him from the rolls?"

Mortimer shifted uncomfortably. "A letter from Brazil arrived. The writer claimed to be Rodger's son. He requested assistance from the family. Well, now, you can see the obviousness of the ploy, yes? One did not have to read between the lines to see this letter for what it really was."

"Which is?"

"Extortion, obviously. Some common vermin who thought he could leech a bit of money off a British aristocrat. Sir Charles fretted this person might even arrive at the Hall—a street urchin demanding a warm bed and a hot meal, and then claim the title itself when he passed on. No, Sir Charles was having none of it. So, he contacted *Atherton's* with a short plea, and they struck Rodger from the register." Mortimer made a piffling noise in the dark.

Boiling at my father being dishonored, and now roiling to hear that my earnest plea from Santarém was interpreted so, I managed to hold my tongue.

After twenty minutes, Mortimer said, "You have heard of the curse, yes? The spectral hound which terrorizes the Baskerville family?" His gossipy tongue was too loose and too eager to allow the affairs of the Baskervilles to grow still.

"I have heard talk around the village of it. I chalked it as local folklore."

"It is not mere myth."

"Dr. Mortimer! We are men of science. Certainly you do not believe a demonic hound loosed from the underworld runs rampant across the moor, mauling any wayward soul it might come across?"

"No. The beast only hunts Baskervilles."

As I wrote earlier, young pink-faced Dr. Mortimer was a foolish kind of medical practitioner, one far more common in the modern world than the profession cares to admit.

"That is why Sir Charles refuses to set foot outside of the Hall at night." Mortimer was twisting his crusher in his hands, as though wringing out a wet cloth. "He fears the hound will hunt him down."

"I was told the curse related to an ancestor's misdeeds from hundreds of years ago. How could one man's sins be transferred to his issue over such a span of time?"

"Don't you see? It was Sir Charles who exiled his younger brother. He took young Rodger to Plymouth. He booked him passage to the New World. He led him by hand onto the ship, and without a word, turned heel and marched down the gangplank, leaving his little brother to fend on his own. He fears the hellhound will claim him for his sins, just as it claimed Hugo Baskerville for his. It is the incarnation of Judgment!"

The image of my father being treated as Dr. Mortimer described sickens me. I never remember my father as anything but an irreparable man. He trusted no one in our fishing village, and they in turn did not trust him. It is no wonder my mother grew to hate him. When I left the tiny shack they raised me in, I too hated him. In turn, I taught him he could not even trust his son.

My father represented the weak and ineffectual men who die leaving only a legacy of tobacco ash and worn shoe leather. The window glass of better society is smudged and dirty from the noses of men like him being pressed up against it. When I left home, I vowed not to become my father. I am ashamed of that now, and I was ashamed of it on that carriage ride home with Mortimer. *Perhaps my father's legacy is repairable,* I thought, *and I the repairman.*

"Sir Charles could repent," I said. "If he were to admit his error and embrace his lost brother—"

"Absolutely not. Sir Charles made a grievous decision, but it was a decision that had to be made. Rodger committed unspeakable acts while in boarding school." He shook his head with the disappointment of a prude. "You will never understand what it means to be the head of a family such as the Baskervilles. Sir Charles cannot only consider his personal well being. He must take into account the family name, title, and estate."

Within the week, I traveled to Ross & Mangles at Brompton Cross in London. There I placed an order for the two black Brazilian *Fila* and the luminescent fungus that grows at the base of palm trees in the Amazon. Uncle Charles feared the hellhound's damning vengeance. Providence shall provide.

Twenty-five

When the two *Fila* arrived from Brazil, I dubbed the bitch Agrippina and her boy Nero. They were fine beasts, sheer black with brindles of dark tawny fur like the stripes of a tiger, only more subtle and visible only in bald sunlight. In the nighttime, they appeared as great black hounds, with a Boxer's musculature, the jaws of a mighty Bullmastiff, the height of a Great Dane, and the girth of…hell-spawn.

Nero's proportions are especially noteworthy. His neck was muscled, so much so there was no demarcation where his neck ended and his head began. His loose skin and pronounced dewlaps made a silky, feline motion as he strode. On hind legs, he was my greater in height and stature. Simply put, he was a bear of a dog, and bore a similarly unflappable disposition. And his eyes…always focused, always engaged and in the moment.

The proprietor of Ross & Mangles peered down on them in their cages with a cocked eye. "They are quite the specimens you've chosen. Took the agent in São Paulo some effort to get this pair arranged for you. He mentioned in the telegram they are bred for hunting. If you don't mind me asking, what in the Lord's name do they hunt in Brazil that needs such a magnificent beast like this? Elephants?" He cackled and hacked, a smoker's laugh.

"Have you ever seen a jaguar? With your own eyes?"

"Shag wire?" he mangled. "Isn't that one of them cats they got down there?"

"A jaguar can crush a turtle's shell with its jaw, much as you used your spoon this morning to get to the yolk inside your three-minute egg. A jaguar will stalk a swamp deer for three days through the jungle before striking. It sinks its twin fangs into the deer's skull and locks them there for minutes, piercing the animal's brain until it is lifeless." I produced a menacing smile for him. "It dines first on the deer's heart, which is a delicacy."

A proprietor of dogs of all breeds and sizes, Mangles was not a fragile man, but my description had left him pale about the edges. "That is quite a cat."

"*Fila* hunt these 'cats.'"

He cleared his throat and regained himself while thumbing through the paperwork. "And this came with it. Your, ah…mushrooms."

It was a package of the luminescent *A. gardneri* fungus, sealed in waxed paper and stored in coconut chips within a small wooden box.

The hounds were quite sullen when I took possession of them. The son Nero was larger than his mother by a half, yet he cowered, with his head pressed to her breast and her comforting paw over his shoulder. She growled when I approached and barked savagely as the men loaded the cage into the bed of my hired wagon. Mangles, hands and forearms in padded gloves, managed to muzzle them both. I had the cage crated up, effectively hiding my cargo from prying eyes and observant employees of the train line.

My schedule had been carefully arranged. We arrived in Devon well after sundown. I took the crate as far as I could drive the wagon into the moor. With them leashed and a training crop tucked under my belt, I led them on foot, careful to avoid the various farms and cottages among the country hills. At Grimpen Mire, I shortened the leashes and swatted their backsides with the crop to keep them close by. All I needed was for one of them to break away, slip into a bog pit, and be dragged down into the burbling muck. And if one dog were to entangle its leash with the other, both would be dragged into the muddy grave, taking me with them if I failed to extricate myself.

My many hours in Grimpen Mire with butterfly net, killing jar, and field microscope paid dividends. I learned the throughways and footpaths with a mapmaker's attention to detail. As my entomological hobby often required searching for specimens in the wee hours, I developed a near sixth-sense to navigating the treacherous mire by moonlight.

It was not my first journey to the tin mine in the dead of night. In the prior weeks, I'd humped in kennels, feed, straw for their beds, and training equipment. Their first night in their pen, Nero moaned and cowered in the protection of Agrippina's motherly breast, who regarded me as just another dictator to placate.

My love for them was planted that night. Nero's trust in his mother was absolute; Agrippina's love for her son was eternal. I'd raised and trained numerous *Fila* at Far Oaks for the Harris family, but none of the dogs exhibited such a strong familial bond. Although I had planned on making the long hike home after kenneling them, I sensed a unique opportunity. I gathered straw in the corner of the abandoned mess hall and made my bed across from them. We slept under the same roof that first night. When I awoke before dawn, Agrippina remained reclined in the rear of the large cage I'd assembled for them. Nero, however, sat on his haunches as close as he could to where I lay. He regarded me with a quiet curiosity.

The training went on for weeks. I learned the basics from Antônio at Far Oaks and refined my technique with Aurelius in Yorkshire. My innovation was to utilize Nero's mother in the training of her son.

With Aurelius, I alternated between love and punishment to capture his devotion. When Aurelius returned with a dead rabbit, I was always certain to reward him with food, strokes, and belly rubs. No rabbit, no love. If he returned with a bird, or another varmint, no love. Dogs fear corporeal punishment, but what dogs dread is being ignored. Ignoring Aurelius for days on end wore him down more than any stick or crop could. When I did return and grant him my attention, he worked doubly hard to satisfy my orders. This give and take created our bond.

And so it went with Nero. *Fila* are more intelligent than most breeds, and Nero adroitly took to my system of calls and whistles. His sharp nose could track fox and roebuck as well as it could jaguar. I could not allow him to roam free, as he would have undoubtedly fallen into a treacherous bog and died tangled in the deep, ropey patches of the underwater plants. This only slowed my progress, but progress I did make.

I made Agrippina my foreman. Where I went, she walked with me. Agrippina received a steady stream of treats and love for her fealty. When I punished Nero, she would not object. Nero would whimper to her, but she remained cold and steadfast at my side. Only when I penned the two in the late afternoon did she lick his wounds and nuzzle his face and give him the love he so craved. My work was doubled, but with it came devotion and loyalty steeped beyond measure.

*

My initial meeting with Uncle Charles grew disputatious at the conclusion of our evening. I immediately worked to patch up the relationship. My goal was to supplant the obsequious Dr. Mortimer as his confidant and friend. As time went on, I gave up in defeat. My uncle simply held Dr. Mortimer in the highest regard, and the best I could manage was to be a reliable friend. I continued to show interest in his dead brother's butterfly collection, as well as interest in the history of our ancestors, which he was more than anxious to share to an attentive young man as myself.

It was Beryl who alerted me to the presence of a young woman in Coombe Tracey, a village near Baskerville Hall. Her name was Laura Lyons, a typist and the daughter of a rather cranky landholder. He'd disowned her after her blackguard of a husband abandoned her. Beryl's nurturing instincts led her to bake bread for the young woman and provide her with household necessities, all with the intention of lightening her financial strain. She asked if we could further assist Mrs. Lyons, and I told her I would see what could be managed.

I confess I first dismissed Beryl's plea. With Nero and Agrippina kenneled in the mire, my spare time was consumed traveling to and fro and training them. Mrs. Lyons' plight, and Beryl's response to it, seemed an utter distraction.

Mrs. Lyons was a fresh woman, but the dampness of the moor, and the bleak prospects of the underclasses there, it grinds down the soul. I found myself immediately taken by her industriousness, and also by her refusal to buckle and accept the life of a destitute woman.

"I am able-bodied and capable of employment," she told me upon my visit there. She made no bones that she did not solicit our charity. "I am a trained typist, which supplies me a reasonable income."

"If you are in not in need, then I will not take any more of your time."

"Wait!" she cried before I reached the door. "Your sister's generosity is most humbling. I do appreciate her gifts and the relief they provide. What I ask of you, I do most hesitantly, as I know it to be well beyond the relief you intended to offer me today."

She asked me to sit with her.

"What I fear most is my husband demanding I go and live with him. He is a vile man and horrible to me. He has the law on his side. He has informed me that, given the right sum of money, he will grant a divorce."

I brought this to Uncle Charles' attention one evening over a game of cards. Dr. Mortimer immediately advised against assisting the woman, whom he regarded as a kind of jezebel. When I demanded an explanation for such harsh judgment, he claimed that if a woman has been abandoned, it must be of her own faults.

"You disagree then, Stapleton," Uncle Charles said to me.

I found Mortimer's petty moralizing disgusting. The proper tack here, however, was to aim positive rather than strike negative.

"The woman capitalizes on her abilities with a typewriter, and is not quick to accept charity," I said. "Sir Charles, I make a proposition: If you will grant this woman fifty pounds, I will find a way to match your donation. Rather than burden you solely, I propose we work as a community to achieve a greater good."

"That is a fine idea," Uncle Charles proclaimed. "Will a hundred pounds be sufficient to excise this blackguard from her life?"

"Alas, no, he's demanded another hundred pounds on top of that. However, with your donation and my match, we might drum up additional contributions."

"What say you, James?"

Dr. Mortimer blanched at being pressed so. "I believe I could contribute a few pounds. If I may change the subject, Sir Charles, I would like again to suggest you consider leaving Baskerville Hall for a period of rest—"

"Not tonight, doctor." Uncle Charles turned to me. "Jack, I hereby name you my personal almoner. I will do your proposition one better. If you can gather donations in the sum of a hundred pounds, I will match it, pound-for-pound, and we will disentangle Mrs. Lyons from this extorting wastrel once and for all."

Later, as we strolled the Hall with snifters and cigars, I decided to test my uncle's view on the family curse. As we passed oaken double-doors leading out to an alley of yew trees, I asked:

"What say we step outside and see the moor? The fog is thin and there is considerable moonlight. Why, it must be magnificent."

Uncle Charles spoke with great hesitation. "I will on occasion stroll there in the early evening for fresh air, but I prefer to remain indoors at nighttime."

Without permission, I flung open one of the doors and allowed in the damp chill. The rustling of the yew trees followed. It was as though I had invited the moor itself inside.

Before Mortimer could protest, Uncle Charles went sallow. He glared out the open door with wide, excitable eyes. I believed he would have dropped his crystal snifter if not for Barrymore intervening.

"Perhaps another time," and I closed the door. If that was his reaction to opening it, imagine his state if he was drawn out into the dark night air.

Uncle Charles needed time to gather himself, but he was right as rain before we adjourned for the evening. Light and cheery from our dip into the brandy decanter, he took me aside, out of earshot of Mortimer and the butler Barrymore.

"I would like to get to know this young lady," he said to me. "Please arrange it."

"She's quite the typist. She and my sister correspond regularly by post. I would not be surprised if she would enjoy similar correspondence with you."

His aged breath was ripe with the old oak the brandy had been barreled in. "I want to see this girl. Not at the Hall. In private."

"As you wish." Once again, I departed from my uncle's residence disgusted with the man—a Baskerville, one of the most well respected names in all of Devon.

Mortimer had quaffed the brandy and consumed a cigar, but he was not so light and cheery on our ride back to the village. "Sir Charles' personal almoner, are we now?"

Beryl leaped into my arms when I returned to Merripit House with my good news. "You have made me very, very happy," she said as I twirled her in a circle.

On the rug, we danced with abandon. A natural with musical instruments, Antônio took up an empty bucket and tapped out a beat for us to follow while singing in Portuguese.

"I am surprised," I called to him over the music. "I thought you would be opposed."

"This is the good in the world I want to do," he said.

"I was growing ill," Beryl said to me as she trotted and twisted to Antônio's beat. "It is not right waiting for an old man to die."

"Now we can direct that money to help people not named Baskerville."

"Including you," she added with a bright laugh. "Mister Jack Stapleton."

As Beryl retired to our bed in lingerie, I again dressed for a night on the moor and mire. Although I had not planned on it from the outset, I had discovered sleeping across the floor from Nero and Agrippina had strengthened our bond immeasurably. For the task I was entrusting Nero to perform, there could be no hesitation, no canine moment of questioning fealty.

"Why tonight?" she complained. "We are celebrating."

"I am on a quest to locate *stigmella dryadella*," a moth of the family *Nepticulidae*. "The moon is right and the air is dry."

"What is out there? You spend all night away, only returning in the morning hours with a kiss on my cheek and a stomach for an English-style breakfast." She sat upright in bed. "You are seeing another woman. Yes?"

"Don't do this."

"Is it Laura? She is quite pretty. You are smitten, yes?"

I kissed her. Her hot bath had left her smelling wonderfully fresh and perfumed. I took her soft, creamy hands. "Moths and butterflies are my work, Beryl. They are my obsession."

"You have filled that entire bedroom with your crawly little insects." She shivered. "I do not like it in there. When I pass through the room, I feel as though they will all break free from their cases and fly at me."

"I cannot explain the mania that comes over me. To possess every species as example…it is a kind of madness, I admit."

She took me by the back of the neck. I believed she wanted another kiss. Rather, she yanked me down so we were touching noses.

"Your madness is more like a passion," she whispered. "Remember: I am your only passion." And she released me as forcefully as she had taken me.

Twenty-six

The collection of alms for Mrs. Laura Lyons, my training regimen for Nero and Agrippina, the endless pursuit of specimens with net and jar…my life grew quite involved, indeed.

As if not enough to manage, I found myself also having to deal with Beryl and Antônio, both of whom were growing restless. Beryl's hatred of the weather, and pining for her family in Costa Rica, made it an almost daily ritual of talking her down from fleeing England. Antônio was less energetic in his complaints, simply weary of playacting the part of my near-mute valet and butler. He yearned for a return to the ranching life. He wanted to marry and raise children. And they both found it distasteful waiting for an old man to die.

"He's not placed me in his will," I explained to Antônio. "This role as his almoner for Laura Lyons is my *entre* to a portion of his estate."

"I do not need his money," Antônio said. "This has gone far enough."

"When the money is finally in your hands, you will think again. A sliver of my uncle's estate is enough to buy your own ranch in the New World. Six more weeks, I promise."

My estimate, and my hectic daily schedule, rushed to a crashing halt one evening when Dr. Mortimer picked me up in his dog-cart for another night of cards and sherry.

"Sir Charles will be leaving for London in two days," he told me in an off-handed way. Mortimer loved being the bearer of Baskerville news, as though possession of it proved his membership in a club. "He has finally taken my medical advice and agreed to get away from Dartmoor."

"What has brought on this decision?"

"I've encouraged him for some time. But it's also the howls on the moor. That great terrible animal sound made when the night is most dark? You've heard them?"

"I hear many things," I said with a dismissive wave. "I do not pay them much attention."

"He believes them to be the demon hound itself."

"Oh, doctor, please!"

"He is not the only one. The men of Dartmoor, they have heard it too. The village is abuzz over it. Fiend or superstition, it's not for me to say, but it is my medical opinion Sir Charles' health will improve in London."

"For how long?"

"Many months. I will be accompanying him. My hope is that he will extend his trip onward to the continent. Anything to take his mind off the moors."

Feeling the panic rising, I said, "Wonderful news. I concur, of course. Time away can only improve his health."

At the Hall, I repeated my agreement to my uncle. "Also, I wanted to tell you I have been successful in collecting pledges in excess of eighty pounds toward the plight of Mrs. Lyons. I do hope, Sir Charles, that we can conclude the business before you leave. Purely so you may travel without the bother of finalizing transactions and such while relaxing."

"I will see to it tomorrow to get the money to Mrs. Lyons. Hopefully, this dreadful affair will be over for the young lady soon enough." He adjusted himself uncomfortably in his armchair. He seemed not to know what to do with his cigar. "I have other news. Since I've made you my almoner, Jack, I suppose you should be privy. James, tell him."

With a tart and smug expression, Mortimer manufactured an obligatory smile for me. "Sir Charles, in his grace and wisdom, has made me executor of his will."

Uncle Charles motioned for Barrymore to top up the sherry.

"A most judicious decision," I said. Months, nay, years of planning, and in one evening, it was nearly demolished. "I confess I always assumed such duties would be delegated to an attorney."

"This is Dartmoor, not London. James here is an educated man, and there are certainly few of them in his area. Oh—I know you're educated too, Jack, but, well, I did not think you would care to be burdened executing my will upon my demise."

What a fool I was—I made my play for administering the Butterfly Pavilion on the assumption administering the entire estate was well beyond my reach. If a town mouse such as Mortimer could be assigned such duties, I could have easily have jockeyed for them myself.

"If I may be so bold, Sir Charles, might I also inquire if you updated your will regarding the project we've discussed over these months?"

"I can't go through with the Butterfly Pavilion, Jack." He spoke out the corner of his mouth while relighting his cigar. "To sell tickets to the common man for entry, well, it has the stench of capital all over it." He motioned about the room. "The Baskerville name is dedicated to our storied legacy and the traditions we hold dear. To employ barkers and guides and bill-posters is, well...It's simply not done, Jack."

"It's not a carnival I'm proposing." It was all I could do to keep my voice even. "The Butterfly Pavilion would be a living museum, an innovation—"

"Does this place look innovative?" Uncle Charles waved his cigar through the air, again motioning to the staid, velvet-walled parlor. "I've made room in my will for you and your sister to receive a modest sum upon my death. I also took your sister's touching letter to heart. She recommended several families and widows deserving of my munificence in the shire, and they will receive as well. Now, let's take a stroll to the chapel. I wanted to show you both a carving I do not believe I've pointed out to you before..."

Returning from our tour of the chapel, Mortimer hastened off to attend to personal matters. Standing before the great shield of the Baskervilles, sensing I had been painted into a corner, I privately gambled my future then and there before the heraldry and escutcheon of my family name:

"Sir Charles...I must make a confession to you."

"Yes? We are all friends here."

"My secret, it has weighed on me ever since joining the community here in Dartmoor. I have held it close to my chest for fear of...well, fear of rejection."

Uncle Charles set a firm hand on my shoulder. "Whatever you have to tell me, I will listen."

Heart behind my ears, I explained in a single burst of rapid language that I was his nephew, Rodger's son.

"I have traveled all the way from the Empire of Brazil to join you. I come to rejoin my family, to claim my seat at the table, and to clear my father's name."

The change in Uncle Charles' encouraging demeanor could not have been swifter or more polar. His comforting hand retracted as though learning I carried a disease.

"It is not a hoax," I continued. "It is I, Rodger Baskerville II."

"I have never heard of such a thing!"

"I admit, I have no evidence of my relation to you, but if given time, I'm certain I could produce documentation from Brazil that would show your brother Rodger married and sired a son. My father—your brother—died recently. But I believe you know that, as my mother attempted to—"

"Barrymore!" Uncle Charles whipped out the handkerchief from his breast pocket. "The evening has concluded."

"I confess I have been operating under a deception while living here in Dartmoor. I did not believe you would accept me if I were to appear unannounced on your doorstep. I hoped to prove to you I am a man of worth and education, a man of respect, and not a charlatan!"

"Have you breathed a word of this to anyone?" he demanded. "To

Mortimer, to anyone?" He was wiping off his hand with the handkerchief.

"Not a soul."

"Then I assure you, if you spread such scandal or innuendo here, or anywhere, I will throw the full weight of the law against you. To come into this Hall and extort me to my face! You call yourself a gentleman and an academic."

"I am asking for nothing but your recognition—my father, he was the innocent."

"Barrymore." Uncle Charles' loathing and anger disappeared in the presence of his butler. He tossed aside the handkerchief as though contaminated. "Fetch Jack's coat and signal the driver." When Barrymore had left us, Uncle Charles' anger returned. "I suggest you get your affairs in order. I will be speaking with my solicitor about you the moment I arrive in London. When he's finished, you will be on a boat back to the Americas."

The next morning, I rushed to Laura Lyon's room in Coombe Tracey. "The financials are near-complete, but there remains a few details. I have learned that Sir Charles will be leaving Devon tomorrow. You must send him your well-wishes now."

"Of course." She inserted a sheet of paper into her trusty typewriter. "If you know his address in London, I would have more time to write him a fuller letter of my deep gratitude."

"I will dictate it to you. And you should write it by hand."

She delicately crossed the room to me. "Did you receive *my* letter?"

Antônio intercepted it before Beryl discovered it among the daily post. He recognized Mrs. Lyon's handwriting, read it was addressed to me, and reasoned the possibilities.

"Your sweet words are most warming," I told her. "We must finish this letter to Sir Charles now, however, before the morning post."

She placed a hand on my arm. "I've come to see you as more than Beryl's brother. You are kind and sincere, and most helpful. Men of your station, they do not speak well to me, or even treat me as a woman. My coarse father is not well-regarded, and his lack of breeding stains me."

"Did Sir Charles ever visit you? Tell me he treated you well."

She laughed imperiously. "He is sweet and charming, in his own way. But he really must learn his age."

"But he didn't—he didn't ask anything of you? Anything untoward?"

"Oh, old men like him suggest much, but they do not have the backbone to carry it through. The scandal of him coming here, an unescorted bachelor in a lady's residence."

"I'm a bachelor," I reminded her.

She tilted her creamy neck back, her flush lips in the air. "And I am in your debt eternal."

"Did he say anything to you that…" How to put it? "I should know of?"

"My sweet protector. Yes. Sir Charles proposed marriage to me. Once the divorce is settled, of course. Oh! But you have no reason to be jealous. I refused."

"You *refused*? You would have stood to inherit the entire estate upon his demise!"

"Do you think me guided by material gain? I am speaking the language of love to you. Are you so absorbed with your butterflies and nets that you cannot see that?"

I gently guided her to the writing desk. "First, we write your thank-you to Sir Charles."

I dictated the letter. There was no time to leave details to chance. In her letter, she thanked Uncle Charles for his charity and suggested they meet at the twin rows of yew trees running from Baskerville Hall to the edge of the moor. It would be scandalous for her to meet him without chaperone, hence the *al fresco* rendezvous.

"A postscript. 'Please, please, as you are a gentleman, burn this letter, and be at the gate by ten o'clock.' And your initials."

She followed my instructions without question until this addition. "Why should he burn this?"

"To avoid scandal, of course."

"And why am I meeting him?"

"Once Sir Charles leaves Baskerville Hall, its affairs and business matters will slip from his mind. He is doddering, and London offers all the delights of the world. If he decamps for London without endorsing a banker's check for you, I fear you will be unable to divorce your husband. Sir Charles will not return for months, perhaps years. And if he were to meet his demise while away—"

My foreshadowing made her distraught. "I will be there at ten o'clock!"

"And be sure to post this letter. Time is of the essence!"

With that, I hurried for Grimpen Mire.

Twenty-seven

On my way to the mire, I stopped at Merripit House and relayed instructions to Antônio:

"Deliver this message at noon to Mrs. Laura Lyons. Tell her my thinking on the matter has shifted. For her sake and mine, I will find a way to cover her remaining expenses and extricate her from her husband's demands. Although I am not a wealthy man, for the sake of self-sufficiency, it is best if she permits me to arrange the final monies. Now, this is important, my friend: You *must* insist she not visit Baskerville Hall this evening. The appointment is off. She should think no more of it."

Antônio managed to locate pen and paper and scratch out my gist. "What's all this about, Rodrigo?"

"I require your complete trust on this."

I hurried across the moor to Grimpen Mire. Maneuvering safely through the bog takes much time, even when possessing as keen a grasp of its geography as I. Nero sensed my eagerness when I arrived, and it enlivened him.

Over the prior weeks, I had begun a habit of taking Nero out on the moor in the middle of the night. It acclimated him to the misty expanse and its many odors and textures and dangers. Through Grimpen Mire, I led him with a tight leash, save he slip into a bog and succumb to its murky perils. On the moor, I allowed him freer rein. The Brazilian *Fila* have a wonderful nose for hunting and tracking, much more sophisticated and versatile than the famed English bloodhound.

Hunting wildlife was not our intended goal, however. Those nights I had taught Nero to howl, not a paltry task. *Fila* will howl out when prey is cornered or captured, but otherwise, it is a rather quiet species. To train him, I led by example. If this journal is a witness to my deeds and motivations, let it also be a witness to a rather silly bit of foolishness: I, Rodger Baskerville, rightful heir to the baronetcy, on all fours on a damp moor in the dead of night, howling and baying at the moon, while Nero looked on with a cocked head and questioning perked ears.

With enough coaxing, soon Nero began baying with me. Eventually, he would howl without any ridiculous demonstration on my part. Nero discovered within himself a throaty vocal baritone. Perched atop the right tor or hill on the moor, his howls would travel miles. After letting him demonstrate his operatic chops for an hour or so, I would muzzle him and we would begin our treacherous route back to the security of his mother and the straw bed at the tin mine.

He was a beast in terms of brawn, but he was a child in terms of his mind. Nero was not, and never could have been, what would be termed "bloodthirsty." Nero sought only approval. He sought it from me, and more importantly, he sought it from his mother.

This night, the night before Uncle Charles planned to travel to London, I leashed and muzzled Agrippina as well as Nero. She would serve to keep Nero's high-strung spirits cool until the right moment arrived.

The three of us worked our way carefully through the mire's treacheries and across the desolate, doleful moor. I marked our way using the luminous *flor-de-coco* grease, ensuring a safe escape into the mire if a hasty retreat was needed. It was a particularly gloomy night, wet and cold. It was sound thinking to bring Agrippina, as Nero was champing at his muzzle and trying to claw it off. She growled and knocked against him to keep him in line.

Besides the provisions I had cached at the old tin mine, my keen mind had prepared one additional contingency. An old stable stands behind Merripit House, with a quaint whitewashed roof much like a country chapel. In the stable floor is a trapdoor leading to a surprisingly large cellar. I had arranged canine provisions down there, muzzles and leashes and such, never knowing if I would need to keep the hounds close by. Quietly, careful not to alert Beryl or Antônio in the main house, I led Agrippina down to the cellar kennel. She was visibly upset at being tied up away from her son, but she complied.

On the moor, Nero's palpable excitement only fueled my own, and I found myself shivering with anticipation. When he strained to be free of the leash, I scolded him. Nero rolled on his back and gave me his belly, acknowledging I was in charge.

As we approached Baskerville Hall, a distinct white light appeared in the window of an upper story. It flashed with regular pulses, much as a sailor uses a lantern at sea to deliver semaphore. Shivery with anticipation, this unexpected turn halted me. A bolt of dread shot through me. In an instant, I feared my entire plan would have to be scuttled. A moment later, the light in the window went dark.

Antônio deserves a great deal of thanks here. While he detested the role he played of my valet and butler, like a fine stage actor, he did play the role to the hilt. In that capacity, he had developed professional acquaintances with the local servant classes, as well as the tradesmen they transact business with, such as the grocer, repairmen, seamstresses, charwomen, and the like.

Antônio had informed me earlier of a convict who'd escaped from the prison in Princetown. The gossip raging among the lower classes in Dartmoor was that the convict, a hardened fellow named Selden, was the brother of Mrs. Barrymore at Baskerville Hall. This connection had the sharp edge of scandal, since it would associate the Baskerville name with the heinous murders Selden had committed.

"Fear has desolated the woman," Antônio explained to me. "She fears his capture as much as she fears his death. The whispers are that she and Barrymore leave food and blankets out on the moor. At night, he scurries from one tor to another, never sleeping in the same cave twice."

Sure enough, from my high vantage, I witnessed a dark, hunched figure scurrying across the moor toward the Baskerville property. He halted at the base of a spindly tree growing askew. Minutes later, the dark figure emerged and hurried off, no doubt in search of a new tor to cower inside and eat his victuals.

Uncle Charles had sent my father off to Brazil to keep the stench of scandal away from the Baskerville name. Would he do likewise to the Barrymores for aiding an escaped felon? Of course he would. He erased my side of the family from the rolls, I reminded myself. He treats my existence as a personal embarrassment. He made the dolt James Mortimer the executor of his will, and he made it clear if any of my father's progeny comes inquiring, they are to be denied and turned away. Some day Beryl would give birth to my child. Uncle Charles would see the little thing as nothing more than a mortal threat to the Baskerville line.

Right before ten o'clock, a figure emerged from oaken double-doors on the side of the Hall. With a spyglass, I verified it was none other than Uncle Charles. He was alone, just as Mrs. Lyon's letter had instructed.

He strolled to the mouth of the alley of yews running in twin lines from the estate. I cursed myself: Did I not strictly instruct him to wait at the far end of the yew alley, at the wicket-gate nearest the moor? His position near the house was inconvenient. If I sent Nero straight at him, all Uncle Charles would have to do was scurry inside and bolt the doors. No, like forcing a rabbit away from the security of his warren, Nero would have to flush him out and chase him away from the house.

Thankfully, after a moment, perhaps needing to screw up his courage, Uncle Charles worked his way down the yew alley to the wicket-gate. He lit a cigar. The time to strike was nigh.

From my coat pocket, I produced a tin of the luminescent grease I'd prepared. I had followed Antônio's recipe completely. Those nights when I trained Nero to howl, I had also used the grease on him to ensure the effect I desired was attainable. I allowed him to run loose on the moor with the greenish-blue glow thickly applied around his eyes, jaw, and hackles. It mixed with his frothy saliva and dripped ghoulishly from his tongue as he charged across the land. The utter darkness of the moor at night cannot be overstated. With his thick black coat, he appeared from a distance as a spectral virescent hound flying ghost-like several feet over the ground.

I scooped a ball of the grease and smeared it over Nero's head. He murmured growls of excitement as I painted him up, my great thespian about to take the stage on opening night. His garish makeup made a green evil grin down the length of his snout. I painted his dewlap and hackles as well. The great secret of Antônio's grease is that it is odorless and without taste. Not only was Nero not tempted to lick it off, it did not interfere with his sense of smell the way another formulation might, such as one containing phosphorus.

What was I thinking at this moment? Of my father as young boy watching his older brother march down the ship's gangplank, never turning to wave goodbye. The sailors cast the lines and he is shipped off to Brazil like freight.

Next I produced the handkerchief Uncle Charles had discarded. I stuffed it against Nero's nose, grabbed him by the scruff, and rattled him up:

Get him boy, get him! Now, now!

Nero bolted from me with nostrils full of Uncle Charles' scent. He bounded for the wicket-gate snarling and galloping like a racehorse.

Out of the fog emerged Nero painted ghoulish green with a mouth dripping hellfire. With a great cry, my uncle dropped his cigar and scrambled backwards. Crazed with fear, he ran the only direction available to him, down the yew alley and toward the moor. It was unthinkable, this elderly man, frightened of a ridiculous curse set upon his ancestor, now charging straight for the very place he vowed never to visit at nighttime.

With a single effortless leap, Nero bounded over the gate and charged down the grass strip along the gravel alleyway. Uncle Charles cried out for help as he retreated. The spectral hound of his nightmares was nearly upon him.

My uncle's trots slowed to an awkward loping. He clutched his left arm above the elbow and convulsed. He stumbled face-first into the gravel path.

He was done for. It was over. Nero hadn't even touched him.

Nero's thirst cooled. He sniffed at my uncle's lifeless body. Yes, his nose informed him, this was the scent he sought, but no, the prey is no longer alive. He returned to my side taking much the same route as his initial charge. He did not sit as before, but rather lay at my feet with long, doleful eyes peering up at me from his glowing snout.

I rewarded Nero with affection and treats. Using a hand towel, I managed to remove most of the last traces of the grease from around his eyes and mouth. We began our march across the moor to Merripit House. With Agrippina joining, the three of us made it back the old tin mine, where I rewarded the both of them.

I was too exhausted to celebrate. It was well nearly two in the morning when I finally kenneled them. I assembled my bed of straw and wool blankets opposite their cages. With a bright, fulfilled smile, I curled up and fell asleep in an instant.

It was over. My father's misery had found its counterweight. As my uncle had denied my claim and purged my existence from all official records, the Baskerville line was now extinguished in kind. Without an heir, the estate would be broken up. The cursed name and title would evaporate and join the mist that crawls upon the moors. I would claim the chunk of money my uncle had guaranteed to me as Jack Stapleton, pack our bags, and lead Beryl and Antônio to the continent, where we could live high in Paris.

Beryl was mutely livid when Dr. Mortimer told her he'd discovered the paw prints of a mighty hound near Uncle Charles' body. She marched inside our house with her arms folded and a pinched-up look on her face, angry and about ready to cry.

Mortimer was confused at her sudden departure. "Ghastly bit of business," he said, as way of reasoning it to himself.

"What is next?" I asked.

"Well, the execution of the will, of course. That should be a quiet affair. Not many claimants, with Charles being childless and all."

"Beryl and I will be happy to assist you."

"Most unnecessary! To save you a trip across the moor, I would recommend you not attend the reading. The amount Charles willed you is quite modest."

It surprised me. "How modest?"

Mortimer told me. Modest was a generous word. It was certainly not enough to sustain a comfortable life on the Seine.

"And you're provided for, I assume?" I asked Mortimer, hoping my bitterness was well hidden.

"I was a long-time friend. He was most kind." He took in a deep gulp of air. "But the big news, old chap, is that we found a proper heir to the title."

I blinked, feeling a distinct flushness growing up my neck. "Say again?"

"Charles' brother? The one who collected butterflies and died young? Well, he had a son after all. Charles never spoke of him. The Barrymores knew, bless their hearts. They'd worked for the Baskervilles for so long, how could they not?"

"No mention of this in *Atherton's Peerage*."

"We've ascertained his relation with more than sufficient confidence."

"Does this nephew have a name?"

"His father's, in fact. Henry." Mortimer breathed an air of relief. "I'll be traveling to London to meet him in five days. Thank the Lord, Baskerville Hall will soon house another resident. We need a regent in these parts." And Mortimer mounted his bicycle and rode off to his practice in Dartmoor village, leaving me to seethe and curse myself.

Twenty-eight

The death of Uncle Charles, and Mortimer's insistence of a spectral hound's involvement, only confirmed to Beryl and Antônio my involvement. The true purpose of my late-night trips across the moor was now recognized.

"Is it a *Fila*?" he demanded. "Is that what's been running around the moors these months?"

Antônio let his opinion be known: I was foolish and wanton, and I would suffer for my actions.

"If they question or accuse me, I will tell them all that I know. I am sorry, my friend. There is no other way."

"Will you tell them about Puerto Limón? And of the Harris clan's reward for our necks?"

"So long as I do not hang in England for a murder I did not commit!"

"No one will hang. After all, there's no evidence of a crime."

Beryl was not so pragmatic. She mourned the death of my uncle, as though he was a great man simply because he was old and gray and rich. I spelled out for her the crime Dell, Carrington, and Lawson had perpetrated, and my uncle's decision to exile my father. I reminded her of my uncle erasing my branch of the family from the books, and how his promises for our financial well-being were hollow and merely to win our approval. And I told her of my uncle's depraved designs upon Beryl's friend Laura Lyons. It made no difference.

At first, Beryl refused to accompany me to London. She resisted my offer to return to the Brazilian sector there and relive our good times at the Café *Dona Isabel*. At the last minute, she changed her mind and joined me. Now I believe she felt it was better to monitor my actions rather than be ignorant and caught unawares once more. I also believe she wanted to warn Henry, the new Baskerville arriving in London. I did not see this at the time, however.

We trailed Mortimer to London. We took residence in a hotel on Craven Street, where I instructed Beryl to remain until I returned. I had two tasks ahead of me, neither of which I divulged to her. One was to locate my cousin Henry's lodgings. The second was to discover if Dr. Mortimer had any other pertinent business in London.

When I rented the cottage in Leicester to interview Carrington and Dell, I had employed a simple disguise when meeting with the cottage owner. I dug up the stage beard and theater gum and used it again in London. I discovered Mortimer did indeed have other business. I followed him to Baker Street, where his visit was so brief, I could only assume it was an appointment that had been cancelled without notice. Mortimer left as he'd arrived, on foot. I noted he'd absentmindedly left behind the walking stick he'd entered holding. It was a foible all-too-familiar. Too often we'd left Baskerville Hall together, only for him to call out to the driver to turn the dog-cart around so he may recover his stick, or gloves, or hat.

As I paid my driver, he mentioned to me, "That's Mr. Sherlock Holmes' residence, if you did not know. Being as you're not from around here and all."

Indeed, I'd picked up the Yorkshire accent while teaching there. Better than being picked out as hailing from Devon, I reassured myself.

This country doctor whom I'd estimated as possessing the acumen of a dormouse now displayed more foresight than I thought him capable of. For all my planning, the only scrutiny I worried of was from the local constabulary in Devon. Charles' skittish heart was well known and would be attested by his personal doctor, a one James Mortimer. So far, the police had accepted this explanation. Mortimer apparently did not.

Following Mortimer also led me to the hotel Henry roomed in. My time in luxury hotels in Panama paid off. A hotel is not merely a business, it is a kind of factory that must stay running all hours of the day. Lolling about the lobby and slipping through service doors as though lost, I befriended a pair of Brazilians and a Portuguese working the laundry. With a crisp banknote slipped to each of them, and some humor involving double-entendres only coherent in Portuguese, I was soon in possession of one of Henry's boots.

At my hotel room, Beryl frosty at my time away from her, I removed the boot from the bag it had been delivered in. Within moments, I was swearing.

"The dandy has bought himself new boots." Its leather was stiff and still smelled of the manufacturer's oil. I would have to pay the crew again to find another article from Henry's room.

"What dandy?" Beryl crossed the room sullenly. "Whom do you speak of?"

"Take a nap, my dear." I had left the laudanum at Merripit House.

"I will not sleep! Tell me what you are plotting!"

"If I could count on the help of you and Antônio, my work would be much easier, but as it stands, I must perform all of it myself."

"I will help you," Beryl said softly. "But I will not help you hurt innocent people."

"These are not innocent people." I shook the new stiff boot at her. "The sole of this boot is as near as its owner will come to the filth of the world." I had her smell the fine, rich leather. "And it is a perfumed world he resides in."

Beryl put a soft hand on the side of my face.

"Who is this man? Who is the owner of his boot?"

"My cousin Henry. He is the new baronet of Baskerville Hall. Another Baskerville I will have to address as 'Sir.'"

"Do not do this. Do not harm this man." She took me by both hands. "Let us leave now. We can book passage to Paris here in London. We will be there in mere days! Let us live in the Latin Quarter and read poems to each other in bed, as we used to!"

"In your father's hacienda," I reminded her. "In the bed he provided me. I refuse to live under another man's thumb ever again."

"This Henry, do you know him?"

"I have never heard of him before Mortimer told me. It is a complete surprise."

"Then why?"

"Because! He's a Baskerville!" I pushed her away. "When will you understand?"

"My love—you frighten me. You loathe a man because of his name. Do you not hear what you are saying?"

I fled. The words I'd spoken to Beryl, they had occupied my thoughts before this. They seemed reasonable enough inside my head. Hearing them aloud for the first time made me vaguely ill. I found myself in a pub ruminating over a Scotch. From there, I allowed myself a long stroll to Russell Square and Bloomsbury whilst smoking cigarettes. When I had cooled and the edge had dulled, I returned to our hotel room.

Beryl was gone. I still don't know where she went. I never asked her.

I took Henry's pristine boot for one more inspection. Knowing Sherlock Holmes was now involved, I supposed I might try and deduce some deep insight into my foreign cousin from this singular clue.

The London bootmaker's insignia was fresh and crisp. I deduced his foot size by comparing it to my own. The tooled design was of a western flower, but I already knew he hailed from Canada. Yes, Watson, we can glean a surfeit of details from this singular boot. He is strawberry blond, well over six foot, and a Freemason, twenty-second order, with an affinity for shag tobacco and American bourbon. He walks with a slight limp, is ambidextrous, and owns a Dachshund…

I threw the boot into a corner. I deduced nothing from it. All I could smell was the fine boot oil rubbed into its leather. It smelled like the musk of other men's sweat and hard work, spent only to keep Cousin Henry in luxury.

Twenty-nine

Henry's arrival at Baskerville Hall sent an electric thrill about the village. The dashing young baronet from far-off Canada was as exotic as an Amazonian flower, but respectable rather than grotesque. His presence in gloomy Dartmoor gave the spinsters something to jaw about, and the maidservants and seamstresses an Adonis to swoon over. When I learned Dr. Watson accompanied Henry and Dr. Mortimer on the train ride, my concerns about Sherlock Holmes' involvement were confirmed.

Watson's arrival meant I could not relax my visits out to the old tin mine, for Holmes' personal terrier might sniff out my comings and goings. For a city man, Watson seemed mighty comfortable walking the moors, both at day and during the nighttime. Only later did I learn he was ex-military and had served in Afghanistan. As such, Watson threw a fear into me. He may be Holmes' fawning biographer, but he is also a man unlike any other in these parts.

One morning, I manufactured a chance encounter with him in the hopes of him revealing his ulterior reasons for coming to Dartmoor. After some back-and-forth about Cousin Henry and the local legends of the spectral hound, I sensed Watson was not loose of tongue. I thought it bold when I asked:

"So has Mr. Sherlock Holmes any theories on Sir Charles' death?"

My question snagged Watson's attention. I held the line taut.

"Come now, doctor. We all know of your association with him. Certainly you can be open about your reasons for being here."

"I am afraid I cannot answer that question."

"May I ask if the detective will honor us with a visit? Hmm?"

Watson cried out and pointed across the moor. In the distance, a pony had been caught by the bog. Trapped, it struggled to free itself from a muddy hole of peat moss and primordial ooze. It whinnied and brayed and fought its fate, but the creature was soon gone.

"That is the edge of Grimpen Mire," I said. "It is a dangerous place. I do not recommend attempting to enter it."

"Have you seen such a sight before?"

"The horse's demise? Yes. It is not unusual in these parts."

"Your accent sounds distinct to me, yet I cannot place it. North of

London?"

"Yorkshire." I had not planned to provide him with a history, and I fumbled to give him one. No one in Dartmoor had made such a connection between my accent and the northern regions, and now the link had been named twice in two days. "I was the headmaster of a school there. Taught a bit of naturalism." I swung around the butterfly net. "Dabbled in my passion outside of the classroom while I was there as well."

The fool I was offering him so much information, and so much of it accurate. No doubt, with a simple telegram, he could have learned a great deal more about me from the authorities in Yorkshire. Or even from the anti-evolutionists who confronted me in my office one morning with a demand to stop teaching Bates' theory of mimicry among the butterflies of the Amazon.

"Why did you give it up? Dartmoor is a fine place, but I would think a York man would find it a tad…well…"

"Dreary? The mire offers much for me and my pursuits." I wagged the butterfly net once more for effect.

A great howl went up across the moor. It was Nero in the abandoned tin mine. He must have worked out of his cage. It was not the howl I had taught him. It was one of pain and sadness. An image arrested me, one of Nero dying in the bog much as the pony had earlier. I could not flee, however, without stoking Watson's suspicions. I could only continue my charade and hope I reached Nero in time.

"That is the weirdest, strangest sound I have heard in my life!" he said, this man who had served on the other side of the world and had tallied Sherlock Holmes' greatest problems. "What do you think is the cause?"

I gave Watson some gab about bitterns, a bird once common to this part of England. It was too much, strolling along amicably and making chitchat knowing Nero might be suffering, or worse. When a butterfly fluttered by—a not uncommon sight in the moors on a fair day—I made off as an absentminded naturalist pursuing his passion. Once Watson was out of sight, I headed straight into Grimpen Mire.

When I arrived at the tin mine, I discovered Nero had indeed freed himself from his cage. He paced around the circumference of the island the tin mine is situated on. He was testing the bog's edge with a delicate extended paw. At least he had enough sense to seek hard land before proceeding.

He was overjoyed at the sight of me. He barked and wagged his rump and jumped up to greet me. When I scolded him, he rolled on his back and exposed his belly to me. I led him back to the kennel and set him in the cage with his mother, where she could lick his face and ears and nurture him. Emotionally exhausted, I was tempted to lie back in my straw bed on the floor and shut my eyes for a moment of peace. No, there could be no hesitation. I hurried back to Merripit House with some haste, hoping Watson had not proceeded on. I did not wish him to meet Beryl outside of my presence, especially if she was suffering another bout of her foul moods.

My fears were realized. "Well, hullo, you've met my sister!" I said to Watson, jovial and out of breath.

"Yes," Beryl said to me coldly. "I was telling Sir Henry it was late in the day and that he had missed seeing the true beauty of our moor."

"I do not believe I did," Watson said softly to her.

Compared to our brittle conversation on the moor, the presence of my Beryl had smoothed over the doctor. Her effect on men, young and old, is profound. Her statuesque figure, her exquisite posture, and her smooth, petite face made her scowl appear dusky and mysterious to other men. Not to me.

"Why, who do you think this is?" I asked her, forcing a laugh to appear amused.

"It must be Sir Henry Baskerville."

"I am not Sir Henry." Watson made a slight bow to her. "I am but a commoner. I am his friend, Dr. Watson."

Beryl grew flush. Her scowl faded into a veneer of annoyed dismay. "We have been talking at cross-purposes."

She strode into the house with arms crossed. Not wishing to appear fazed by any of this, I offered Watson a chance to examine my collection of *Nepticulidae* and *Cyclopides* common to the environs. He refused, and after a brief goodbye was on his way.

Beryl again had locked herself in the bath and refused to answer my knocks. Antônio had spotted Watson's approach and quickly changed into his manservant outfit. When I entered the house alone, he sourly undid his tie's knot and threw the tie aside.

"She is reckless, Rodrigo."

"She thought him my cousin. It was an easy mistake."

"I listened from the window. She warned him to return to London. She was all but ready to confess you were responsible for killing Sir Charles."

I admitted something to him I was having trouble admitting to myself: "It burned when I heard her call him 'Sir Henry.'"

"Titles and honors. It is all you concern yourself with." Antônio flopped into a chair across from me. "This time with you, running from men with guns, and dogs sending men to their grave, it is making me an old man."

From the washroom, while I cleaned up, I yelled across the house to Antônio. "I am to meet my cousin tomorrow morning. He wants to discuss the circumstances of Uncle Charles' death. I suspect he will also want to know of the hellhound of the Baskervilles."

"And you will tell him?"

"I'm a man of science. It's rubbish, through and through."

Another cold dinner, and another cold bed to sleep in. Early that morning, I surreptitiously met Mrs. Laura Lyons at her apartment. At the sight of me, she burst into tears and was beside herself. She grieved hard for my uncle.

"Why did you dictate that letter to me—? And then tell me not to meet Sir Charles—?"

"Have you told anyone of your letter? I've told you before, you must not speak of it."

"I've not told a soul."

"It will only make you appear suspicious in the eyes of the law. If Sir Charles followed your instructions, he burned the letter and the police will never know of it. That is for the best. You are innocent, after all. There is no harm and no foul."

"But *you* wrote the letter!"

"To clear your mind. Was there a single sentiment stated you disagreed with?"

"I never would have told him to burn it!"

"For your protection. As I explained, I will ensure you receive the money to divorce your foul husband. But I cannot give you the money if you are suspected of murder. So, for your sake, you must keep quiet about this. It is perfectly moral what I am suggesting. You did nothing wrong. You should do nothing to endanger yourself falsely. Agreed?"

On my way back to Merripit Hall, I discovered the most sickening sight I could imagine. Cousin Henry and Beryl walked side-by-side on the moor with the slow stride of a man wooing a captivated woman. He was entranced. Worse, she appeared smitten.

Without a second thought, I descended upon them and broke up the rendezvous. Beryl's tranquility was shattered upon my arrival. On the spot, I devised a reason for Beryl to return with me to Merripit House, some nonsense about a chicken cooking on the stove. Henry took Beryl around her waist and produced a list of formal objections to my intrusion, as though I was rustling the horse he was grooming. Her slight contortions to worm out of his grip went unnoticed by him. It only enflamed me further.

From the little I'd heard from my cousin to date, he had only spoken with an unmistakable Canadian accent. Here I recognized the patronizing tone of my uncle and my father gradually shoring up his lazy North American tongue. His objections were clipped and militaristic, spoken as though in command of all rational facts, treating me as little more than an old-fashioned nuisance. The more he spoke down to me, the tighter he held Beryl, utterly oblivious to her shamed hanging head and her womanly resistances to his touch.

Was it the money? The estate? No. It was the title. It's the coachmen and the carriage drivers saluting him, and the women in Dartmoor village curtsying as he passed. He arrived in London a Canadian, smelling of maple trees and beer, and he left London as the perfumed Sir Henry. Do not tell me people never change. People will change immensely if they're suddenly treated as a better, or an inferior.

When I was about ready to strike him in the Adam's apple, and his dullard brain realized fisticuffs were a possibility, Henry released her. Without hesitation, Beryl moved to my side. Her mute willingness to abide only made me appear the worse in his eyes. I am certain we left Henry thinking me the possessive and commanding brother, and Beryl the obedient sister.

"Why?" I demanded of her.

I expected a story of a chance meeting on the moor, or of Henry's arrival at Merripit House to greet the commoners now living under his gracious aegis.

Instead, Beryl merely said to me, "I owe you nothing."

"You owe me an explanation."

"I am done with you."

"Done? I have brought you up from *nothing* and you are done with me?"

"Nothing? I lived well in my father's hacienda!"

"Beaten for talking back, no less. Married off according to his plans. I've given you freedom. Self-determination. A boundless world. When we reach Paris with Uncle Charles' money, we will live well!"

"I will live ten times as well as Lady Henry Baskerville."

I raised a palm to strike her—and stopped myself.

"No." I lowered my hand. She remained in an instinctive cower. "I will not divorce you."

"Divorce! I am your sister. The boat captain who married us—he has sailed off with whatever wind carried him away. There is no paper of our wedding. There is no ring on my finger. You did not even buy me a simple band when we arrived in England. Nothing!"

She declared:

"Your uncle is dead. The men who broke your father, they are all dead as well. You have your revenge. Henry has done you no harm. Go now to Paris. Take Antônio with you. I will remain in Dartmoor. On my honor, I will not tell anyone of what you have done. Of that I swear."

No: I would not give up Beryl quite so easily.

Thirty

Antônio grew slack in his assistance. He loitered about Merripit House and studied books in the diminutive but sensibly stocked library provided with the house. The upkeep of the house suffered from it. He was not completely lax during these days, however.

"There is another man on the moor." He pointed off through the window. "He lives among the tors, just as our escaped convict does."

"Another prisoner from Princetown? Perhaps they fled together."

"I do not believe so. Selden has been scurrying about the moor for some time now. This second dweller, he is newer." He raised an eyebrow. "He appeared around the time Dr. Watson arrived in Dartmoor. Also, the tittle-tattle in Coombe Tracey is that the inn there hosts a new lodger, a singularly gaunt man of few words."

"And?"

"I would not be surprised if Dartmoor's new visitors are one and the same."

There and then I knew what Antônio was suggesting. I now had one more busybody to worry about, one more set of eyes upon the moor attempting to ferret out the truth of the situation. Long walks at night with Nero were now out of the question. Into Grimpen Mire I plunged, but only when necessary and only under the cover of deep darkness.

It was also Antônio who intercepted a perfumed note delivered for Beryl. With great agitation, I tore it open, knowing well its sender.

"Canadian swine," I murmured. "Gentlemen of repute and standing, presuming they may simply demand the presence of whatever woman strikes their fancy."

"He will persist," Antônio said. "We cannot keep him away forever."

I rapped the paper note against my other palm. "We need to get ahead of this. My outburst before Cousin Henry can be a pretext for a tête-à-tête and an explanation of my behavior. I will make certain he never comes around again." At my writing desk, I jotted off an obsequious note to Henry inviting him to join me for an evening constitutional. "Get this to Baskerville Hall promptly," I told Antônio. "We will end this tonight."

He pulled on his jacket and knotted his tie. "Is it wise to host him here, in Beryl's presence?"

"You will take Beryl into the village this evening. Any pretense will do—tell her Mrs. Lyons needs a shoulder to cry on." They both still grieved for my uncle. "Make sure neither of you return until well after ten. That will give me enough time to settle matters with Cousin Henry."

Antônio had little trouble inducing Beryl out of the house, as she always bristled at our efforts to keep her inside. I waited for dusk to fall, and scrambled into Grimpen Mire.

By eight o'clock, a wet gray mist was drifting out of the mire and crossing the moors. With taut leashes and both dogs muzzled, I led them out of the fens and underbrush and across the bald hills toward Merripit House. In the privacy of the cellar beneath the stable, I worked up Nero into a lather, using Agrippina's devotion to me as a wedge between his sense of belonging and security. Soon he was in a froth. The hour of Henry's arrival was imminent.

With Agrippina tied up in the cellar, I led Nero out. We waited atop one of the tors. From the flat stone plank emerging from the hillside, I could survey the path running between Baskerville Hall and Merripit House.

It was a desolate evening, grim and raw, a night no sane man would abandon the creature comforts of his home to explore the wet marshes. Dr. Watson might be prowling about again, but I saw no evidence of him from my vantage. Nor did I spy the second man Antônio had warned me of. Nero pawed at his muzzle and growled his disapproval. He struggled against me. I took him by the scruff and reminded him who was the top dog. He meekly rolled on his back, belly exposed and paws in the air. His temper was only superseded by his understandable need for attention.

And then the time was right. Across the moor wandered a man from the direction of Baskerville Hall. He walked with some urgency in the moonlight, as though not keen to be upon the moor at such a time at night. Perhaps Henry too had succumbed to the dire warnings of the family curse? Do the hoary tales of the ghastly hellhound weigh upon him as they burdened Uncle Charles? Peering through my collapsible lens, the dim moonlight was sufficient to determine he wore a tweed suit and sharp hat. He was neither of Holmes' height nor Watson's girth. No, this was Cousin Henry of the groping paws, eager to sniff at Beryl once more.

Taking Nero by the scruff, I shook and agitated him until he was frothing once more. I was frothing myself from Henry's overeager and lusty expression in the presence of my dear Beryl. With more of the luminescent grease smeared across his face and through his hackles, Nero, my spectral Burbage, was prepared to tread the boards once more.

From a bag, I produced Henry's used boot. After the mix-up at the London hotel, I had to pay the Portuguese-speakers again to pilfer a well-worn one from his room, as the first one was newly purchased and did not bear his scent. This boot I crammed into Nero's nose. Crazed, he bounded off toward the lonely silhouette crossing the moor.

In the distance came a cold scream. Through my collapsible lens, I witnessed the events unfold, which they did in a way eerily mirroring the events at the yew alley. The tweed-suited man attempted an escape, but in no way could he outrun Nero, who was bounding at him as a racehorse would the finish line. In his confusion, the man stumbled over and down—and I lost sight of him. Nero dove into the nighttime mists as well, disappearing as though racing toward the very gates of Hell.

Would Cousin Henry have carried a pistol? He might. He had lived on the western Canadian frontier much of his life, and men in those parts were as comfortable with a sidearm as any rancher in the Amazon. I heard no report, however. I waited, blind in the dark and confused, until finally Nero appeared with his greasepaint ablaze. Calmly, almost businesslike, he trotted across the moor and joined me where I stood.

With considerable haste, I wiped the grease clean, muzzled him, and hurried him back to Merripit House. With no blood in evidence upon him, I could only assume a similar fate had befallen Henry as my uncle. Perhaps he shared some hereditary weakness of the heart, an ailment that seems to have skipped me. I left Nero in the loving affections of his mother, who licked the greasy residue off his face while he rested against her breast.

It is done, I told myself with a great sigh of relief. The Baskerville line was extinguished. We could leave this place, perhaps poorer than we arrived, but at least I could claim an ounce or two of personal dignity mixed with a half-pound of satisfaction.

From a dark window at Merripit House, I peered across the moor with my looking glass. Activity began to stir out there. Two figures emerged from the tors upon the hills and descended upon the site of Henry's death. It would be Dr. Watson and the mysterious Sherlock Holmes, who finally decided to reveal himself now that his client was dead. So much for collecting his fee; hopefully, he required a nonrefundable deposit for his services. Cigar lit, I strolled over the moor to the silhouetted men huddled over Henry's corpse.

Suddenly, the taller of the two began dancing. It stopped me cold. He was dancing and singing words I could not make out. What could this be?

When I arrived, Holmes' jig had ceased. Coming into their presence, I detected a smug countenance upon him. The doctor, on the other hand, was stifling an intense anger.

"Dr. Watson? Is that you? This is not a night I would expect to find anyone upon the moor. And who is this—somebody hurt?"

Lying face down beyond the outcropping they stood upon was Henry in tweed.

"It is our friend, Sir Henry!" I rushed down the outcropping and knelt beside him. "Did he fall? He does not know the moor well, he should not have traveled alone at night—"

With a great crashing sensation, I realized my mistake. The man bore a scraggly beard, the result of living weeks on the moor scurrying between the caves and the tors. He was bony and emaciated, as his only sustenance was the over-salted scraps and bland leftovers Mrs. Barrymore had put out for him, just as yard dogs are fed every evening from a bowl at the rear door.

Aware I must feign the blithe innocence of a bumbling naturalist, I demanded, "Pray, who is this?"

"It is a man known as Selden," Holmes announced. "A convict who escaped from the prison in Princetown."

"How did he die?"

"He appears to have broken his neck when he fell over these rocks. My friend and I were crossing the moor when we heard his cries."

"I heard them as well." I rose and joined them atop the outcropping. "That is what drew me out. I'm worried about Sir Henry."

"Why?" Watson demanded. "What about Sir Henry in particular concerns you?" The good doctor, sworn to the Hippocratic oath, appeared ready to take a swing at me.

"I suggested he visit me this evening," I said, fumbling. "Naturally, I grew concerned for his safety when I heard the man's cries."

"Did you hear any other cries tonight?" Holmes asked. "Any other weird noise that you cannot account for?"

"I am aware of the legends of the hound patrolling the moor. I heard nothing of the sort, however. Do you believe he was attacked by such a beast?" I peered down at the corpse lying before us. "Is there evidence he was mauled by a hound?"

"No evidence at all," Holmes said.

"He has been living on the moor for a great deal of time," I said. "Perhaps exposure led him to lose his head. If he was rushing about the moor on a night such as tonight, it's no doubt he would fall and hurt himself."

"And that is your theory?"

"It seems most reasonable. Don't you agree, Mr. Holmes?"

Holmes displayed nothing. "You are quick with identification."

"We have been awaiting your arrival. Unfortunate such a tragedy would coincide with your appearance."

"Yes. Indeed. I will take an unpleasant remembrance back to London with me tomorrow."

"You return tomorrow? I hope you will be able to cast some light on these unfortunate events besieging our little village on the moor?"

Holmes shrugged off my question. "I do not dabble in local legends, only verifiable facts. This case has been most lacking in them."

To be in the presence of Sherlock Holmes is a singular experience, even under the odd circumstances of our meeting. His sudden change of tone and emotive expressions, to see him shift from dancing and singing to somber frankness and concession, and in only a matter of moments. It is all quite disarming.

"We cannot leave this poor soul out here," I said. "The sight would give my sister a great fright. Otherwise, I would suggest carrying him to our house. Perhaps we could—"

"Leave him," Holmes said. "We will cover his face with a cloth and come for him in the morning with a cart."

It was outrageous. Holmes had danced over Selden's corpse, most likely erupting when he and Watson determined it was not my cousin Henry lying there dead. Now this pair was ready to leave his body exposed to the elements of the moor, a place built for devouring the dead. Meanwhile, they board and dine in the house managed by the poor man's sister, ordering around the Barrymores for hot water and fresh linen while her kin decomposed. When would they deign to inform the poor woman? In the morning, as she served them their coffee and toast?

The pair made their way to Baskerville Hall with little talk between themselves. No doubt they waited to draw out of earshot of me before conversing. Not a twinge of guilt nagged at their consciences. Not a single doubt hindered them. I could not carry Selden alone. I left him on the moor too, and for that I am guilty.

Thirty-one

The funds we managed to take from Yorkshire were sufficient to board ourselves at Merripit House and enjoy a modicum of comfort. Those funds had dwindled, and with Uncle Charles' promised money held up by Dr. Mortimer, our time at Merripit House was drawing to a close. Now Holmes' presence in Dartmoor was overt. The judicious course of action was to depart at once for the continent.

Beryl's actions in the morning washed away my regretful decision to leave England. When she returned from the village, she brought with her an impassioned rage:

"Mrs. Barrymore's brother was killed last night!" she yelled at me. "Why did you—?"

She pushed me away when I tried to comfort her.

"An angel of hell!" she screamed at me in Spanish. "You are the Devil himself!"

"He fell in the dark," Antônio told her, not convincingly. "It was an accident."

"I do not believe you! And I will never believe anything you say again!" she said to me.

"We're leaving," I told her. "Tonight we travel to Paris."

"Thank the Lord," Antônio murmured from off to the side.

"No." Beryl was resolute. "I will remain here with Henry. I will give you both two days to flee. If I learn you are still in the country, I will go to the authorities."

"You would not."

"I will."

"You will come with me to Paris. You are my wife."

"I am not your wife! No more!"

I backed her into a corner. "From this moment forward, you will never contradict me."

"Do not touch me! Stay back!"

"We should sedate her," Antônio called from behind me.

When I came close, she slapped me across the jaw. "Do not lay a hand on me—"

As she went to slap me a second time, I caught her wrist.

"I will not strike you," I said with as even a voice as I could manage. "I made a vow on the ship, and I am a man of my word." I released her hand. "I am your husband."

She had stormed into the house with such fury, she had not taken the time to remove her bonnet. I pulled it free and held it to her face.

"There is another who never contradicts me." I pushed the bonnet into her nose. "He takes one whiff and he will do anything I say." I caught her arm before she could take the bonnet from me. "I will hold on to this."

She fled the room crying. Upstairs, the bedroom door slammed.

"We cannot take her to Paris, Rodrigo. She is lost to you now."

I gently folded up the bonnet and placed it aside.

"In time," I told him. "In time."

*

As though a man cursed, the imprecations upon me continued when Antônio noted that Henry had sent his regrets missing our tête-à-tête the evening before, but would be delighted to sup with us the next. The mistake of loosing Nero upon Selden took a comical shape: Selden's death was not merely due to him wearing the baronet's donated clothes, and thereby carrying the baronet's scent, but also due to the baronet's finicky scheduling. The aristocracy seemingly invents new ways to burden the common man.

"Perhaps we should send *our* regrets to Henry. We can flee tonight, Rodrigo, you and me. You heard her. She will give us two days to leave the country. That is more than enough time—"

"I am not leaving Beryl. She is my love."

"Does she love you?"

"She will never love Henry, that much I assure you. No, we will host Henry tonight. Make preparations. The meal should not be overly lavish. Don't 'toff it up,' is how I think these English say it. Cigars, wine, and coffee after dinner."

"For what purpose? You wish to keep Beryl from him, yet you invite him into this house?"

"I have my reasons. Make the preparations. I will handle Beryl."

Henry's message also included a tantalizing detail: Watson would not be dining with us, as he and Holmes were returning to London immediately. Holmes had mentioned this detail as we conversed over Selden's corpse. I did not take him for his word then, yet this seemed to confirm it.

To Antônio, I said, "Travel to the station immediately. I need to know if Holmes and Watson are leaving Devon. I smell a game being played here."

"I believe there is, and it is not a game you can win. Why would Mr. Holmes leave now?"

"Because his famed skills of detection rely on the examination of physical evidence, of which there is none. Neither my uncle nor Selden died with so much as a mark on them. If Holmes could prove any of it, he would be here now with the law. Antônio, you have trusted me this far. You must trust me once more. I will see us through this."

"I do not share your ill will toward your cousin. He has done me no harm."

"Remain here after I am gone, then. Wait until he takes Beryl's hand in marriage. Beryl will then have no need for you, yes? She said she will denounce us both, and you will be taken away in handcuffs."

"Under what charges?"

"Charges? You ask about 'charges?'" I burst out laughing. "This man is an aristocrat! Even if he is fresh and raw to the ways of the English, he bears a sturdy family name and a title! He hails from North America, we three are from South America, and yet somehow we are the foreigners here. There will be no 'charges.' There will only be *punishment.* And it will be summarily dispensed."

Antônio sagged. "I give up," he said softly. "I have allowed you to place me in a position where I am utterly dependent on you. Yes. Claim your misguided revenge. This business is a bottomless bowl, and you will not stop until you've devoured the meal and yourself with it. You will have your evening with Sir Henry, and your cigar and port as well. Upon serving dinner, I will leave the house."

"When will you return?"

"I would not count on it." And he made begrudging preparations to visit the train station to lookout for Holmes and Watson.

Out to Grimpen Mire, I traveled once more. There I roused the spirits of Nero and Agrippina. I napped with them until the sun drew low. I muzzled and leashed both and began the demanding process of leading them out of the mire. The timing was right; when we emerged, darkness covered the moor. A bite in the air, which I had grown familiar with since moving to Devonshire, suggested a stiff incoming fog.

With Agrippina secured in the stable cellar, I made one rearrangement to my usual mode of operation. Henry's arrival complicated much. Leaving Nero with Agrippina was impractical. Nero had to be available at a moment's notice. So, after giving him the opportunity to say goodbye to his mother, I took him to an old outhouse on the edge of an untended orchard on the eastern side of Merripit House.

With Nero locked up, I returned to the house and assisted Antônio with the evening's preparations. Although his cooking skills were honed over campfires, he was a savant in a modern kitchen as well. I helped him in the final stages of the supper he'd planned. He had fetched from Grimpen village the last bottle of fine port the grocer stocked. We toasted in the kitchen after the meal.

"My father's family hails from Porto," he said in Portuguese. "I was raised in a household where a bottle of port was on the side table every evening."

The drink we shared…I sensed it would be the last between us. With the brandied wine came a surge of fond memories shared: The smell of bananas ripening on the tree in Santarém; the rain and mud and thickets of the Amazon; living high in the best hotels Panama City and Colón offered; and the glorious sun of Puerto Limón. We reminisced all of it over that tidy drink.

Antônio also shared his news. "It is confirmed. Sherlock Holmes and Dr. Watson were indeed at the station today. They met a third man on the platform. I did not recognize him, although he patently knew the two of them."

"Did they board the train?"

"I had to return to prepare for Sir Henry's arrival."

"What? Did you see them with bags?"

"They appeared dressed for travel, but I could not tell you more." He clapped me on the shoulder. "*Adeus.*" And he exited the house.

Beryl was not in our bedroom, and the door to the bath was not locked. After traversing every room in the house, I discovered her in the least likely place, my collection room.

From the first butterfly I gathered in Brazil, my collection had ballooned over the years until I was able to construct a little museum of my own. Cases on tables and trays lined the walls and formed a minor maze through the center of the otherwise bare room. Of all my material losses, I count my collection as the greatest.

I discovered Beryl hunched over one of the cases. She was tapping the glass top with a sharp fingernail, as though attempting to wake one of the moths pinned crucifixion-style to the mounting board.

"It is morbid how you keep your pets."

"I see a beauty in them that some people refuse to perceive."

"They are beautiful when they are free and dancing about in the air. Here they are cold and desiccated. You killed each one and filed it away in one of your little cages."

"I cannot let them fly around in here. They have to be preserved. If my uncle had kept his word, I would be the administrator of the Butterfly Pavilion. Imagine the children of Devon being able to experience what I experienced growing up in the jungle. To walk among a flurry of the God's most elegant creatures. To have a richly decorated *Nymphalidae* land upon their shoulder and—"

"Enough. You and your buttery dreams hold sway over me no more. Antônio told me Sir Henry would be dining with us tonight. What do you plan on doing to him?"

I value my friendship with Antônio above all others, but in this case, I am sorely disappointed he did not warn me of his indiscretion.

"Will you hurt him? Will you sic your hound on him—?"

I intercepted her hand before it struck my face.

"I will warn him of your plans," she taunted. "I will tell him all of your history. How you are the bastard son of a Baskerville who was sent away because he shamed the family—"

"I am the final rightful heir. I should be living at Baskerville Hall, not him."

"—I will tell him you are a petty thief and a confidence trickster—"

I intercepted her other hand before it reached my chin. "And you are a cheap enough woman to fall in love with a man like me."

I smashed my mouth into hers. I came back with a bloody lip and a string of red between our mouths.

"I'm going to let you hear what a staunch and upright gentleman my cousin Henry is," I said. "Tonight you will learn how love is negotiated by the aristocracy. That's right. Tonight I will inquire of Henry's intentions. You wish to marry him? You wish to be Lady Henry Baskerville? You will learn your exact price."

I had entered the room prepared, with a length of rope tucked into the back of my pants. Her alarm intensified when she realized my own intentions toward her.

"Call as loud as you want," I said over her screams. Within a minute, I had her secured to the baulk of a supporting timber awkwardly set in the center of the bedroom. "I sent Antônio away. You know full well no one can hear."

I opened a vent set in the floor. It permitted warm air from the fireplace below to heat the room.

"You listen as the men gather to discuss the womenfolk," I told her. "You will learn the truth of Cousin Henry tonight. And then you will know why all the ladies of the aristocracy wear chokers about their necks."

Thirty-two

Henry was punctual. He told his driver he would be walking home, and sent the trap back to Baskerville Hall.

"Come inside," I said with a warm smile. I took the opportunity to glance about outside. "No one else joining us tonight?"

"It is only myself this evening," he said, rather stiffly.

"I was surprised to read in your note that Watson and Holmes would not be joining us. I looked forward to their company."

"They've returned to London," he said, again, stiffly. "I'm quite dissatisfied with their investigation. This Holmes fellow was most uninspiring. He's so absentminded, he wired from London to say he left behind his pocketbook. Why would such a fellow choose criminal detection for a profession?"

It seemed most unlike the Sherlock Holmes I had read about, what with his magnificent powers of observation. Still—could a man fake a telegram from London? I dismissed the line of thought to focus on Henry.

"Well, you picked a rather chilly night to walk the moors," I told him. "Even the born-and-raised of Dartmoor wouldn't venture outside on a night like tonight."

"It's good for the constitution." A stiff man, stiff in diction and stiff in gait. "In Canada, I made sure to walk at least ninety minutes each day. With the sea voyage and the business over the estate, I've fallen out of my routine."

"And you are not concerned about the family curse?" My grin was mocking now, I imagine. "The spectral hellhound sent to savage any Baskerville who dares to cross the moor alone?"

"I am…of two minds on the matter." His expression betrayed a greater doubt. "Your home here. I am told it has a history worth hearing?"

Over supper, I relayed what I knew of Merripit House, which had been relayed to me by the owner the day we leased it. Henry inquired about my manservant; night off, I explained. He made a special point to ask about Beryl; visiting friends in Torquay, I assured him. He expressed disappointment, and told me flatly if he knew Beryl would not be in attendance, he would have given his regrets and requested another evening.

We retired to the sitting room, where I had started a healthy fire. After pouring the *café noir* and the port, we lit cigars and continued our conversation.

Henry, without fail, turned each path of our conversation back to himself and his accomplishments in the New World. Henry's stories of his personal successes always centered on the sheer might of his determination and his pluck in new ventures. With Uncle Charles, I allowed his stories of gold speculation in South Africa to drag on without interruption. Feeling plucky myself, I needled Henry for clarification, and received it:

"Well, yes, the loan my timber company obtained was secured by the Bank of London," he said with note of complaint in his voice.

"Why would they secure it? You told me you had not yet signed for the timber rights."

"Not that it's your business, as you plainly do not comprehend the—" He drew deep on his cigar and caught his temper before it let loose. "I contacted a great-uncle-in-law in Exeter, and he acted as a go-between with the bank here in London."

"You mean you called in a favor."

"What are you edging at?"

"It must be nice to possess such clout, even in a far-off place like Canada."

He looked at me squarely. "Family is important. A good family takes care of each other. Do you come from a good family, Stapleton?"

"I should say I do not."

"Shame. And shameful. Every family is responsible for caring for their own. It's a core component of the social contract. These Socialists—" He waved his hand as though throwing salt over his shoulder. "Blowing up Europe with their bombs and issuing their saber-rattling manifestos, they would have it that the *state* is responsible for—"

"Port?'

"Why, yes," he said through teeth gritted about his cigar.

"I would like to ask of your intentions toward my sister." I raised my voice so it would carry through the vent in the ceiling.

"Ah. Yes. Beryl. Beautiful girl. Perhaps her absence tonight is a blessing, then. It will give us a chance to speak of her future, man-to-man."

While he was extolling her beauty and virtues, a distinct *snap* sounded from beyond the room's walls. Frozen, I worried Beryl was working through the ropes and sheets I'd bound her up in. The sound had come from outside the window, however. It was futile to peer outside. The gaslight and fire only made the window a black mirror. If a prowler was edging about, it was best to meet him outside, and without Henry's awareness.

"Sir Henry, you must excuse me a moment."

Through the servant's door, I escaped into the cold night air. A great gray fog bank crossed the moors toward us, a veritable cumulus cloud smothering the low hills. Now my designs to keep Henry occupied into the evening took on a new dimension: If he were to walk home in the pea soup, he would have no advantage, even if he carried a pistol, which I had not detected so far.

I saw no one prowling about. If only I had been more thorough in my search! I was a circus juggler that night, what with Beryl upstairs, and Henry unawares in the den, Agrippina patiently waiting underground, and Nero locked up in the old outhouse, a tight and unfamiliar enclosure no doubt causing him much anguish.

I jogged off to the barren orchard, unlocked the door, and joined Nero inside. He was muzzled, which kept his whimpering to a minimum, but he had been clawing at the door. I calmed him; the hour for his blind rage would come soon enough. My presence did much to relieve his distress, and he nuzzled my face as I whispered reassurances.

When I returned to Henry, he was pacing the floor and checking his pocket watch.

"My apologies," I said. "Please. Let us continue."

Henry, lawyer-like, made a few more token appreciations of Beryl's goodness and figure before demanding I name a price for her hand in marriage.

"When I arrived in London, one of the first things I did was buy new suits," he said. "If I am to squire in Devon, I must dress accordingly. Likewise, if I am to carry on the family name and tradition, I must have a fine woman at my side. Before we continue, I must know of your family background. It is apparent you come from good stock. Your accent gives you away. You run about with your nets and killing jars, but your manner of speech tells me you are a most educated and refined man. Your sister, though…I do not expect her to have the intellectual command you possess. Her social graces are her true value. But there is something about her I cannot put my finger on. Tell me, Stapleton: Is she a half-sister? Out with it. You are fair and Anglo-Saxon, but she is swarthy like a Mediterranean."

"There is a dark streak in our family."

"No hint of bastardization? These are questions that must be asked."

I made the assurances he so desired to hear. "I do confess, our family has seen better days. If Beryl is wed, our family would certainly hope for due consideration."

He laughed, arching his back. He blew smoke up toward the vent in the ceiling.

"I like you, Stapleton. You and your tweedy ways, flitting about the landscape in search of your precious insects and pupae. You speak with a refreshing forthrightness. Well, growing up abroad has taught me the value of a dollar. If you want good value, you must pay for it. And I will most certainly pay to have it."

And from there, we negotiated Beryl's price as though horse-trading. I will not detail the exact figures we arrived at. What's important is, Beryl learned, for the first time in her life, her value down to the farthing. With the named price came my assurances of *hymen intacta*, stipulations that if she failed to produce a male heir within five years, the divorce would not be contested, as well as other sundry requirements regarding her physical and moral fitness as a wife and a mother.

"It's agreed, then. I will have the papers drawn up."

After helping him with his coat, I showed him to the head of the footpath. He bade me goodnight, and began his march across the fog-laden moor. The sudden change in temperature from raging fire to the damp chill of the moor, and the sliver moon made a-glow by the mists, dampened his spirits. He proceeded down the path with a notable trepidation. His long glances up and across the hills were focused in the direction a hellhound might travel when it caught the scent of a Baskerville loose on the moor.

Time was precious. Upstairs I fled, two steps at a time. I kneeled before her and pushed up the mask I'd wrapped around her to keep her quiet. I asked her what she thought of Sir Henry now. She was crying.

*

Quickly now, I hurried to the orchard and released Nero. I smeared the *flor-de-coco* grease around his eyes, down his snout, and across his hackles and dewlap. I carried with me two items in bags, which I now produced.

One was a tuft of hair I had brushed off his mother that afternoon. I thrust it to his nostrils. He whimpered and pawed at my leg to let me know he wanted to see her.

On bent knee, I whispered into his ear in Portuguese, "Know that I love you fully, my friend."

From the second bag, I produced Henry's boot. He recognized it from the night prior. The odor memory sent him into lather, the thrill of the hunt unfulfilled by the lack of a kill. This was another chance to prove his worth to me, and thereby to his mother. He wrestled my grip, ready to charge.

I cried: *Go get him!*

Nero leapt with a snarl. He charged headlong into the pale fog bank settling across Grimpen village. Full of venom and vigor myself, and smelling victory at hand, I raced across the dale in his wake. Growls and yips sounded across the moor. The bluish-green dripping flames were but otherworldly smears floating apparition-like through the mist.

Moments later, a human scream ripped through the air. The unmistakable throaty gargle of Nero launching himself onto his prey went up—

What then came I can only describe as the most sickening series of sounds. Years of ambition crashed down in a moment.

"Now, Watson!" came a shriek through the misty curtain. "Your gun!"

Two gunshots rang out, followed by several more in quick succession. In between them all came a piteous yelp of a dog crying out—Nero's sickening last cries for his mother.

"We have him!" It was Watson's voice.

The game was over. *Fila* can withstand all manner of adversaries, even the ferocious jaguar of the Amazon, but like all of God's gentle creatures, it must answer to fearsome Man, the only amoral animal to exist.

No sanctuary waited for me at Merripit House. The local villages would be searched soon enough. No train out of Dartmoor until morning. No horse or transportation to call my own. My plan of last resort was now my only resort. I threw aside Henry's boot and hurled myself across the moor and into the foul embrace of Grimpen Mire.

And so I reach the moment where this journal commenced: Retreating to the old tin mine, licking my wounds, and planning my revenge on Sherlock Holmes.

Enough planning. The time has arrived.

Thirty-three

London is too much to comprehend at once, and the cold, wet people, too much to bear for this São Paulo native. London wears me down as no other city does.

I had a note couriered to 221B Baker Street. The message was intentionally provocative:

> *Mr. Sherlock Holmes,*
>
> *I am a hardworking citizen of London and a union man. I come to you with hat in hand bearing information I presume to be of interest to one such as yourself.*
>
> *Three weeks ago, as I passed Mitre Square early in the morn, a man was fleeing the square itself with a great and untidy haste. Thinking him a cutpurse, I attempted to halt his escape. He was fleeter of foot and evaded me, although I assure you I did attempt chase.*
>
> *When the bobby whistles sounded and word got round that the tart killer had struck again, I came to comprehend the man fleeing Mitre Square was likely the culprit. Perhaps he is the fiend responsible for the other ladies o' the night meeting their demise in likewise fashion?*
>
> *Mr. Holmes, could we not meet at a neutral place of my choosing, so I may offer a full account of my memory? It would not do if my name was to reach the newspapers, and my wife would not take kindly to learning my whereabouts that night. In any case, I do not trust the police. They are most unkind to union members. I ask you attend alone, as I dearly wish to preserve my privacy. Would you consider meeting me at Mitre Square at ten o'clock, under the conditions requested?*
>
> *– A concerned citizen*

I arrived well ahead of my proposed meeting time, in disguise and with my Colt at the ready. Mitre Square is an out-of-the-way place, and was especially quiet. I made particular care not to enter the square itself, for fear of exposing myself to Holmes and any police in hiding he may have summoned to his aid.

Here I make a list of those I witnessed passing through or near the square:

1. A grocer pushing a cart of pears and carrots.

2. A man and a woman groomed and well-dressed, moving with some haste through the square and down Mitre Street. Within minutes, they had a hansom cab and were away.

3. A vagrant lying among his own filth in an alley up the way, using newspapers for blankets and a bottle of gin to stay warm.

4. Two boys in school pants hurrying along, no doubt out later than allowed.

5. A rather tall and gaunt man lingering in the threshold of a tobacconist's. He spent a considerable amount of time preparing his pipe before lighting it.

6. A stout man with a limp and cane. He strolled the square whistling a bawdy French tune.

The gaunt man captured my attention. He was all the more suspicious for lingering before the tobacconist's for such an interminable duration. I dared not approach him, as if he were Holmes, I feared he would recognize me instantly. My disguise was not foolproof in close quarters, although the dark October night was only to my advantage.

"Farthing?" was all the vagrant was capable of saying to passersby. Last I noticed, he was leaning against an alley wall near his bower and urinating.

I grew most suspicious of the stout whistling man. He was wrapped in scarf and woolen coat, and his hat was pulled down tight around his ears. He could easily have been Dr. Watson incognito, perhaps working with Holmes on some kind of snare, or scouting the area forward of Holmes' arrival.

With the time of our meeting nearing, and then passing, I despaired Holmes would never arrive. When eleven approached, I resigned. I abandoned hope of returning to Holmes exactly what he had delivered to me that fog-soaked night on the moor.

Upstairs in my hired room, I removed my coat and holster. At the basin, I prepared for the arduous task of stripping off the beard. Remove it in haste, and the spirit gum would tear the disguise and render it useless.

From below came a commotion, a kerfuffle amplified by the woman of the lodging house herself. She was screaming in the thick accent of the lower classes that she did not "Cotton such riff-raff off the street, no liquored-up vagrants allowed in here I tell ya, particularly those as rank as yourself—"

I'd been had—I snatched up Colt and coat and bolted from the room. Only one proper exit, down the stairs and past the front desk where the commotion was transpiring. Sure enough, from my brief glance down the stairwell, I made out Holmes in his vagrant costume trying his best to maneuver past the old woman, who was beating him back with an umbrella.

"Madam, it is a matter of great importance—your lodger, I believe he is the Ripper!"

I crashed through the door of a neighboring room with gun up. The man and woman in bed screamed and scrambled back. With the butt of the Colt, I smashed their window open, and ran its barrel about the perimeter of the frame to clear off the remaining glass. Unlike my room, which offered a twenty-foot drop to the street below, theirs was over a fenced-in garden. It was likely maintained by the same woman now battering Holmes with a parasol.

Without so much as a goodbye, I climbed down the sill and landed among the potatoes and leeks in the soft soil below. My frantic energy was such I was over the fence and on the street in no time, dark and desolate save for a couple growlers wheeling past. With a speed I did not think myself capable of, I rounded the corner back to the lodging's entrance—Holmes believed he trapped me, but I had trapped *him*.

The poor woman, who'd done her best to beat back the drunken, urine-smelling vagrant, stood at the desk in an appalled daze. Holmes had managed to get past her and reach the top floor. He was now mostly likely in my room. I charged inside brandishing my Colt, fully prepared to rush up the stairs and shoot Holmes down.

"Got you." From behind me, two capable hands landed on my shoulders. It was the voice of Dr. Watson, who'd remained inside the front desk out of view of the doorway. "Holmes! Our lodger is down here—"

Dammit all, so close and yet outmaneuvered once more!

I swung around flashing steel in his face. Watson stumbled backwards, his hands protecting him from a pistol-whipping. The Colt went off in my hands. The muzzle lit like a photographer's flash powder. Half-blind, deaf from the shot gone wide, I stumbled out the front door and escaped into the misty midnight. Oh, I'd been outplayed, and thoroughly so.

I have not run so hard since Nero's death. The boggy mire of Grimpen, and the foul wet terrain of London, they do not seem so different at night. Both are mined with dangers, and both were designed as fiendish mazes to trap the unprepared within.

Thirty-four

Within sight of Merripit House, lurking in the early morning shadows, I waited tens of minutes for any sign of a watch or a surreptitious monitoring of the property. Holmes had tricked me twice now. If I did not learn from such mistakes, I am unworthy of my name.

Upstairs, I discovered my butterfly collection had been raided and turned over, as though Visigoths had sacked the place. How such chaos could be reported as "police work" only confirms the slipshod practices of law enforcement.

In the master bedroom, Beryl slept soundly. Or so I thought. As I neared, she sat up and commanded I halt. Only after assuring her it was I, Rodrigo, did she relax. With the lighting of the oil lamp came the revelation she wielded a short but lethal knife.

"The people of Grimpen hate me now," she told me. "I fear they will come for me in the night and lynch me. The English, they say they do no such things, but I do not believe them."

"Nor do I." I kneeled before her. I kissed her hand and up her arm. "I have missed you so—"

She murmured *No…no…no* until she forcibly retracted and pushed me back. "It is over."

"It is not over. I love you. I have come for you."

"Comc for what? To get me killed?" With the terror of a sudden understanding, she brandished the knife again. "To silence me, yes? I told them nothing!"

"Beryl—I have come to take you away from this, and start a new life with you."

"A new life? Yet another? No. I am not like Antônio, that coward."

"Where is he?"

She had not set aside the knife. "He went on an errand. To Princetown, I believe. After he returned, he went to the men of Dartmoor and told them all he knew about you. All he asked was to be sent home. They secreted him to Plymouth. I believe he is on his way to Brazil as we speak." She rejected my continued advances. "Do not. You sicken me. You are an infection. You filled me with your disease and have made me complicit. Who will you go after next? Dr. Mortimer? Mr. Holmes in

London?"

Exhausted—exhausted at what I was hearing, but also exhausted from the past three days—I collapsed on the floor beside her bed.

"My love is like a spring," she said. "It never stops running. But when you became ugly and spiteful, my love had to flow elsewhere. And it found its home with Sir Henry."

"Did you not hear what he said about you? The night we talked in the den—?"

"Yes, I heard Henry's disappointing words. They stifled not an ounce of my love for him." She collapsed back into her pillow. "I am weak. I fall in love with men who see me as nothing more than a carnation on their lapel."

"I never thought of you like that—"

"As long as I supported you." She sighed. "There was a time I thought you deserved to be reunited with your family. To live at Baskerville Hall, to play a part in your family's affairs. The closer you drew to their estate, the sicker and fouler you became. I no longer recognize my Rodrigo. It is as though you are dead. I can only think of you in the past."

"So you do not love me any longer," I said from the floor. "And Henry, the man you do love, he does not reciprocate either."

Then she decided it was the right moment to announce this to me:

"There was a question made by the men of Dartmoor to the parish priest, or whatever these English dogs call their holy man. This holy man asked Sir Henry what his wishes were if, by an act of God, your body was found in the mire."

"How did Henry respond?"

"He said if your body was found, there would be no recourse but to bury you as a Baskerville. That, he declared, was 'a prospect most intolerable.' I believe there is some kind of understanding between the men of Dartmoor and Sir Henry regarding your fate."

She let me brood over that for a long while. She lowered the lamplight until darkness consumed us both.

"Leave me." Her voice pierced the void. "I will return to my father. He will beat me mercilessly, but he will take me back. I will marry the man he selects for me, and I will produce offspring for them both. And so the cycle will repeat."

"What do I have to do to prove my love for you? I risked life and limb. And not once have I been unfaithful."

I returned to kneeling before her in bed. She considered my sorry words for a long moment. She made an imperious laugh and said, "To think, for a moment, I dared to imagine a life with you again. The men from London told me you were dead. They said the mire claimed you.

They were not wrong. You are dead. Here in this room stands a ghost to haunt me. Fly away, ghost. You scare me no longer."

She rose and led me across the room. The waning moon cast its gray light across our faces. In her white lace nightie, she appeared spectral, as though gliding over the floor. From the window, we overlooked the old stable at the rear of the property.

She pointed down to the stable.

"Your fate awaits you there, Rodrigo. There you will find the crop of nightshade you have sown."

Thirty-five

With aid of neither lamp nor lantern, I opened the stable door and slid inside, Colt up. Although no equine had been stabled there for decades, the pungent stench of horse and hay haunted the building, which was no larger than a country church.

As soon as I lifted the cellar door came a raucous barking and growling. Up from the depths rose a distinct foul stench of excretion and stale urine, as well as something evil. It was the ripe odor of rotting flesh.

I kept a spare lantern hanging on a peg in the stable. I risked lighting it for my descent. It was as Antônio had warned me: Agrippina remained tied up down there. I never intended to hold her there for more than a few hours. Food was scattered everywhere, much like a prisoner throws his meals against the walls in protest of poor conditions. She stood on all fours, eyes blood red, hackles raised, snarling and daring me to come near.

I descended the stairs with comforting words and *sssh*'s and a calming tone of voice. Thinking her anger would subside when she could smell me, I dared to approach with a hand out. She leapt at me, slicing open the back of my hand with a fang.

In the shadows lay Nero. The bastards had dragged her son down the stairs and left him to rot before her. Her nostrils would be saturated with the scent of his fur, his blood, his childlike nature, and memories of his desperate love for her.

Voices rose from above. Truly I had trapped myself down there.

Scrambling up the stairs, I bolted into the nighttime without caution. Men's voices intensified from all directions. Calls came in the dark, and police whistles were shrilled.

Out from the old orchard sprang a young man named Smith, whose father raised ponies. The expression he wore was one of utter resolve. I did not wait for him to raise a firearm. With a quick flick, I unleashed the Colt into his chest. He fell backward and rolled on the ground screaming.

Once I stripped off my wool overcoat, I gained speed. The time lost gave another man a leg up on me, a man named Harmon who produced chickens and potatoes. With another quick flick, I unloaded on him, sending him to the dirt with a face full of his own blood. Rifle shots sounded behind me, but they failed to make their mark. I fired off one more round into the dark crowd behind me as warning.

Without the coat, speed was on my side, but now all my spare ammunition was lying useless on the moor behind me. More alarums were raised. More voices cried out behind me.

Just as I had the night of Nero's death, I scrambled into the mire, and did not let up until convinced my pursuers had given up the chase.

Thursday, the Twenty-fifth of October, Eighteen hundred and eighty-eight

Thirty-six

This journal I write with a vain and naive hope to correct the record. To correct a record yet to be produced, in fact. What will Watson write of me? No, no, no—scratch that out. What will he write of the others?

Holmes' role in this adventure is, of course, simple to predict. Watson will be his faithful but confused assistant sent off to Dartmoor, until Holmes makes his dramatic appearance among the tors. Uncle Charles will be kindly and generous, as the English consider all gentry with royal title and broad wealth. Henry, blessed with handsomeness uncommon in the Baskerville line, will be the rugged frontiersman from Canada who adopts the civilized mien of an aristocrat within hours of his arrival in England. James Mortimer will be the concerned country doctor. And the Barrymores will be loyal and obedient lifelong servants, as the British always like to think of their indentured underclass.

Beryl? The suspicious raven-haired beauty of obscure foreign origin and loyalties. Antônio? I wonder if Watson will even bother to mention him. Creative license, and all that.

And I, "Jack Stapleton"? A secondary character at best, unpresuming, uninspiring, only revealed in the last moments as the prime mover of all the tale's mysterious events. They will accuse me of all manner of unsolved crimes in this county, as a dead man cannot complain of the baggage he's given to carry into the afterlife.

I believe that is how Watson will construct his story. Who will protest otherwise?

*

I grew up taught I was English. England taught me I am Brazilian. Perhaps I am neither. What is a mutt, other than a breed no one bothers to name?

A sleepless night has me left considering anew Antônio's advice to make a run to the Plymouth docks. If the men of Dartmoor truly are keeping my survival under their hats, then I stand half a chance of boarding there and sailing to freedom in the New World.

Perhaps I will pay a visit the Harris clan's relatives in Mississippi. I will introduce myself as a Kentucky Colonel, and introduce to them my Colt Single-Action. Or I will settle in Mexico and take the guise of a wealthy landowner removed from my native Alta California. When I dream, I dream of the silver in California's hills. There I will don a new name and elaborate a new history I can wear about San Francisco like a stiff musky pair of boots.

Beryl, I cannot leave her behind as easily as she has me. And to run without Antônio at my side, it is like navigating without a helmsman. Her affection, her energy, it motivated me. His cool council, it tempered me. I miss them very much. Reminiscing leaves me empty. Perhaps I am a steam engine at the end of its line. The fire in my belly has gone cold.

*

From the edge of the mire this morning came the voice of men organizing. Their dogs were a cacophony of barks and howls. The men dare not enter Grimpen, though. The bog will devour them alive. Hiding in this cave is losing a war by attrition, but it is my most promising strategy to date. How many losses to the bog-mire are they willing to suffer?

What I witnessed makes me quite ill. The men of Dartmoor have come for me, indeed. On drawn cart, quite difficult to navigate across the moor, they transported Agrippina in a cage. She is as vicious as ever. They transported with her Nero's decaying corpse to feed her fury.

No doubt they are preparing to release her into the mire. She is a wonderful tracker, single-minded in purpose, thirsty in her execution. The overcoat I discarded during my escape, they offer it to her by river pole.

I have so much more to write, and so much more to experience. My life has been full, but it remains nothing more than a rough draft of a complete one. I wish to see it all with my eyes and taste it all between my teeth. The bowl of meal I was given, it is not enough. I would like seconds.

Agrippina's howls echo across the mire. The men of Dartmoor taunt her and egg her on. They do not respect her. They could not muster the courage or the shrewdness to take me on, so they send a female grieving her lost son. Where reason and planning have failed, they turn to unbridled instinct. It is the wisest decision these yokels have made yet.

*

This morning I discovered *A. iris*, a purple emperor, among the leaves of a whortleberry bush. Its broad indigo wings shone iridescent in the early light. With cupped hands, I captured it alive. I hoped I might have a chance to admire its beauty before releasing it, just as César taught me to admire butterflies in the Amazon so many years ago. I wished to hold the *Nymphalidae* in my palms as he held the *Mariposa tigre* in his, wings open so I may admire its delicate palette.

When I opened my hands, I found it dead. I do not know what I did to kill it.

I have pressed its corpse between the end pages of this journal.

*

Barrymore left me Uncle Charles' nickel-plated hunting rifle and two rounds. Lying flat on my belly, I peered down the rifle's sight into the thicket of men about the cart. Judging for distance and allowing for the wind, I loosed a bullet. A heartbeat later, one of the Dartmoor men flailed backwards. The others scrambled for cover.

As I reloaded, one screamed epithets at me. He promised I would die a vicious death. That he made such bold claims while in hiding, and preparing to send a dog into the mire rather than take me on himself, struck me as an apt summation of my encounters with these men of Dartmoor.

I trained the bead upon Agrippina's head. She was frothing at the mouth, thick foamy bile about her gums, so much rage, so eager to be released from her kennel. When the wind settled, I took a deep breath, held, and tightened the trigger. One more bullet would end their plans.

What stirs a man's soul is as mysterious at what gives him pause. Beryl and Antônio gave up on me, but I did not give up on them. So it is with Agrippina. Perhaps when she reaches me, we will reunite like old friends, as Augustus and I did in the Amazon years ago.

I've returned to my cave. From the shouts across the mire, I know they've released her. She is approaching. I will use these minutes to tidy up my journal.

*

From the earth I came, to the earth I return.

She is close now.

The stone placed over my head should bear my given name. Not Stapleton. Not Vandeleur.

I hear her. Soon she will be upon me.

Let my stone be inscribed thusly:

"Here lies

Afterword

Forty years before Rodger Baskerville landed in Dartmoor, English naturalist Henry Walter Bates traveled up the Amazon River cataloging and observing the stupendous selection of species hosted there. He spent time near Óbidos and Manaus, locales not far from Santarém. When he returned to London in 1861, he brought with him a fresh theory of natural selection that remains of service to biologists today.

In Brazil, Bates discovered *Heliconius* butterflies exhibiting the shapes and colors of unrelated butterflies inedible to birds and amphibians. This discovery was as key to Batesian theories of mimicry as Darwin's finches were to his own research.

The mimicry of the *Heliconius* is so accurate, they even travel among the butterflies they are imitating. So self-assured of their disguise, Bates witnessed these butterflies dancing and flaunting merrily before the very predators who could devour them in an instant.

Truly miraculous, Henry Walter Bates must have thought, *to find such a perfect imitator here in the Amazon.*

*

Years ago, while traveling Japan via its *Shinkansen* bullet train, I found myself without a book to read. An ebook reader I'd installed on my phone came with a free sample to whet the reader's appetite. That book was Arthur Conan Doyle's *The Adventures of Sherlock Holmes*, a collection of the earliest Holmes short stories.

The collection stands as a record of a remarkably creative streak. So remarkable, if Doyle were to have stopped writing after its publication, we would still be talking about his literary creation and storytelling prowess. The titles of the stories within are as familiar as the books of the Bible: "A Scandal in Bohemia," "The Red-Headed League," "The Man with the Twisted Lip," "The Adventure of the Speckled Band." Perhaps the only missing short story title of comparable infamy is "The Adventure of Silver Blaze," published in *The Memoirs of Sherlock Holmes* a mere two years later. *In toto*, they represent the height of Doyle's powers and inventiveness.

None of this inspired me to write *A Man Named Baskerville*. As exciting and inventive as a great Sherlock Holmes story can be, never have I entertained the question that has dogged countless other producers of Doyle homages and pastiches: *Could I write my own Sherlock Holmes story?* Honestly, the thought has never crossed my mind.

*

After consuming the first collection in a rush of reading, I used the opportunity of a brief train stop and some free wireless Internet access to download more Sherlock Holmes books for our continued journey. I had read a little of Doyle's work before, and never found much interest in it. They were too Victorian for my tastes, too concerned with Empire and upright decency and British morality. My California upbringing, and the plain-speaking tastes I inherited from my parents, led me to the hardboiled school of Chandler, Hammett, and Cain. Nathanael West's grotesqueries and William Gibson's cyberpunks are a better fit for me than Holmes' Irregulars.

On that train ride, my interest in Sherlock Holmes kindled. Holmes may not have walked Chandler's mean streets, but he did present a more compelling moral force than I'd sensed before. As with the hardboiled school, Holmes time and again must balance his own sense of justice against the British legal system's notion of the same. Doyle wrote for an audience who would understand those boundaries implicitly. A hundred and ten years later, I viewed Holmes' sense of justice through a different lens. This came to a point when my reading reached *The Hound of the Baskervilles*.

The book was first serialized in 1901, ten years after that auspicious run of early short stories. Doyle had killed off Holmes in "The Final Problem" (1893) hoping to rid himself of the literary creation upstaging all his other work. An appalled public demanded more stories featuring Holmes, and publishers increasingly pressured Doyle to satisfy the market's cravings.

Inspired by a trip to Devon and its local folklore of wisht hellhounds roaming the countryside at night, Doyle produced *The Hound of the Baskervilles*. To avoid what we today call "continuity problems," he retroactively dated its events to October 1888, three years before the publication of his earliest stories. This places the story square in the middle of the Autumn of Terror, when a serial killer dubbed Saucy Jack terrified London, while, across the Atlantic, the Empire of Brazil was warily beginning its dissolution.

One overlooked quality of Doyle's writing is that his knack for concise storytelling in the short form executes equally brilliantly in the longer form. I've seen adept short story writers get fouled up when they attempt to tackle the novel. The pacing and breathing cadences that permit a runner to win the 100-meter dash do not sustain when attempting a marathon. Yet Doyle's economical style holds up with *Hound*, making for dazzling quick cuts between crucial scenes, and exposition that does not lead the reader to impatiently flip ahead. Doyle had a gift for paring down prose to its vital emotional and informational elements without stripping it of that uniquely English sense of mood and atmosphere. One also sees in *Hound* Doyle's assiduous control of pacing. The early chapters draw out their scenes, while the closing chapters barrel headlong toward the conclusion. The movement becomes so breathless at the end, it takes pure inference on the part of the reader to detect scene changes.

Readers either love or hate this no-business approach to storytelling. Either way, the final output of his opus on the moors is consistent with this quality, and obviously has held the public's interest for well over a century.

None of this inspired me to write this book, either. I grew to admire Doyle's writing while traveling by bullet train, but I never craved to imitate it. The first fourteen chapters of *The Hound of the Baskervilles* served to reaffirm my growing estimation of the man's talents, but not to pick up a pen.

*

What did inspire me to write *A Man Named Baskerville*? The fifteenth and final chapter of the book it derives from.

All detective mysteries deal in sleight-of-hand. Keeping the perpetrator out of the narrative limelight until the moment the solution is announced is a tried-and-true technique for maintaining the element of surprise. In response, savvy readers have learned to guess whodunnit by evaluating how much "screen time" the author gives the suspects. The most obvious suspect is never culpable. The suspect we've read the least about is quite often guilty up to their eyeballs.

And that's pretty much the case in *The Hound of the Baskervilles*. The perpetrator is one we hear precious little about, an absentminded collector of butterflies and moths named Jack Stapleton who lives with his sister (the nineteenth-century equivalent to rooming in your parents' basement, apparently). He's not the least elaborated-upon character in the book, but he is pictured as far removed from the crimes and the curse of the Baskervilles. When Holmes and Watson finally suspect his guilt, Doyle spends no time speculating on his motivations in favor of keeping the story moving at a brisk clip.

Doyle knew the reader would eventually demand to know why Stapleton posed under an assumed identity to murder his uncle in such a contrived way, and then attempt the same on his cousin. To sew things up, in Chapter 15, Watson calls on Holmes to explain the background of Jack

Stapleton. Holmes launches into fourteen pages of exposition, a matter-of-fact recounting of Rodger's life from the New World to Devonshire, England.

Much detail is omitted, of course, but Holmes' reckoning of Rodger's life is a far more plumbed-out biography than I think any reader expected. After all, Holmes could have simply stated, "He was raised abroad and returned to England to kill his uncle and claim his estate." Yes, that could be worded more artfully, but Doyle stretched himself to fill in the blanks.

I don't know why Doyle felt the need to so thoroughly detail Rodger Baskerville's life. I'm not sure anyone does. In my research for this book, I never located a definitive answer to the question. Perhaps in Doyle's papers, or in a complete treatise on his life and work, an answer may be found. Perhaps it was a modernist faith in the triumph of reason—all things must be explained that can be explained—that led Doyle to stretch himself, much as he uses many pages to lay out the backstory in *A Study in Scarlet* and some of his short stories.

What I do know is, reading those seemingly superfluous fourteen pages of Rodger's life struck me as a kind of boggy sinkhole in the tale. It felt Arthur Conan Doyle had wanted to write *two* books, Rodger's life story and *The Hound of the Baskervilles*. Unable or uninterested in writing the first, he wrote the latter and included a précis of the former in the final chapter.

Fascinated, I made copious notes of Holmes' reckoning of Rodger's life. Later, I transferred and organized them on my computer. A bell tinkled in my mind, a Pavlovian reaction all writers develop: *Is there a novel here?* I let the idea stew. Holmes' reckoning might appear a rich vein to mine, but once I started digging, it might yield little more than a couple of small gems.

And how would readers react to Rodger as a main character? Yes, everyone says they like stories about villains—but too often those so-called villains are more like lovable rogues or bad boys with a soft spot. Was I trying to humanize Rodger Baskerville? That's exactly what a novel does: It humanizes. Would it be a Victorian "Sympathy for the Devil"?

Maybe, I thought, I should just write the damn thing and see what comes out of the keyboard.

I made a private agreement with myself: I would not write yet another pastiche of Sherlock Holmes, of which there are plenty to pass around. The book would be told in Rodger's voice and not in imitation of Doyle's Watson. Of course, that didn't excuse me from the challenges of writing a historical novel, which include diction, grammar, tone of voice, colloquialisms, and historical accuracy. Nor could I write such a book without featuring Holmes and Watson at some point.

Mostly, though, my doubts centered on originality. Certainly *someone* had executed on this idea since the publication of Doyle's book. Internet searches yielded nothing of the sort.

It became a secret too juicy to keep to myself: In the final chapter of *The Hound of the Baskervilles*, Arthur Conan Doyle embedded a working outline for a novel—a rousing novel, in my estimation—that had been overlooked for over a century. It took me five years to set aside my private doubts and write it.

Yes, it was exhilarating to liberally borrow from a master's synopsis and expand it into this novel. No, having said synopsis to work from did not make my job any easier.

*

Holmes' reckoning of Rodger's life brims with contradictions—not errors of logic, which even a casual reader would seize upon, but cultural contradictions.

When Dr. James Mortimer expresses that remote Dartmoor is a place where people of all stripes "are very much thrown together," he adds that with the exception of himself, Sir Charles, Stapleton, and one more, "there are no other men of education within many miles."

Yet there's no indication in Holmes' reckoning that Rodger Baskerville enjoyed a proper education. Given the (mostly unmentioned) circumstances around his father's departure from England, he presumably did not have the family's fortune at his disposal. (Besides, the Baskerville fortune is described as having been restored by Sir Charles upon his return from South Africa, well after Rodger reached manhood.) Lacking money and cut-off from his family, I fail to see how a young Rodger would have received an advanced education in mid-nineteenth century South America without some Horatio Alger-like munificence falling into his lap. Yet this oversight on Mortimer's part is never corrected in the book.

(And if Rodger flees Costa Rica after "purloining a considerable sum of public money" as Doyle describes, I also don't see how that comports with a gentleman raised among the leisure class, without falling into the Hollywood trope of the stuffy overbred scoundrel, e.g., a Terry-Thomas type.)

Mortimer commits the sin of assumption that bedeviled Western culture back then and bedevils us now: *An intelligent person is an institutionally-educated person*, followed by the sin of transitive logic, *An educated person is a person of proper values and high worth.* Rodger's successful impersonation of an educated Englishman of high character is a rather damning failure of the assumptions of Holmes' time…assumptions continuing to this day, in America and elsewhere.

Another assumption is the "like father, like son" logic of Holmes' reckoning of Rodger's life. Rodger Sr. left England under a cloud—a "cad" is the innuendo here, I believe—and, hence, his son naturally followed. To compound the issue, Rodger is identified as looking strikingly like the original Hugo Baskerville, the pillaging brute on whom the family curse was first laid. For Rodger to follow in Hugo and his father's footsteps is a *fait accompli.* No alternate possibility is explored. The Rodger Baskervilles are British Jukes, and criminality is in their blood. Again, this goes unquestioned, even in a rational age of Darwinism and Batesian mimicry.

There's a few ways to read Doyle's myopia. Rodger can't be written off as a superlative mimic and a deft confidence trickster. Holmes acknowledges Rodger's impressive expertise with butterflies and moths. He was a schoolmaster to boot, not an occupation one associates with con men and hucksters.

I think the myopia is Doyle dog-whistling to his readership that Rodger simultaneously was "one of us" and "not one of us"—an Englishman raised by an English gentleman, but a fallen one, and raised in the wrong part of the world. I suppose to a reader of Doyle's time, this Schrödinger's cat of identity made a great deal of sense. In my experience, this unintentional cross wiring of signals indicates a cultural blind spot.

When I planned this book, I failed to see how a man with Rodger's background would not bring to Dartmoor one or more Central or South American dialects along with his impeccable upper-class English accent. He would also bring with him a rich and varied New World culture as his starting point of reference.

Once in England, around his neck would be the weight of several albatrosses: His father's suspicious exile; his "ethnic" upbringing and foreign tongue; his lack of secure income; his marriage to a dusky woman most un-Anglo-Saxon. Only his upper-crust accent would save him. It would work in the British Isles like a charge card with no spending limit. After all, he didn't merely fool the English into thinking he was one of them; he fooled them into thinking he was *better* than most of them.

Of course, by their own reckoning, Rodger really was better than most of them. He was a Baskerville, direct heir to a baronetcy, scion of a family with a storied history reaching back to the English Civil War. Henry's arrival from Canada is treated auspiciously, as was Sir Charles' return from South Africa, but Rodger's foreign background is a stain to blot away with soda water and a clean rag. If Rodger were simply to approach Uncle Charles and ask to be accepted into the family, there would be an accounting. The damage his presence would make to the family name and reputation would be weighed. A Christian reconciliation of a prodigal son returning home to a joyful father (or uncle) strikes me as beyond remote here, and yet Rodger's only Original Sin is that his father many years earlier had "fled with a sinister reputation to South America." Henry arrives from Canada a rough frontier man, yet after a single London shopping trip, he becomes the dignified and aristocratic Sir Henry. Rodger would have to hustle and deceive to achieve a similar transformation, all while forever denying his language, his culture, his father, his past—his own self.

It seems to me the world is consumed with competing narratives: The Gospels versus *The Antiquities of the Jews* and the Midrash; Karl Marx's history of class versus Adam Smith's history of nations; the 9/11 Commission versus the 9/11 Truthers; Stop the Steal versus the Big Lie; and on and on. Much of the competition deals with barring certain narratives—and narrators—from the playing field. Sometimes more time and energy is spent disqualifying than narrating.

I imagined a Rodger Baskerville particularly sensitive to this competition and its rigged rules. His journal is more than a recounting of his life. It's a corrective to the tale he predicts Watson will write when the time comes. A man in his position, with his intelligence and insights into human behavior, knew Watson's account would muddy his own past while circling the wagons around the Baskervilles' reputation, just as the modern mass media protects established power. While many particulars of Rodger's situation are unique to an England of 1888, changing just a few surface details would place Rodger in the same situation in America circa 1888, or even 2022.

Freud's narcissism of small differences is an underappreciated observation of the continuing human condition. As long as people lift themselves up by cataloging their differences with outsiders, there will always be Rodger Baskervilles walking among us.

*

The problem with a Victorian "Sympathy for the Devil" is that the Devil remains, no matter how sympathetic his situation.

Like humans, dogs come into the world with an undeveloped understanding of right and wrong. They are impressionable and easily conditioned to normalize acts we would find reprehensible.

Rodger trains Nero, Agrippina, and the others without regard for their well-being. Try as he might in his journal, he cannot manage to hide the plain truth that he abused these dogs.

No matter what I've written about Rodger Baskerville, in no way do I condone animal abuse. Training dogs for blood sport or with the intention to incite harm is evil. Abusive violence on dogs is unacceptable.

Jim Nelson's novels include *Bridge Daughter* (Kindle Press, 2016), *Stranger Son*, and *In My Memory Locked*. He divides his time between San Francisco and Tokyo.

MX Publishing

We have been publishing Sherlock Holmes books since 2008 and have become the largest imprint of its kind in the world, with more than 600 titles and 150 authors writing fiction and non-fiction. As a social enterprise, MX Publishing has raised over $150,000 for good causes to date across the UK, USA and Africa. Our two founders, Steve and Sharon Emecz are mentors and advisors to several charitable organisations and in 2020, Steve was part of the World Food Program (WFP) team that was awarded the Nobel Peace Prize for works combating hunger. You can find all our books on our website mxpublishing.com and through all major bookstores.

Our new books are featured here –
https://mxpublishing.com/pages/new-books

Our Hound related books include:

Non-fiction

- Hounded - My lifelong obsession with Sherlock Holmes And The Hound of The Baskervilles (Vince Stadon)
- The Hound Of The Baskervilles – A Sherlock Holmes Reader (Nick Reekie)
- Bertram Fletcher Robinson: A Footnote to The Hound of the Baskervilles

Fiction

- Mark Of The Baskerville Hound (Wilfred Huettel)
- The Hound of The Baskervilles – A Sherlock Holmes Graphic Novel (Petr Kopl)
- The Official Papers Into The Matter Known As The Hound of the Baskervilles DCC143589 refers (Kieron Freeburn)
- Hound of The Baskervilles - The Play (Simon Corble)

www.ingramcontent.com/pod-product-compliance
Lightning Source LLC
Chambersburg PA
CBHW030426310726
48979CB00009B/1640/J

9781804246054